Deep Water

www.**kids**at**r**and**om**house.co.uk

Also by Debi Gliori

PURE DEAD MAGIC
PURE DEAD WICKED
PURE DEAD BRILLIANT
DEEP TROUBLE

DEEP WATER

Debi Gliori

DOUBLEDAY
London • Toronto • Sydney • Auckland • Johannesburg

DEEP WATER
A DOUBLEDAY BOOK 0385 60630 3

Published in Great Britain by Doubleday
an imprint of Random House Children's Books

This edition published 2005

1 3 5 7 9 10 8 6 4 2

Text and illustrations copyright © Debi Gliori, 2005

The right of Debi Gliori to be identified as the author of
this work has been asserted in accordance with the
Copyright, Designs and Patents Act 1988

Papers used by Random House Children's Books are
natural, recyclable products made from wood grown in
sustainable forests. The manufacturing processes conform
to the environmental regulations of the country of origin.

Set in 12½/16pt Palatino by
Falcon Oast Graphic Art Ltd.

RANDOM HOUSE CHILDREN'S BOOKS
61–63 Uxbridge Road, London W5 5SA
A division of The Random House Group Ltd

RANDOM HOUSE AUSTRALIA (PTY) LTD
20 Alfred Street, Milsons Point, Sydney,
New South Wales 2061, Australia

RANDOM HOUSE NEW ZEALAND LTD
18 Poland Road, Glenfield, Auckland 10, New Zealand

RANDOM HOUSE (PTY) LTD
Endulini, 5A Jubilee Road, Parktown 2193, South Africa

THE RANDOM HOUSE GROUP Limited Reg. No. 954009
www.**kids**at**randomhouse**.co.uk

A CIP catalogue record for this book is available from the
British Library.

Printed and bound in Great Britain by
Clays Ltd, St Ives plc

This one's for my boys;
setting sail into deep water.

Contents

Dramatis Personae

THE FAMILY

TITUS STREGA-BORGIA – thirteen-year-old hero

PANDORA STREGA-BORGIA – eleven-year-old heroine

DAMP STREGA-BORGIA – their two-year-old sister

SIGNOR LUCIANO AND SIGNORA BACI STREGA-BORGIA – parents of the above

STREGA-NONNA (AMELIA) – great-great-great-great-great-great-grandmother (cryogenically preserved) of Titus, Pandora and Damp

SOMEONE ELSE ENTIRELY – The unborn baby Strega-Borgia

DON LUCIFER DI S'EMBOWELLI BORGIA – evil half-brother to Luciano

MALVOLIO DI S'ENCHANTEDINO BORGIA – Strega-Nonna's grandson

APOLLONIUS 'THE GREEK' BORGIA – mapmaker, cartographer, Great-Great Etcetera

THE GOOD HELP THAT WAS HARD TO FIND

MRS FLORA McLACHLAN – nanny to Titus, Pandora and Damp

LATCH – StregaSchloss butler

MARIE BAIN – possibly the worst cook in the western hemisphere

MISS ARAMINTA FRASER – new nanny to Titus, Pandora and Damp

THE BEASTS

TARANTELLA – spider with attitude, and now, family

NOVELLA, EPISTOLIA, ANECDOTA, TRILOGIA, EPICSAGA, EMAILIA, DIARYA – daughters of the above

SAB, FFUP, NESTOR AND KNOT – mythical dungeon beasts

TOCK – crocodile inhabitant of StregaSchloss's first-floor guest bathroom

MULTITUDINA AND TERMINUS – free-range StregaSchloss rats
THE SLEEPER – Scottish unreconstructed-male mythical beast
ORYNX – salamander and escaped slave
VESPER – Damp's bat familiar

ASSORTED MEMBERS OF THE CAST

RAND MACALISTER HALL – member of Titus's band
MUNRO MACALISTER HALL – hideously expensive lawyer and
Rand's father
LUDO GRABBIT – estate lawyer from Slander, Defame and
Grabbit, W. S.
DETECTIVE SERGEANT BILL WATERS – CID sergeant
DETECTIVE CHIEF INSPECTOR FINBAR McINTOSH –
senior CID officer

THE IMMORTALS

ISAGOTH – demonic defence minister and castaway
S'TAN – First Minister of the Hadean Executive
DEATH – as himself
THE CHEF – angelic being from the Other Side

ARGYLL HERALD DISPATCH

UNIDENTIFIED MAN SURVIVES STORMS

Argyll Police are endeavouring to establish the identity of a man found unconscious on the western shores of Lochnagargoyle. Thought to be aged between 45 and 50, the man was wearing a black Gore-tex jacket with battered chinos over a pair of lace-up paratrooper's boots. His unconscious body was found by local fisherman Archie McIntoul during the early hours of Wednesday morning.

LUCKY TO BE ALIVE

'It's a miracle he's not dead,' said Mr McIntoul, whose speedy intervention probably saved the life of this unidentified man.

'I saw something on the shore when I was hauling in my creels, so I motored over to investigate.' The fisherman's lobster boat *Time and Tide* has been a familiar sight sailing up and down Lochnagargoyle for the past 40 years.

MAN'S BODY SHOCK

'Imagine my shock when I realized that it was a man's body lying there,' said Mr McIntoul (63). 'In all my years of fishing on this loch, I've never seen anything like this. His face was all covered in wee red spots and the way he was lying made me scared to move him, so I covered him with my jacket and radioed for assistance.'

RAPID RESPONSE FROM HMS COAST-GUARD

Within a very short time, the man was airlifted to the local hospital in Auchenlochtermuchty, where nursing staff confirm that he is out of danger but still unconscious. Moments after arriving at the hospital, surgeons operated to save the man's legs, which had both been broken in several places.

BAFFLED

Hospital sources admit that they have no idea how this man could have survived prolonged exposure in sub-zero temperatures. Police are asking any witnesses to this incident to come forward.

Memento Mori

At four o'clock on the afternoon of the first of October, police cars drew up at each of the three main gates to the StregaSchloss estate and effectively cordoned off the area.

As a further precaution, a launch sped up Lochnagargoyle, cut its engines and dropped anchor just out of sight of the StregaSchloss jetty. Radios crackled, then fell silent as moments ticked by, marked by the rain drumming on the roofs of the police cars and turning their windscreens opaque.

Inside the cars the policemen waited for the rain to stop, enviously imagining what it would be like to have so much money that

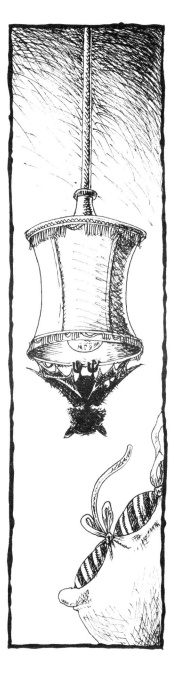

you could afford to live in a huge house like StregaSchloss.

'*How* many did you say, Detective Sergeant?'

'Fifty-six chimneys, sir.'

There StregaSchloss lay, its turrets and chimneys thrust aggressively into the sky; a vast, unattainable, immeasurably expensive chunk of real estate bigger than all the policemen's houses put together.

'Surely that rust bucket can't be their only car, Detective Sergeant?'

"'Fraid so, sir – apart from the butler's wee Japanese jobbie.'

Outside StregaSchloss, parked on the rose-quartz drive, was the Strega-Borgia family car, badly in need of a wash and bearing a scrawl to this effect on its rear window. With a pair of high-power binoculars the DCI could just about decipher the message:

Pure Dead mingin' - please wash me

In Titus's opinion a wash was not enough. He'd written this considered criticism on the car's rear window months ago, but it had failed to bring results: the car still hadn't been washed, and a season spent trekking Titus and his sister Pandora back and forth along a rutted muddy track hadn't improved the car's general state of decrepitude. Nor had his little sister Damp's habit of littering all the car's internal horizontal surfaces with a combination of peanut butter, glitter and a selection of the dried-up furry bits from the insides of several disembowelled felt pens. No, Titus thought, a grin appearing on his face, a wash was *not* what their car required. It needed some kind soul to disengage the hand brake, put the gears in neutral and push the car straight into the moat, where, with luck, it would vanish from sight into the deep mud at the bottom; the same forgiving mud that had swallowed so many unwanted things over the years.

Then they could buy a decent car. Something fast. Something sleek and powerful. Something – Titus's smile faded – something highly unsuitable for a family of two adults, three children plus another one due to appear round about Christmas. By which time the parents would either tie Titus and Pandora to the roof rack to make room for the new baby, or go and buy something truly hideous with bus-like rows of industrial seating, the motor equivalent of an elastic band under the bonnet and a name that would make Titus cringe every time the parents referred to it. Like, er: *'Go and get my bag out of the Nipply, would you, darling'*; or, *'I think I'd better get petrol for the Sopha while I'm in town'*; or even, shudder, shudder, *'Yeah, but it's not as big as our Urse TDi.'*

Still, Titus decided, anything, even an Urse TDi, had to be better than having to *walk* to Auchenlochtermuchty. He hardly noticed when several wet figures ran across the rose quartz and applied themselves to the front doorbell with great urgency. Had he not been quite so preoccupied, Titus might have spotted that two of the scurrying figures were dressed in identical damp black serge with checkerboard detail round the epaulettes: the uniform of the Argyll and Bute Police.

Meanwhile in his bedroom in the attic, the StregaSchloss butler, Latch, was not enjoying an afternoon nap. He'd spent the hours since lunchtime trying to evict a bat. In vain had he opened skylights and made shooing noises; unsurprisingly, given the rain outside, the bat was having none of it. Latch had no desire to harm the little creature, but he most emphatically *didn't* want to share the same room. After several abortive attempts to flap it out of the window using a pillowcase as propellant, Latch had given up and was now sitting on his bed, trying to reason with the intruder. The bat hung upside down from the lampshade and ignored him.

'Look,' Latch said, 'it's dead simple. This is *my* cave, not yours. The only person I want to share it with lies fathoms deep at the bottom of Lochnagargoyle, and frankly you, pal, are no substitute. Though undoubtedly heaven-sent, the love of my life had no visible wings and definitely wasn't covered in black fur.'

The bat blinked and extended one leathery wing.

'Please,' Latch said, blowing his nose and wiping his eyes, 'leave me alone. Go and do your bat-thing somewhere else. You remind me of death – as if I needed reminding.' He closed his eyes, shutting out the sight of the spartan bedroom; a room that bore no evidence of anything other than solitary bachelorhood and utter loneliness. There were no photographs, no letters, nothing to show for the love he'd found and lost. Even his memory of her was dimming as the days without her ticked by; days he spent scanning the loch shore, willing the water to return her to him, his mermaid, his selkie, his loved and lost Flora.

The bat extended both wings and cleared his throat with a discreet cough. 'I hate to intrude on your grieving, sir,' he whispered. 'Forgive me for interrupting. I'm not looking for you, actually. Any chance you could point me towards the witch?'

He waited, refolding his wings like organic origami, his pale eyes blinking in the fading light.

'The *witch*?' Latch's voice emerged as a strangled squeak.

'The real witch,' the bat insisted. 'Not the big one, nor the medium one, but the little one – oh whatsername: Wet? Clammy? Moist?'

'Damp,' Latch said. 'Down eight flights of stairs, hang a left and third door on the right along the corridor.'

'Damp,' the bat said in an awed voice. 'D-aaaaa mmmmmmp.'

'Indeed,' said Latch, his tone indicating that his patience was running out alongside the bat's welcome. To further this impression he opened the door leading onto the attic corridor, and stepped back to allow the uninvited guest to make his exit unimpeded.

'I'm much obliged,' the bat squeaked, unfolding one wing after the other and giving both a good shake. 'Really sorry about your sad loss.'

'Quite,' muttered Latch. He turned aside and crossed the room to stand gazing sightlessly out of the window; as clear a signal as one could wish for that the conversation, such as it was, had come to an end. When his swimming eyes were able to focus once more, he realized that the distant white blob parked across the north gate to StregaSchloss was a police car, but by then it was too late.

The table in the StregaSchloss kitchen was heavily dusted with flour along its entire length, as were the motley assortment of kitchen chairs; the shelves and crockery on the dresser; the hotplates of the range; the flagstone floor, and every horizontal surface within a five-metre range of where Ffup the teenage dragon was holding a one-sided conversation with something deeply unpleasant in the bottom of a mixing bowl.

'Come *on*,' she begged. 'Upsa-daisy – arise arise – allez oopla – hey ho and up she rises.' The dragon closed her eyes, held her breath for a count of ten and then peered hopefully into the bowl where, to her disgust, her diet-approved no-carbohydrate bread dough still lay irretrievably lumpen, stubbornly inert and flatly unrisen.

'Rrrrright,' she muttered. 'Time for desperate measures. I'm desperate and you're not measuring up to your picture in my recipe book. Don't say I didn't warn you.'

Brushing flour from his leathery hide and pulling a hideous face behind his fellow-beast's back, Sab the gryphon dropped his newspaper onto the table and sighed pointedly. 'What *are* you on about, woman? I can't think loud enough to drown out your insane mumblings. Tell me, why are you talking to a mixing bowl?'

There was a subdued *whumph* like an under-powered firework, then the kitchen filled with the smell of burnt offerings. Ffup burst into tears, hurled the red-hot bowl into the sink and fled to the kitchen garden. In the ensuing silence there was a hissing sound as the bowl rapidly cooled down in the washing-up water, followed by a long ring from the front doorbell.

'*More* interruptions,' growled Sab, rattling the pages of his paper. 'Get that, would you, Tock?' The gryphon absentmindedly shredded a ballpoint pen as he considered the horoscope page, wrinkling his leathery forehead with annoyance as some thought-less visitor rang the doorbell again. Where *was* that crocodile? '*Tock?*'

'The crocodile is out,' said a languid voice from somewhere on top of the dresser. 'He is a not-in reptile. He's gone see-you-later-alligator. He's in an ongoing in-a-while-crocodile situation.' The voice paused and its owner gave a deep sigh. 'Actually, he's dredging the bottom of the river Chrone for quartz pebbles. Remember? Tock's moat renovations? He wanted lapis lazuli, but that was going to cost more than the *house* so he had to downsize to quartz—' The voice broke off and emitted an exasperated *'Tchhhh'*, and when it spoke again, the sound came from nearer the floor.

'Though why,' it continued, its tone becoming increasingly shrill, *'why* anyone would see fit to construct a quartz-lined channel and then fill it with w-wa— Oh Lordy, I can hardly bring myself to pronounce the word, let alone think of it – fill a quartz-lined channel with *water* – gag, urk, yeurrrch – is *quite* beyond my understanding.'

This last comment was delivered at a deafening volume, then, apparently exhausted by the effort of projecting her voice so far, the owner limped across Sab's field of vision and dangled herself from his ruined ballpoint, positioning her tennis-ball-sized abdomen between the gryphon and his newspaper.

'What star sign am I then? Hmmm? Go on, guess' – the voice emerging from the tarantula's cherry-red mouthparts was once again languid, chilled and ever so faintly smug – 'oh come on, team. You do know this one.'

'I have no idea,' Sab muttered. 'I didn't even know spiders *had* star signs.'

'Rrreally.' Tarantella narrowed all her eyes simultaneously. 'Well, you live and learn, huh? What did you *think* we had? Serial numbers? Bar codes?'

'Don't be so touchy.' Sab returned to the study of his paper, running a talon along the list of horoscopes and, to Tarantella's annoyance, ignoring her completely.

'For your information, *I* was born on a cusp,' she hissed, her mouthparts snapping shut after delivering this nugget of information.

'Hmm?' Sab managed to convey just how lacking in interest he found this bit of spider lore.

'A *cusp*,' Tarantella insisted. 'Which, in case your studies in astrology haven't grasped such advanced concepts, means the point of overlap between two star signs; where the influence of both is equal – the word *cusp* coming from the Latin *cuspis*—'

'Was that the doorbell? Again?' Sab's voice was tinged with desperation. 'No, Tarantella, don't get up. I'll go.' He leapt up and bolted out of the kitchen, the heavy slapping sound of his footfalls rapidly swallowed up by the vastness of StregaSchloss.

'– meaning point, as in the sharp bit at the end of a spear,' the tarantula continued to the empty kitchen. 'Or, if you prefer Pliny's version, it's the pointy bit at the end of a bee; its sting, in other words—'

'I prefer Ovid, where *cuspis* refers to the sting of a scorpion,' piped a small rat, emerging blinking from the darkness under the dresser.

'Damn,' squeaked an older, fatter rat, squeezing out of the cereal box and wheezing with the effort. 'Do you have to be so revoltingly clever, Terminus? I can't stand it when my kids make me feel like, feel like, like duh—'

'Precisely,' muttered Tarantella, glaring at the whiskery rodent waddling out from the shadows. 'I rest my case. Like "duh"? What sort of sentiment is *that*? And Multitudina, while we're assassinating your character, when did you last wash? You're covered in dust and fur-balls. Please. Do us all a favour. Go and ablute.'

'*What?*' The whiskery rat stopped in her tracks and scratched her bottom thoughtfully. 'What's a bloot?'

Tarantella rolled all her eyes and was on the point of delivering the final crushing verbal *coup de grace*, when from outside the kitchen came the sound of male voices raised in anger. Tarantella shut her mouthparts with a snap, and scuttled for the safety of the dresser, from where she routinely eaves-dropped on the household; occasionally calling in when she sensed the family had need of her wisdom.

Like now, for instance . . .

The Camera Does Not Lie

T he sound of the doorbell barely penetrated the master bedroom of StregaSchloss, where Baci Strega-Borgia stirred under a Siberian goosedown quilt that was as heavy as a meringue, three times softer and probably impossible to tell apart in a blind tasting. Thinking of meringues made her stomach growl loudly and she sent an unspoken telepathic apology to the tiny baby currently curled like a comma in her tummy – the tiny baby that was probably deafened by her digestive excesses.

Wedged up against Baci's ribcage, the baby narrowed its dark brown eyes. *Whatever was she on about* now? *'Gabble, gabble, sorry, always have had an embarrassingly rumbly tummy, especially when I'm pregnant, dear wee baby, sorry it's so loud in there, love you, can't wait to see you, aaargh, I'm ravenous . . .'* What a racket. *When would Mama learn to keep quiet?*

Baci's eyes sprang open. Across the darkening bedroom her husband Luciano had fallen asleep with a calf-bound copy of Dostoyevsky's *Crime and Punishment* across his face. Baci sighed. On the off chance that Luciano might wake up and offer to make her a cup of tea, she sighed again, this time with feeling. Nothing happened. It was no use, she was going to have to get up. Bother, bother, bother . . .

There she goes again, the baby groaned. Pressing its feet against its mother's spine and wedging its head against her navel, it rolled around in time to Baci's heartbeat – a manoeuvre that caused the majority of its mother's internal organs to register their extreme disapproval.

'Right, stop, ouch, OK. I'm getting up.' And doing a passable imitation of a beached whale, Baci rolled out of bed and landed on the floor with the grace and elegance usually associated with sacks of concrete.

Finding itself abruptly tilting downwards, the baby adopted an upside-down position and was just about to go back to sleep when it heard the faintest of voices whisper: *'Scratchy jumpers.'*

Neither word made sense since there was nothing

in the baby's world that scratched or jumped. Yet. What had caught the baby's attention was the voice itself. Even though it was only just audible, it was crystal clear, unlike Baci's muddled communications. Whatever or whoever had said *'Scratchy jumpers'* spoke the baby's language fluently. *Thank heavens – there was intelligent life on earth after all.*

The unborn baby's eldest sister Pandora was hunched over a cauldron she had filled with developing fluid. The unborn baby's other sister, Damp, was mentally adding developing fluid to a list of things to be avoided – along with scratchy jumpers, soapin myes and hairybrushes; the new addition included after she had unadvisedly dipped a thumb into Pandora's cauldron and sampled its contents. Now Damp sat in a corner of the darkened laundry room and thought dark, stinging, scratchy thoughts, while above her Pandora waited for her photographs to appear, as if by magic. In fact, Pandora thought, the whole photographic process was decidedly magical; starting with the overlooked and unlabelled birthday present she'd opened to discover that someone had given her a non-digital 35mm camera. When Pandora had examined it closely, she found the maker's name embossed in the camera's hidden interior:

i-caramba

it said, in tiny letters, reminding her of previous magical gadgets she'd come across – artefacts like the i'mat, the Multiplimuffin and the Alarming Clock. Recalling these, Pandora knew exactly who had given her this present.

Two months before, presumably after she had wrapped the i-caramba and hidden it with Pandora's other birthday presents, the children's beloved nanny, Mrs Flora McLachlan, had disappeared into the waters of Lochnagargoyle. No explanations could be found for this, no suicide notes, and unusually, no body was recovered from the loch. To say that the family was devastated was to understate the full horrific impact of the nanny's disappearance. Pandora still cried herself to sleep each night, only to wake every morning hoping that it had all been a nightmare. She couldn't believe that Mrs McLachlan was gone for ever, even though each passing day served to reinforce a message to the contrary; for had the nanny still been alive, surely some word of her continued existence would have made its way to the grieving Strega-Borgias. There had been a brief flicker of hope when Titus and Pandora found evidence of the nanny's survival engraved on an antique map; enough proof to lighten Pandora's despair temporarily and allow her belatedly to open her birthday presents and find Mrs McLachlan's magical gift. At least Pandora *assumed* that the i-caramba was magical, even if she hadn't yet discovered in what form this magic would manifest itself. Certainly it allowed her to take better photographs than she'd ever thought possible . . .

. . . Like this one, for instance. 'Look, here it comes,' she breathed, gripped, as she had been each and every time, by the wonder of the process that made captured light visible, by the alchemy that produced pictures on blank sheets of paper. Developing films and printing her own photographs made Pandora feel like a real photographer, but the chemicals necessary to the whole process had proved to be impossible to obtain locally. While waiting for more supplies to arrive by mail order, Pandora had been forced to send off several films to be developed commercially. As she looked, she saw that one piece of paper was floating on the surface of the liquid in the cauldron, a sheet on which an image of StregaSchloss was beginning to appear, its turrets and crenellations swimming into view in the developer. Damp stood up and tottered across the laundry room to stand beside Pandora, leaning into her big sister's leg, her hot, wet thumb temporarily removed from her mouth to facilitate speech.

'Up,' she muttered, remembering, just in time, the magic word, 'Now.'

Pandora bent down and scooped her up with some difficulty, since at two and a half Damp was no longer a small bendy baby but had metamorphosed into a wriggly, dense bundle with a determined agenda of her own.

'Let Damp see,' she demanded, her eyes wide in the red glow of the safety light.

'There, look. There's our house, Damp.' Pandora fished the print out of the developer and dropped it into the fixative, an even nastier-smelling liquid sloshing around in an antique soup tureen. 'And there's Mum, and Dad and— Oh *dear*. Well, never mind, I can always crop that bit out. How did he get in there?'

Damp leant closer, examining the photo carefully before deciding, 'Poor, poor Titus. Why mouth gone all funny?'

'More to the point,' said Pandora, 'how come I didn't see him standing there pulling that *awful* face? Good grief, his mouth is the size of a letter box and his eyes . . . What a complete moron. Surely they found him under a bush. Tell me we're not related—'

'Trees,' Damp interrupted, as if encouraging Pandora to stick to the point. 'Trees got man in them.'

Pandora dragged her gaze off the image of their brother-as-gargoyle and stared at a patch of deep shade indicated by Damp's pointing finger.

'A man?' Her brow furrowed. 'Are you *sure*?' She peered more closely at a shadowy blur to the right of the ruins of the old ice house at the edge of the photograph, but with little success. 'Nope, sorry. I can't make it out – or should I say *him*?'

'In trees. *Look*,' Damp insisted, her thumb creeping closer to her mouth for comfort. 'Hobbible man.' Her voice rose in pitch and volume as she continued to stare at the picture. 'Not *like* it, that MAN.'

'OK, OK. Calm down.' Sensing that Damp was on the edge of throwing a wobbly, Pandora flipped the photograph face down in the soup tureen and said with false heartiness, 'There. It's gone. The man's gone now,' adding under her breath, '*If* he was ever there in the first place . . .'

Temporarily reassured, Damp wriggled and squirmed in her big sister's arms, until Pandora was obliged to put her back down on the floor.

Vowing to examine the offending photograph later with the aid of a magnifying glass, Pandora tried to remember when exactly she'd taken it. In the print the trees were in leaf, her mother's pregnancy was enormously visible, Damp was— Hang *on*. Her thoughts skidded to a standstill. Damp was wearing a swimsuit and her golden glittery wellies; a combination that shrieked *Summer in Argyll*. As Pandora's body began to fill with ice she remembered the day that Damp had insisted on wearing this striking costume. She also remembered her parents' doomed attempts to persuade her to change into something more suitable. It had been the day when a professional photographer had showed up at StregaSchloss; the same day that Mrs McLachlan had disappeared. A day that would be engraved on Pandora's memory for ever. But – she shivered – a day many weeks *before* the i-caramba had come into her possession.

Therefore this photograph was impossible. It should not, could not exist. She must have made some sound, some involuntary whimper or sob, because Damp leant heavily against her legs and gazed up into her face. Trying to disguise her feeling of mounting hysteria, Pandora reached out and turned the photograph face-up in the tureen – and caught her breath. She'd missed the most important detail in the picture. Her hands began to tremble uncontrollably. In the photograph, the front door of StregaSchloss lay open, the hall beyond too shadowy to make out much detail save for . . .

Save for two figures in partial silhouette.

A middle-aged woman, her shape so achingly familiar that Pandora felt tears of longing well in her eyes: Mrs McLachlan bending slightly at the waist as she embraced a young girl . . .

A young girl who, in the here and now, held a dripping photograph in her wildly shaking hands – a photograph that shouldn't . . . couldn't exist.

For, Pandora's mind insisted, that photograph had to have been taken weeks *after* Mrs McLachlan had gone. Pandora had not possessed a camera before then. There was no possible explanation for— She blinked. There were numbers, very faint, like a date-stamp in the corner of the print. At least, she could see a five and an eight, which would be about right. It had been the fifth of August when

Mrs McLach— Pandora closed her eyes and took a deep breath – and groaned. *Repeat after me, Pandora,* she told herself. *There is no possible, logical explanation for the existence of this picture in my hands.*

The distant ringing of the front doorbell drew her back to the real world. Pandora opened her eyes and stared at the photograph. Looking at the tiny image of Mrs McLachlan made her chest hurt. Slowly she slid the print back into the tureen and blew her nose on a nearby pillowcase – an action that she *knew* Mrs McLachlan would have viewed with extreme prejudice. Pandora crossed the room and opened the shutters that had temporarily turned the laundry into a darkroom, and realized that the day was nearly over. In the distance the doorbell rang again; a long insistent ring, as if whoever was outside was growing impatient. Unaccountably, Damp burst into tears and fled across the twilit room to cling to Pandora's legs as if she never wanted to let go.

An Innocent Man

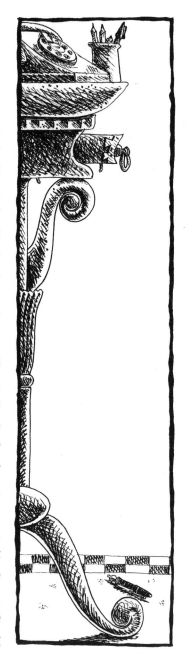

The policemen stood shoulder-to-shoulder on the doorstep of StregaSchloss, with jaws firm and their faces set in the Police Academy approved neutral-with-an-undertone-of-menace expression.

'Shall I do the honours? Sir?' the DS hissed.

'Let's just see who opens the door first, shall we, Detective Sergeant? No point in launching into your *spiel* if it's not your man, is there? Keep your powder dry, there's a good chap.'

The DS coloured. *Obviously* he wasn't about to caution a member of the suspect's family or staff. What did the Chief take him for? He was treating him like a moron, making out like the Highlands were policed by complete idiots whose heads buttoned up at the back. To which was added the injustice that this weasel-faced high-heid yin, this big cheese from Glasgow's Serious Crimes Unit had just swanned in and taken over *his* case.

Some of his resentment must have shown on his face because the blond DCI from the SCU raised his eyebrows and enquired in a whiny Glaswegian accent, 'Who rattled *your* cage, pal?' just as the front door was opened by a creature that looked as if cages might have been its specialist subject – and no, it didn't rattle them, it *bent* them like lengths of overcooked spaghetti. The creature stood about three metres high and appeared to be upholstered in well-seasoned dark leather. The policemen's first impression was that the door had been opened by a mutant lion, but as the creature turned its back to them and roared something incomprehensible into the interior of the house, they all caught sight of a perfect set of wings in co-ordinating battered leather, folding back against the beast's spine.

This, of course, was before the crocodile appeared behind the policemen, its teeth exposed in what might have been a smile of greeting, but, on the other hand, might not.

Hands stole towards weapons; the DS, who was woefully unarmed, clenched his fists so hard he drew blood.

Summoned by the leather creature, a boy

appeared at the top of the stairs, gracefully slung one leg over the banister and slid to the bottom, where he dismounted to slouch across the hall towards the front door.

'They're utterly harmless,' he said, following this complete fiction by turning to the two beasts and explaining, 'It's OK, guys. Chill. These are policemen. They won't do us any harm. They're here to protect us.'

Unfortunately, in this assumption Titus was entirely wrong. As Luciano came downstairs, alerted by the sound of voices in the hall, Titus realized how badly he'd misread the situation. As he was to remark later to Pandora, it would have been a far better idea just to instruct Sab and Tock to *eat* the policemen before . . . well, before they went ahead and arrested Luciano Strega-Borgia for murder on several counts.

'WHAT?' the suspected serial killer roared. 'Don't be bloody ridiculous. Do I *look* like a murderer? You're making a hideous mistake.'

The DS stepped forwards, cleared his throat and met the suspect's astounded gaze head-on. This was *it*. The moment he'd been waiting for. All those years of training. 'I must warn you, sir, that anything you say may be taken down and used in evid—'

Luciano batted at the air in front of his face as if brushing off an cloud of insects. 'Oh for heaven's sake, *Constable*, save it for some real criminals. Calm down. Now, come in out of the rain while I phone my lawyer.' Then he turned his back on the policemen and strode across the hall to where the telephone was balanced on a rickety pedestal table bearing the pockmarks of the battle it was losing to woodworm.

'Da-aad.' Titus's voice, which was passing through an unpredictable phase pitch-wise, chose this moment to swoop up an octave, causing him to blush horribly.

'Titus, would you be so kind as to put the kettle on and make a cup of tea for your mother? I'd rather she didn't come downstairs right now. No point in worrying her needlessly in her present condition.'

'DAD.' This came out as a deep growl, manly and gruff, showing a potential depth of which, had circumstances been otherwise, Titus could have been justifiably proud. Luciano was raking through the table drawer, scattering woodworm-generated sawdust in a hunt for his address book just as Titus reminded him of the pointlessness of such a search. 'Dad. *Dad.* Your lawyer's dead, remember? Uncle Lucifer shot him? Come *on.* Surely you haven't forgotten?'

Luciano froze, shock and fear replacing his previous expression of mild annoyance. No lawyer? What about that one he'd known years ago? What *was* his name again? Loopy? Lido? Surely there must have been more than *one* lawyer down there in the offices of Slander, Defame & Grabbit, W. S.? Did he still have their phone number? Granted, they weren't criminal lawyers, which was probably what was needed: S, D & G were tweedy types with overtones of beeswax polish; decent chaps, the fly-fishing-off-to-bed-at-nine-and-up-with-the-lark kind, slow and methodical estate lawyers. The sort of chaps, Luciano decided with a sinking feeling as a policeman's hand descended on his shoulder, *exactly* the sort of chaps who would rather *eat* their dusty law books than engage in the cut and thrust of legal debate in a criminal court. Nor, he realized, looking at his watch for confirmation, would Messrs S, D & Grabbit be *in* their dusty brown Auchenlochtermuchty offices at 4.30 p.m. on a Sunday afternoon in October. Chances were, they'd be in the clubhouse of the Auchenlochtermuchty Golf Course, talking incomprehensible twaddle about mashie niblicks and swapping tales of the ninth hole. Oh Lord, Luciano realized with a lurching sensation in his stomach, I think I might be about to spend a night in a police cell till this gets sorted out.

'*Titus*,' he squeaked, 'get Latch. *Now*.' And turning back to the policemen, he tried to smile innocently at his would-be captors, especially the weasel-faced blond one with the gratingly nasal Glaswegian accent and the hand that gripped his shoulder with quite unnecessary force. '*Please*.' Luciano laid his hand on top of the policeman's. 'Officer, there's no need for that. I'll come with you willingly. Answer all your questions. I'm an innocent man. I have nothing to fear—'

'Are you Luciano Perii Strega-Borgia, owner-occupier of StregaSchloss House, Lochnagargoyle, Auchenlochtermuchty, Argyll and Bute?' This was from the middle-aged policeman who'd made an earlier attempt to read him his rights. Irrelevantly, Luciano noticed that he'd missed a patch of grey bristle on his jawbone last time he'd shaved. And his mouth was moving, lips drawn back, teeth in shadow as the unbelievable words – lies and slanders – spilt forth.

'You are charged with the murder of the following . . .'

Names, a list of people, most of whom he'd never heard of, until, like a blurred picture coming into focus, Luciano began to recognize words, names, and started to see faces appear in the lens of his memory.

'. . . Vadette Kyle, Vincent Bella-Vista . . .'

Luciano almost smiled. This was ridiculous. He remembered *them*. A local builder and his girlfriend. Luciano had been in bed, with Baci, staying in a hotel, with witnesses, three miles away when *they'd* met their unfortunate ends—

'. . . Hugh Pylum-Haight, Ffion Fforbes-Campbell . . .'

Heavens, were they dead too? What a lot of murders they were trying to pin on him. On *him*? Ridiculous. What a waste of police time this was all turning out to be. He'd soon prove his innocence – or was that wrong? Wasn't he, Luciano Perii Strega-Borgia, innocent *until* proven guilty? Hah, he thought belligerently, just let them *try*.

Then, as if someone had pulled Luciano's plug, all his confidence and righteousness flooded away, leaving him beached, stranded and very afraid. One name was all it took.

'. . . Mrs Flora McLachlan.' The DS stood back and folded up the warrant for Luciano's arrest, using the fingernails of his thumb and index finger to give the document a wholly unnecessary knife-edge crease. He looked up and across his face flashed an expression of utter contempt for Luciano and everything that he stood for.

Luciano entered free-fall. 'But . . . but . . . no, NO, this is *wrong*,' he wailed, clinging to coat stands, door handles, stone statuary and suits of armour, abandoning all dignity as the policemen dragged him out of his house. His ears filled with a static hiss as he rolled past his white-faced son, and he felt his balance shift and tilt as he was dragged outside to the waiting car. Too late he saw Latch running towards him, the butler's long face made even more cadaverous by the police car's blue light, which was bathing the south face of StregaSchloss in its cold flash of alarm. Bundled into the back seat, Luciano began to weep hopelessly as Latch disappeared behind the rapidly accelerating car.

In a slew of rose quartz, the car skidded away

down the drive, hurtled along the track and was soon no more than a twin-beamed light below a flashing blue pulse; then it was swallowed up by darkness.

A Man Betrayed

Supper that night was a sombre affair; even if it had been edible, no-one would have had much appetite for it. Baci dabbed her eyes with a shredded tissue and sniffed continuously until, in a rare moment of parent/child role-reversal, Pandora passed her mother a sheet of kitchen roll and muttered, 'Don't *sniff*. Blow.'

Pale and silent, Titus for once didn't demand pudding, nor did he tilt his chair backwards until it crashed into the dresser when he stood up. He even cleared the table, stacked the dishes and began to wash up without being asked.

'Titus . . .' Baci's voice wobbled. 'Darling, leave those. They're Marie Bain's job.'

Titus ignored this, reasoning that he was there, in the kitchen, while Marie—

'Where *is* that woman?' Baci stood up, pushing her chair away from the table with such force that it crashed backwards into the dresser.

Pandora looked up from the table; she'd been repeatedly stabbing a rubbery oven chip into a pile of tomato ketchup and using it to polka-dot her plate with little daubs of scarlet condiment. 'Who cares?' she said under her breath. '*She* can't cook either.'

'MARIEEEEEEE!' Baci roared, causing Titus to upend an extravagant quantity of green washing-up liquid into the sink. Sighing mightily, he added a torrent of hot water from the tap, with spectacular results.

'Pretty,' Damp decided; she slid off the pile of lumpy cushions that brought her up to table height, and wobbled over to the sink to examine Titus's bubble-fest.

Baci swept across the kitchen radiating ire. '*Today* of all days,' she spat, dragging open the door. 'Not only am I forced to cook dinner, but we're expected to clear up afterwards? Why do we employ a cook? Where *is* she? This isn't her day off. MARIE! This is simply *not* on. Not only is she an absolutely rotten cook—'

Out of Baci's earshot, Pandora gasped, clutched her chest theatrically and rolled her eyes at Titus, who whispered, 'Do the words "pot", "kettle" and "black" ring any bells with you?'

Baci meanwhile disappeared into the gloom of the corridor and then came a slow thump-slither, thump-slithering sound, as if something very large and heavy was dragging itself downstairs. Thuuuump-slither, thummmmmp-slither – and then came their mother's voice: at first precise and icy – her Siberian-wind-chill, her nothing-can-withstand-this-temperature-and-live, her don't-mess-with-me-pal voice; the one she always used when she was assured of being right. The thumping sound speeded up – thumpthump-slither-thumpthump – and now Baci's inflection thawed somewhat; held the promise of ice melting; snowdrops poking through snowdrifts; an I'm-sure-we-can-come-to-some-agreement-or-*else* kind of tone.

A look passed between Titus and Pandora, and as one they crossed the kitchen to eavesdrop at the open door, leaving Damp sploshing happily in the soapily enhanced washing-up.

'Marie, come now, I'm sure we can work something out. Please? I need your help. Especially since Signor Strega-Borgia has been temporarily . . . detained. Here, let me help you back upstairs with your suitcase.'

There were more thumps now, and the unmistakable sounds of a struggle.

'Non, non, my mind ees make up. I go now, seenyora. Pliss to leave my valise alone.'

'Marie. What has come over you? Whatever is the

matter? Is it money? Do we need to review your salary? When Signor Strega-Borgia returns I'm sure we can come to some arrangement about an increase, a bonus – if you could just wait until my husband is released then we—'

'Non. Ees amposseeble. I 'ave, how do you say zis, grassed heem up, non?'

'I'm not sure I underst—'

'Monsieur Borgia. Eet was I who telephone the *gendarmes*. It was I who tell to zem your husband has keeled all zose—'

'Marie?' Baci's voice had shrunk, lost several decades of sophistication and elocution, and emerged as the raw howl of an abandoned child. 'Marieeeeeeee. Nooooo . . . Ohhhh, help . . .'

Titus and Pandora rushed to her assistance, leaving their little sister unattended in the kitchen. Damp blinked, seized a spoon and spun it wildly above her head. The bubbles in the washing-up bowl rose to the ceiling like a tornado, twisting upwards, spinning faster and faster until the soapy spiral began to bulge and distort, breaking free as Damp tried to summon the best help she could think of. In the centre of the blizzard of bubbles the faintest shape of a woman appeared, albeit briefly. Flora McLachlan, conjured in soap bubbles, looking as if she lived in a snow shaker. The phantom nanny opened her arms wide and Damp leant forward, eyes wide open, words tumbling from her mouth.

'*Not* say ba-bye. *Not* go away.'

For one brief, blissful instant she was embraced in warm arms, fell into the softness of pillowy chests, was surrounded by a fading scent of lavender . . . and then, as if by design, the bubbles all burst at once, making Damp wail as soap stung her eyes and her mouth filled with the bitter taste of detergent. Coughing and sobbing, she abandoned her attempt to conjure up a soapy phantom and ran for the flesh-and-blood comforts of her family.

Baci clutched Marie Bain's arm in a desperate attempt to delay the cook's departure, to understand what madness had overcome her, but to no avail.

'Ees no good you crying,' the cook hissed. 'I ees going now. I not vish to stay in zis house weeth a murrrrderrrrrerrrrr's *famille*. You all evil, here. You keep vild *animaux* een your basement. You ees all insane. Who knows, maybe I be your next veectim, *moi*. Maybe eef I not go, zey find *my* bones in ze mud at ze bottom of ze – ze – laichh.'

'*Loch*,' muttered Pandora.

'*Lake*,' Titus corrected.

'MOAT!' yelled Baci. 'Oh my God. Tell me you *didn't* say to the police that Luciano buried his victims at the bottom of the *moat*? Oh, you *stupid* woman. What have you *done*?'

'I haff told ze truth.' Silhouetted in the light now spilling from the downstairs WC, Marie Bain stood beside her outsized suitcase, her shoulders hunched and her head swivelling from side to side like a

44 ⎯⎯

cornered animal wondering from which direction death would strike.

'Shall I just toast her now and have done with it?' demanded Ffup, appearing behind the twitching cook. The dragon loomed over Marie Bain, her slowly unfolding wings adding a whole new dimension of menace to the tableau of cook and would-be cremater. The cook turned a ghastly shade of grey and staggered against her suitcase.

'Or . . . um . . . I *could* just asphyxiate her,' Knot said, emerging from the WC with a look of faint apology on the woolly expanse of matted fur that passed for a face among his fellow-yetis.

'AAAAAAAAND, if all else fails,' roared Sab, dropping out of the skies and flapping down to tower over the stone steps beyond the front door, retracting his wings with a finality that boded ill for the now sobbing Marie Bain, 'I could just remove her head from her worthless body and slam-dunk it in the loch.'

'Just GO!' Baci screamed. 'Get *out*. You faithless, betraying, lying—'

The cook needed no further invitation. She fled out of the house, half-fell, half-ran down the stone steps and vanished sobbing into the darkness. One minute later, to everyone's immense satisfaction, they heard her fall into the moat with a loud splash.

Familiarly Damp

Damp waited until the *schlep-schlepp* of Baci's mules had died away down the corridor before she opened her eyes. Despite having sobbed inconsolably for more than an hour following her attempt to reincarnate Mrs McLachlan in soap bubbles, and even after having had a grand total of five picture books read to her by assorted members of the family and beasts, and notwithstanding the soporific effects of a bath laced with camomile oil, Damp was still horribly awake.

Adults have a number of strategies lined up for those long dark nights when sleep is impossible and melancholy moves in to

take its place. Had she been a grown-up, Damp might have abandoned any hope of sleep and crept downstairs to the kitchen for the comfort of hot chocolate and a brainless bestseller, or even a stiff nightcap followed by a couple of pages of the writings of long-dead Roman philosophers. However, at only two and a half years old she had little choice but to lie awake in the dark and wonder when she might stop feeling sad. Damp didn't really understand the workings of time yet. She'd heard mention made of years, but if you've only been in the world for two and a half years, the concept of a period of time that encompassed almost half your life was – well, it was for *ever*. Or half of for ever, which is still an awfully long time. 'Soon' and 'later' and 'hang on a minute' and 'in two ticks' were equally incomprehensible when all you wanted to hear was 'yes, right now'. The past was 'once upon a time', the future was 'in a little while' or 'tomorrow', but to Damp, only 'now, right here and now' was real.

And, in Damp's opinion, right here and right now was really awful. Her eyes stung from soap and from crying so hard. Her head throbbed in time to her heartbeat. She was too hot, so she kicked off the quilt, then she began to shiver as the cold air dried her tears. Once upon a time there had been Mrs McLachlan's warm arms to hold her, gentle hands to stroke her cheek and a soft voice murmuring lullabies and stories to soothe her to sleep . . .

. . . there had been lavender water and ironed linen sheets . . . teddies stacked neatly on shelves, holes in tights mended and books and toys put away at the end of the day. There had been laughter and jokes, sunshine spilling in squares of gold onto the lemon-waxed nursery floor, light caught in spinning prisms in the window and scattering rainbows across the walls and ceiling. There had been nursery teas by the fire, toast fingers, soft-boiled eggs and homemade cakes. Downstairs had smelled of fresh bread, vanilla and lemons . . .

A sob caught in Damp's throat. Now StregaSchloss smelled rank. Like mould. Like slimy autumn leaves and old drains. Latch still lit the nursery fire every day, but no-one had the heart to unearth the toasting fork, or to soft-boil the eggs for tea. For some unaccountable reason the range in the kitchen appeared to be sulking and consequently Pandora's cakes either failed to rise or suffered such over-leavening that they flowed out of their pans and turned to carbon on the oven floor. Lemons rotted in the fruit bowl; Titus spilt the vanilla essence and no-one thought to replace it; freshly baked bread became a fading memory. In the dwindling light of autumn there wasn't even enough morning sunshine to set the rainbows spangling across the nursery.

Damp rolled on her side and stared at her bedroom floor – what little she could see of it beneath a tangle of discarded toys. Fuzzy felt and glitter speckled the floorboards like infant confetti thrown for the bizarre marriage of headless Barbie to legless Action Man. Also present were assorted Sylvanian Family members in varying states of undress, a selection of antique teddy bears with matted fur and mites, and a small velvet dog with a well-chewed foot – an item that bore evidence of having been loved almost to destruction. In the shadows lay disembowelled felt pens, toothmarked Lego, annoyingly redundant bits of sticky plastic which had once been shoes for small dolls, all of whom now lay footless and naked under Damp's chest of drawers.

Hanging from the curtains and surveying the chaos, the little bat squinched his wings in closer to his body and shuddered fastidiously. Not only was this new cave a complete tip, but his new mistress was leaking. Wet stuff sounds completely different to dry stuff when listened to via echolocation. The bat emitted a series of high-frequency squeaks and then concentrated fiercely. There. Well. That *was* a relief. Only leaking from *one* end.

Unaware that she was under surveillance, Damp rolled over, presented her back to the nursery chaos and turned her face to the wall.

'Whoops, no—' The bat squeaked in alarm. In his experience, when humans turned their faces to the wall, it wasn't in order to examine the wallpaper. It was a sign of surrender, or losing interest in life; a prelude to death. He panicked – 'No! No way, ma'am. Not when I'm on dooty. Code *Red*. Repeat. Code Red. I'm going in' – and launching himself into space, plummeted from the curtain rail, in his haste unfortunately omitting to unfold his clenched wings before take-off.

'Mayday, mayday!' he squawked, tumbling wings over toes, falling in a squeaking, shrieking bundle onto an oversprung ottoman, and from there bouncing straight onto Damp's bed.

'I'm down!' he yelled, somewhat unnecessarily, his high-pitched shriek just within range of Damp's hearing. 'OK, team. Here we go. I'm going to try and establish contact with the ur-witch.'

'Go 'way,' Damp muttered, not deigning to turn over and see whatever had flopped onto her bed and was now making noises like something in dire need of a spot of axle-grease.

The bat's eyes glowed and he upped his squeaker volume somewhat. Extending his wings, he heaved a sob of gratitude. 'Finally, they *unfold* – oh let my joy be unconfined.' Then he hobbled and flapped across the patchwork quilt, scrabbled up onto Damp's shoulder, wrapped his toes round a lock of her hair and abseiled down to land right on a horribly soggy patch of pillow in front of her face. Understandably, Damp's eyes widened and her mouth opened in preparation for a good howl, but before she could emit as much as a squeak, the bat wrapped one wing round her lips and said, 'Please. No. Ma'am. *Don't*. Don't *scream*. I come in peace, humanchild.'

Damp blinked, her lips moving under his wing.

'Pardon me, ma'am? Oh, I'm sorry. We haven't been introduced, and here I am taking liberties with your face. I'm Vesper, at your eternal service. Familiar, friend and flying consultant.' The bat fluttered away across Damp's pillow, scrabbled up to the top rail of her bedstead, wrapped his bony toes around it and effortlessly swung upside down. He dangled from this new perch, apparently unaware that he was sharing it with a pink fun-fur Incy-Wincy and a glow-in-the-dark star.

Damp gazed up at the visitor and Vesper blinked back. He certainly wasn't the first bat the little girl had encountered; living at StregaSchloss ensured that the Strega-Borgias and their staff were accustomed to meeting small flying creatures navigating the many corridors and stairwells in the house. Indeed, bowls of decomposing fruit were left out as food for the fruit-eating species, and Tarantella regularly donated sun-dried bluebottles and houseflies for the enjoyment of the insectivorous types. Nor was Damp perplexed by *this* bat's command of English: her age group regarded talking animals as hardly worthy of comment; children's literature leads the young to *expect* their pets to chat. Nor was she in the least bit frightened at the prospect of sharing her bed with a winged mammal so beloved of the writers of horror movies; fortunately she was too media-innocent to know that tradition demanded that she should now run screaming down a darkened corridor, clutching a guttering candelabrum and pursued by a flapping bat.

Damp attempted a tentative smile and wriggled into a sitting position. 'Show me,' she demanded, adding, after a second's pause, 'Please? Now?'

'Heavens, ma'am,' Vesper gasped. 'You humans don't hang about, do you?'

'Yes. Want it. Want to hang about.' Damp stood up, the bedsprings creaking in protest. 'Wantit, wantit, wantit—'

'Right. OK. Calm down, ma'am. Rome wasn't built in a day and all that classical jazz. One thing at a time. If you want to hang like a bat, first you've got to learn toe control, right? Nunna that "This little piggy" nonsense. I'm talking toes that're just as happy picking up grains of rice, one at a time, as clinging to a windswept twig. Got me? Then we move on to headstands, yeah?'

Damp nodded, her eyes gleaming, her mouth upturned in a wild grin. If she'd been asked what was different between right here and right now and the once upon a time of, say, ten minutes before, it was that for the first time in two months, ever since Mrs McLachlan had disappeared, she was free of the big heavy hurt inside her chest.

Lost in Time

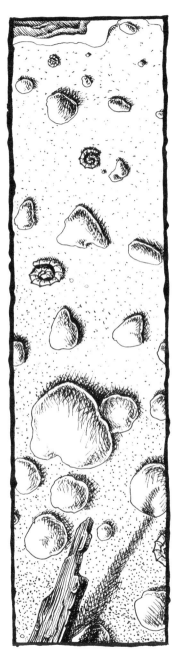

A chilly mist rolled in from the sea-loch, swallowing the shoreline and bejewelling the island's few trees with pearls of dew. As the sun faded behind the mist's grey veil, the temperature plummeted. By Mrs McLachlan's reckoning, today marked the beginning of the third month they'd been here. In an attempt to make sense out of the confusion of these days, she'd been marking time ever since they'd arrived on the island. At the end of that first awful day, when all was lost and she could barely see for the tears that threatened to drown her all over again, she had found a large piece of driftwood by the shore and carefully embedded it in the sand above the high-tide mark. Since then, she'd been arranging pebbles around it in an ever-increasing spiral, one laid in place at sunset every day. Her fellow castaway watched her in silence, picking his teeth with a sharp twig and huddling closer to their little driftwood fire. Mrs McLachlan bent to place a rose-quartz pebble on the outermost arm of the spiral and paused, struck by a persistent but fading memory.

A house . . . that was it . . . a huge sprawling extravagance of a house . . . surrounded by a pink sea of rose-coloured stones, just like this one she was holding in her hand. Stone steps lead . . . up to a door which lies half-open, inviting the eye into the shadowy spaces beyond. She hears the far-off murmur of voices; a peal of laughter; the upraised carol of children playing. There is warmth on her back, late summer's sunshine turning trees to golden lace. She looks down to her hands and sees that in one she holds a silver thread, and in the other . . . a child. A girl. Not the little one, but her sister. She needs to tell the girl something important. To explain why she has had to leave so abruptly. To comfort the girl, for the child's eyes have the bruised appearance of the grieving. Don't worry, she wants to say, I still breathe. But the girl turns away and now Mrs McLachlan is running, away from the house; the sky darkens and she is in woods, running and running; the light flickering on-off, on-off through the slender birch trunks. She is weaving a path, just as she weaves a silver thread through the trees. She must not let go. No matter what else is lost, she must not let go and lose the thread.

The rose-quartz pebble falls from her hand to land in the middle of the spiral, clattering against the driftwood in the dead centre. And now it is followed by a tear, and then another, for Flora McLachlan has paid a high price for her journey to this island. Her memory is fading rapidly with each passing day. The images of everyone she loved slip through her mind like sand through her fingers. Even the names of the children in her care have washed from her memory, as if she'd written them in the sand at low tide. She has tried so hard to bring their names back; but try as she might, she cannot retrieve them. Yet she feels their absence like the phantom limbs of an amputee . . .

An exasperated hiss came from the direction of the figure hunched by the fire and she hastily put the fallen pebble into its proper place on the spiral's perimeter. There. Fifty-seven pebbles. Fifty-seven days and counting, wondering for what felt like the millionth time where on earth she was. Was she dead? She couldn't be. Immortals don't die despite their best attempts at suicide. No, she wasn't dead, but Death was taking ages to answer her summons. In times gone by Flora had courted Death by various means; not through a desire to end her life, but because suicide was the quickest way to call Death to her side. On previous occasions she had travelled light, with no luggage and no travelling companion. This time the journey had been entirely different, her travelling companion a demon and her luggage, such as it was, lethal. It consisted of one small stone, no different from all the myriad others on this island; no different save in one respect – that this stone had always been in existence. Always. With this stone the ebb and flow of Time began. The Earth in which it is buried came much, much later. Aeons after the stone, after the Earth had cooled, and long after the ice had retreated, mankind arrived and in its ignorance sought to pin a label to the mystery, calling the stone names by which they might know it: Chronostone, Pericola d'Illuminem, even Ignea Lucifer. In its name men spilt blood and destroyed countless lives, fuelled by a desperate desire to own it, this diamond-like gem which, had they but realized, could not be possessed by anything mortal.

The Chronostone was a neutral source of un-imaginable power, in itself neither good nor evil; neither magical nor divine. Like a humungous battery, it could be used to enable the kind of spells and enchantments that could cause whole galaxies to implode; to make stars ignite and the heavens fall to Earth. The Chronostone could alter the balance between the powers of Light and Darkness, and for this reason Mrs McLachlan had flung herself and it into Lochnagargoyle in the hope of depositing her dangerous luggage in the safety of Death's realm. At least this had been her plan back then, fifty-seven days ago. Being immortal, she had anticipated washing up some hours later on the shores of Lochnagargoyle, mercifully minus stone and with a convenient but minor memory loss . . .

Unfortunately, she hadn't reckoned on having a travelling companion along with her luggage. When Flora had thrown herself into the loch, she'd been accompanied by a creature which had issued from Hades, intent on killing her and retrieving the Chronostone for its Master. The demon Isagoth, emissary from His Satanic Majesty, S'tan. Isagoth, the hunched and shivering demon who now huddled by the driftwood fire and moaned continuously about the weather, the lack of variety in his diet, the uncomfortable nature of his heather bed, the weather, the tastelessness of fish, his aches and pains, the weather, his recent bout of insomnia, the absence of toilet paper . . . The insufferable demon Isagoth who, by use of his vocal cords alone, was turning this little corner of a foreign island into a new Hell.

Almost as if she'd spoken this thought out loud, Isagoth snickered and looked at her. He waved her over, patting the heather beside him, inviting her to join him.

'Hey, c'mon, Flora,' he said. 'Take a load off. Relax. Pull up a tussock.' His face creased up in a grin that seemed almost human – until Mrs McLachlan reminded herself that she was sharing this island with a *demon*. Whether Isagoth was being genuinely friendly or fiendly was hard to tell; after so much time spent in the demon's company she was becoming less certain where, on a moral litmus paper, black would cede to white. It appeared that even demons had their angelic moments, even if such occurrences were rarer than snowballs in furnaces.

'Cold, huh?' Isagoth complained, hunching his shoulders and shuffling so close to the fire that Mrs McLachlan feared he'd set himself alight. Staring into the flames, he sighed heavily, gnawed at a hangnail, and then, not waiting for a reply, said, 'D'you know, I woke up this morning and for a moment I couldn't remember my name.' The demon's expression was one of acute melancholy. 'Every day we're here I'm growing weaker – more forgetful. At first I thought it was just the aftermath of drowning; you know, even for an immortal like me, that *was* pretty tough. But then I realized I was forgetting all sorts of small things: my shoe size, what I take in my coffee, the best route between Purgatory and Perdition – all trivial stuff – but this morning, for a second, I forgot who I was, or what I was doing here. It felt as if we've always been here, with me staring into the flames while you play hide-and-seek with the stone.'

At the mention of the Chronostone Mrs McLachlan sighed. Here we go again, she thought.

'You may as well give it to me, you know,' Isagoth began wearily.

'Oh, dear me, Mr Isagoth. We've been through this before, many times. I cannot give it to you. Not even if I wanted to. I do not remember where I hid it. You are welcome to try and find it among the many millions of other similar stones on this island. But even if you do find it, you won't be able to use it—'

'Yeah, yeah, yeah. Because this place is out of Time; it's, er, a limbo in which memory fades, powers dwindle to nothing yadda yadda, blah, blah, blah. Yup. Heard it all before.' Morosely, Isagoth kicked at the edges of the driftwood fire with one boot. Sparks flew up into the air, peppering the darkening sky with pinpoints of light which flared and dimmed, drifting back to earth as smudges of carbon.

'D'you know, Flora, right now, if I *had* a soul, I'd trade it for a little black cigar.'

Mrs McLachlan tutted disapprovingly. 'Then, Mr Isagoth, you must regard your present sojourn on this island as a health cure. Even though your soul is as black as pitch, there's no need to have co-ordinating lungs.'

With a heartfelt sigh, the demon climbed to his feet and stretched his arms up to the sky, flexing his long fingers and glancing at Flora. 'I don't think we'll be stuck here for much longer,' he said gloomily. 'I was supposed to return that stone to Hades no later than the autumnal equinox or . . . face the consequences.' Isagoth fell silent, his expression betraying just how ghastly he imagined those consequences would be. 'I don't want to go back without the stone,' he murmured. 'It would be . . . messy.'

Mrs McLachlan tutted sympathetically, drawing her cardigan tighter around her shoulders; though whether this was against the misty chill rolling in from the loch or in reaction to the implied awfulness of her companion's fate it was hard to determine. Isagoth was in full flow now, lost in horror at his Boss's fiendishness, his corrupt black-heartedness, his innate evilness, his natural-born malevolence—

'What's that?' Mrs McLachlan interrupted. 'Look, out there. In the mist.'

Isagoth's eyes narrowed. Surrounded as they were by a dismal shroud of grey, it took him no time at all to spot a faint yellow glow out on the water. The light bobbed and wobbled, growing brighter by the moment, drawing nearer until they both heard the dip and creak of oars and, finally, a faint voice calling, 'Land ahoy. I say, can you hear me?'

Ahead, the grey parted like curtains on a stage, drawing back to reveal a man standing in the bow of a black rubber dinghy. Behind him, two hooded figures plied the oars that pulled the boat to shore. Nearer it came, until both Mrs McLachlan and Isagoth could clearly see what lay ahead.

The dinghy was full of holes – its fabric rotted away to a perished mesh that was about as buoyant as a lead brick. The oars were full of worm, their paddles long gone, eaten down to two poles with which the hooded figures punted to shore. Mrs McLachlan's gaze skidded across the shadows that lay beneath the hoods of the oarsmen; shadows whose black depths she had no wish to explore. Instead, she met the familiar grey stare of the man in the bows, who extended a hand in greeting.

'Flora, my dear. Enchanted as ever. Is it time?' And leaping from his ruined craft, Death came ashore.

The Loveliness of Teenagers

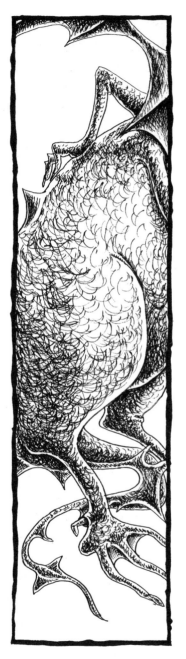

The morning following Luciano's arrest dawned warm and sunny, lending an atmosphere of faint cheer to the devastated household. Sunlight glinted on the crystal glass of orange juice on Baci's breakfast tray. Tiny rainbows danced across cream porcelain dishes embossed with tiny bats, dappling toast and marmalade alike and decorating her linen napkin with myriad speckles of colour. Latch balanced the tray on one hand and knocked on the door of the master bedroom.

'Moddom?'

Silence rolled along the corridors of StregaSchloss, pounding at the butler's ears, filling them with the sound of his own heart, its beat rapid after climbing the stairs between the great hall and his mistress's bedroom. Then came a muffled sob and Latch's thudding heart clenched with pity. The poor Signora – he well understood what it was to lose a partner.

'Moddom?' he whispered, his mouth against the door. 'It's nearly, ah, eleven o'clock . . .' He paused, uncertain how to continue, trying to rise above the sadness that threatened to overwhelm him. 'I thought perhaps some breakfast – to fortify you for the day ahead . . .'

At the sound of renewed sobbing, Latch clutched the tray in both hands and slumped against the door, at a loss for how to proceed: sobbing mistresses and arrested masters did not feature largely in a butler's command of etiquette. Suddenly the problem was taken out of his hands. Literally.

'I'll have THAT,' a voice roared, and before he could utter so much as a bat squeak of protest, Baci's breakfast tray was scooped out of his hands: with a fiery blast Ffup barged into the bedroom, crockery clattering, toast flip-flopping to the carpet in the dragon's haste to arrive, snorting, beside Baci's bed. And such was Baci's absorption in her own misery that she failed to look up and pay attention to the vast dragon who was hunting for a level surface upon which to lay down the breakfast tray.

'Oh, please. Come *on*,' Ffup roared, clearing a space on the dressing table with a swift and catastrophic sweep of her tail. 'No-one needs *that* many moisturizers' – *crash, tinkle, smash* – 'Come on, woman. Get a grip, would you? Quit wallowing and sit up' – *chingg, thud, choink, tinka* – 'Here, have some toast. I try to avoid it myself, but carbohydrates are good when you're feeling blue.' And reaching down to retrieve them from the carpet, Ffup sanitized the slices of toast by blowing on them, unfortunately forgetting to turn off her nasal flamethrowers. 'OOPS!' she squeaked, dropping two flaming toast triangles to the floor, where they smouldered cheerily on top of an irreplaceable silk kilim.

Standing outside the open bedroom door, Latch could take no more. Holding up one hand to prevent his eyes from witnessing his mistress in a state of partial undress, he rushed into the room and extinguished the burning carpet by smothering the flames with the first thing that came to hand.

'My cashmere shawl . . .' Baci moaned, her grief over losing Luciano replaced, albeit temporarily, by a far sharper and more immediate anguish at the sight of her favourite garment being reduced to cinders. 'No – no, NO. Please, Latch, use this instead.' Forgetting her vastly expanded waistline and perpetual state of nausea, Baci fell out of bed, hauled herself upright and, with a moan of dismay, threw up on both burning carpet and cashmere with a commendable lack of favouritism.

'Oh heck,' whimpered the dragon, as the first whiff of toasted vomit wafted past her nostrils. Staggering slightly, Ffup compounded the damage by leaning over Baci's recently vacated bed and following her mistress's example.

'Blaark,' she explained incoherently, wiping her mouth with the scaly back of her paw. 'I was just about to tell you-arrpfllll.'

Latch closed his eyes in denial. No. Surely this wasn't happening to him?

The dragon interrupted his meditations with an encore. 'Been feeling grim for a couple of w-halllp.'

It was insufferable, Latch thought. As the last remaining domestic servant at StregaSchloss, he would land the unwelcome task of mopping up huey.

But Ffup had the last word on the subject: 'Looks like Nestor'll have a wee broth-arrrgh, blaark.'

Latch fled downstairs, slamming the kitchen door behind himself and leaning back against it, wild-eyed and panting. Such was his state of panic that it was some moments before he realized that an unknown teenager was giving him the thousand-mile stare from across the kitchen table. Titus's head swam into view from behind the open door of the fridge.

'Ah, yeah. Latch. Rand. Um. Meet Latch, our, um, ah, yeah, well . . .' Horribly embarrassed at having to admit that his parents employed staff, Titus came to a halt and emerged from the fridge with a jar of mayonnaise in one hand and a baking tray bearing the congealed oven chips from the previous night's supper in the other. A painful silence fell when it became apparent that Titus's friend was ignoring this opportunity to be introduced to the butler.

Shy, thought Latch kindly, bending at the waist in an attempt to make eye contact with Rand, who sat with his head down, face shrouded in a veil of hair, apparently utterly engrossed in picking at a splinter on the table. Latch sighed. Now here was a young man for whom the word 'sullen' might have been invented. Obviously a newly conscripted member of Titus's fledgling band, the appositely named Alien Brothers. Latch frowned, trying to remember who it was that Sulky was replacing. Unwashed? No, he left ages ago. Grunty? Yes. That was it. Dear Grunty. Runt-like in stature, *that* poor adolescent had barely come up to Latch's armpits, but what he had lacked in height, he'd more than made up for in Neanderthal utterances. Drums? Bass? Or had he sung? Surely not, Latch mused. Singing involved words, and he'd never heard Grunty speak more than a single syllable at a time. What had it been again? *Unnh.* Yup. That was it.

Latch's speculations were interrupted by Titus, who was still trying his hardest to be polite, even if his efforts were accompanied by the gruesome sight of his semi-masticated mouth contents, which popped into view every time he opened his lips.

'And yeah, um, this is Rand, our new, um, er – hey, just what would you call yourself, huh?'

The teenager in question looked up from his study of the grain pattern on the kitchen table and Latch bit his lip to stop himself from voicing his disgust at what he saw. Rand's entire face was punctured in countless places: his eyebrows were wrapped in so many surgical steel loops that his very skin appeared to be made from metal. His nose was studded with multiple gold dots, so that he appeared to have suffered an attack of pricelessly valuable acne. His lips and chin were also pierced and his ears were cuffed, chained and a-dangle with crosses, ankhs and tiny daggers. As he began to speak, Latch noted that the teenager's top molars were inset with tiny diamonds and, horror of horrors, there was even a piercing on both his tongue and – Latch blinked – his eyeball, but ... how ...? The butler closed his eyes in sheer disbelief.

However, the worst obscenity was the boy's words. Words that pierced and wounded far more than any backstreet tattooist.

'I'd call myself a musician, Titus, actually.' The voice was cut-glass, confident of its owner's worth, educated enough to calculate that worth down to the last troy ounce, which was why there was no excuse for what came next: 'That is *if* I ever spoke to servants. Which I don't.'

It was at this point that the kitchen door opened and Pandora came in, her hair wrapped in a towel and her face pink and shiny from the shower.

'Um, yes. I mean, *no*. I mean *what*?' Titus's voice wobbled, betraying his deep desire for the earth to rise up and swallow him. He'd had no *idea*. Rand was behaving like a – like a total—

'Who's your punctured pal?' muttered Tarantella, dropping down from the dresser and announcing herself as another witness to Titus's discomfiture. 'Doesn't his face set off the metal detectors at airports? Let's deport him anyway, shall we? Like, back to the seventeenth century where he belongs?'

Latch opened his eyes and looked at Titus. He gave a stiff little bow from the waist and said, 'Will that be all for now, *sir*?'

'Ex*cuse* me?' Pandora laid a hand on Latch's arm to detain him. 'Did I miss something here?'

Silence greeted her query until, finally, Tarantella took it upon herself to translate for Pandora's benefit. 'Sieve-features here' – she flung out a furry leg in Rand's direction – 'has just announced that not only is he utterly stupid – witness his facial perforations – but he also does a nice line in condescension bordering on bigotry. In short, he's a perforated plon—'

Whatever she'd been about to say was lost to posterity: Baci Strega-Borgia appeared in the kitchen, her recovery testament to the miraculous curative properties of inhaling burnt cashmere when suffering from morning sickness.

'Titus, what was that man's name?' she demanded, unaware that she'd walked into an atmosphere so poisonous one almost required breathing apparatus in order to survive.

Unobserved, Tarantella scuttled back up to her dresser-top vantage point and began to apply lipstick to her mouthparts as Baci babbled on. 'That man – the lawyer one on the radio the other day. Oh come *on*, Titus. We all heard him. That Edinburgh one who'd never lost a case. Remember? Sab said' – Baci closed her eyes, grimacing as she tried to recall the exact words – 'he said if *he* was ever in trouble, that lawyer would be the one he'd want. Oh, if only I could remember . . .'

'Munro MacAlister Hall.'

Baci peered gratefully at Titus through eyes that swam with tears. 'Darling. Thank you. And thank heavens for your good memory – you certainly didn't inherit *that* from my side of the family—'

'Mum. It wasn't me who spoke,' Titus broke in. 'It was Rand. Munro MacAlister Hall is his dad.' And *that*, he thought to himself, is probably why Rand is such an insufferable snot-bag. He'll have to go, Titus decided, automatically reaching for the comfort of food. He shovelled cold oven chips onto a plate and decanted a quivering globule of mayonnaise on top. There. First, this modest snack, I think, followed by a short practice and then I'll pluck up the courage to give Rand the boot. He may be an outstanding key-board player, but that doesn't make up for treating Latch like something he'd found stuck to the sole of his shoe. Titus crammed a handful of cold chips into his mouth and chewed. He had to find a replace-ment for Rand. The question was when.

He looked across the table: Rand was trying to pretend he wasn't watching Pandora dry her hair over by the range. Yeah, well, Titus thought. There was *another* reason Rand had to get the heave. It was becoming horribly obvious that he had a thing about Pandora. Ugh. Titus shuddered. It was just so *embarrassing*. He was gazing at Pandora as if she was the first girl he'd ever seen and he couldn't quite believe the evidence of his eyes.

'Let's go,' Titus mumbled, keen to put distance between his sister and his about-to-be-ex keyboard player. 'C'mon. Rand?'

Ignoring this and turning to face Mrs Strega-Borgia, Rand shrilled, 'My father's the top criminal lawyer in Scotland,' thereby demonstrating that his face jewellery wasn't the only piercing thing about him; his voice was as high-pitched and squeaky as it had been when he was an infant.

'*Rand*,' Titus insisted, pointedly holding the kitchen door open. With obvious reluctance and a last lingering glance at Pandora, Rand climbed to his feet and slouched out, humming under his breath with an expression of deep inward con-centration on his face. Titus tried not to laugh. If he

wasn't stopped, Titus suspected that Rand would begin to compose love songs in which his sister's name would feature heavily. As he followed Rand into the corridor, a grin crept across Titus's face. Rand, he decided, had still to discover how impossible it was to find a decent word that rhymed with Pandora.

Brains Over Brawn

As the first chords of *She Wore a Fedora* rattled windows and dislodged StregaSchloss roof tiles, Baci replaced the telephone handset, superstitiously crossing her fingers and hoping she'd Done The Right Thing. Over two months had passed since Mrs McLachlan had vanished, and with Marie Bain now gone and Luciano temporarily imprisoned, Baci had been left with little choice. She had a sneaking suspicion that Titus and Pandora wouldn't agree; would in fact throw synchronized wobblies and refuse to speak to her for at least a week, but eventually they'd get over it.

Course they would.

Wouldn't they? Baci looked around Luciano's study as if she could gain assurance from her husband's possessions in much the same way as she used to from his continuing presence in their lives . . . She shook her head, blinking rapidly. She simply *must* stop thinking about Luciano in the past tense. He'd be home just as soon as—

Baci took a deep breath, closed her eyes, opened them and stared at the pewter-framed photograph on the desk in front of her. There they were, she and Luciano, long before the children were born, impossibly young and totally, utterly, rapturously in love, walking hand-in-hand across the Piazza Maggiore in Bologna. Doves broke from the shadows, flying up on either side of them. The photograph captured that single moment for ever, a second in their lives, all those years ago. She'd woven tiny cream rosebuds into her hair that day and Luciano still had all his hair then. Oh, but they looked so young and happy in that long-ago Italian springtime of balmy, blossomy promise . . .

Baci's eyes began to swim and she shifted her gaze to the huge window overlooking the meadow. Leaden skies promised more rain, and the wind had stripped the branches of the sweet chestnut planted many years ago by Luciano's great-grandmother. Drawing strength from the shades of Borgias long dead, Baci vowed to overcome this rather grim phase of their family history. That morning she'd engaged the services of a man who was reputedly one of the best lawyers in Scotland. This had been marginally less stressful than her next task, which she'd been unable to postpone any longer. Ten minutes ago she'd taken the first steps towards finding a new nanny for the children. It's *not* a betrayal, she told herself firmly. I am not giving up hope that Mrs McLachlan will . . . be found. Alive. Not at all. But right now I need to hire a temporary . . . replacement. Bleakly, Baci considered how impossible it was to replace Flora McLachlan. She'd been so much more than a nanny. Flora had been a friend, a confidante, a big sister, a teacher, a mother almost . . . At this last, Baci laid her head on Luciano's desk and was on the point of bursting into tears when she was rewarded with a stiff kick in the ribs from her tiny passenger, the unborn baby Borgia, outraged at the sudden shrinkage in its accommodations.

Also suffering from a major down-sizing of his living quarters, Luciano Strega-Borgia was gazing in disbelief at what passed for lunch *chez* cell number three below the High Court in Glasgow. His lunch tray, slid through a hatch cut into the vertical bars of the cell door, bore one smear of dubious meat-product sandwiched between two curling slices of white bread; a plastic knife of such flimsy construction that it wilted in the heat from Luciano's hand; and one tiny carton of tropical fruit drink. This, when opened, scored a direct hit on Luciano's jacket with a squirt of indelible orange fluid that had no connection with the tropics or indeed with any fruit grown on earth. However, these crimes against gastronomy faded to beige beside the horrors lying in wait inside a white polystyrene cup. This held possibly the foulest, nastiest liquid ever to pass Luciano's lips since the *gluhwein* Marie Bain had prepared for a StregaSchloss drinks party some years ago, ad-libbing ingredients with catastrophic effect. To that day Luciano had been unable to look at a tube of Araldite without twitching uncontrollably, and he still had nightmares about watching a local farmer trying to prise his lips apart after quaffing what amounted to superglue diluted in hot claret; a sight Luciano was unlikely to forget. Ever.

But the contents of that cup, masquerading as *cappuccino* ... Tears came to Luciano's eyes as it dawned on him that this vile liquid might be the closest he was going to get to coffee for some time. He'd tasted better bathwater. Peering morosely at his reflection in his pretend coffee, Luciano's morale sank to an all-time low. Looking around the cell, he sensed that 'low' was a relatively elevated position when compared to the depths to which his cell-mates had fallen.

Slouched on the bench opposite was a pallid mountain of human flesh propped up on one side by what Luciano initially took to be a bundle of jaundiced sticks. He blinked. The sticks folded themselves into a different arrangement, revealing as they did so that they were the limbs of one of the most skeletal human beings he had ever seen. The sticks gave voice, rubbing their tonsils together in such a fashion that Luciano feared they'd set their owner on fire.

'Right, big mawn,' they rasped, 'seez a cup a coffee. A'm that thirsty ah cud spit.' And with this logic-defying statement, the sticks toppled backwards onto the bench. The man-mountain heaved and shuddered, stretching out one vast arm towards the cell door, where another tray had been pushed through the hatch.

'Err yiz go, Malky,' said Man-Mountain, flashing Luciano what might have passed for a polite smile in shark society, then snapping his teeth shut before continuing, 'Ah wiz gaggin' fir this, me.'

Luciano smiled nervously; he prayed that this hadn't been an utterance requiring an answer, since he had no idea what had just been said. In his confusion and embarrassment he bent his head and took a large gulp from his coffee cup before he remembered how bad it had tasted. Halfway through an automatic swallow, he tried to apply reverse thrust and succeeded only in spraying his front with regurgitated coffee-*faux*.

Across the cell Malky and Man-Mountain watched with interest, pausing only to take long slurping mouthfuls of their own identical beverages. When Luciano's splutters had ceased and he could once more draw breath without choking, Malky stretched out a scrawny arm in his direction. Puzzled, Luciano held out his hand, wondering if even in *this* place good manners were still the norm.

'Naw, naw,' Malky grated. 'Ah don't wan' ter shake yer haund. Ah'm no wantin' your *germs*. Geez yer coffee if yer no wantin' it.'

Luciano obliged, passing across the cup with a hand that he could not stop from shaking.

'Awwww. The wee man's feart,' observed Malky; he drained Luciano's cup and narrowed his eyes with pleasure, though whether this was at the joy of drinking more execrable coffee or of realizing that he'd successfully intimidated Luciano it was hard to tell. 'Eh, Big Brian,' he continued, sinking an elbow into his companion's considerable gut, 'see if the wee man's got any snout on him. Ah fancy a smoke, eh no?'

Luciano shut his eyes in horror. He *was* going to die. He just knew it. Here, in a filthy cell below the ironically named Courts of *Justice*, he, Luciano Perii Strega-Borgia – an innocent man, a man who paid his taxes on time, a man whose family's considerable tax burden had probably helped *build* this hell-hole, a decent man who had never laid a finger on another being with harmful intent, a kind man who rescued spiders from baths and loved his wife and children to distraction . . .

'Aw look, Brian,' the hateful rasp continued. 'The wee man's cryin'.'

Luciano opened his eyes and saw that if he died now, the last written words he'd ever clap eyes on were: Tongs ya bas natcherl born Killers scrawled in what looked ominously like blood on the wall behind Malky's head. Taking a deep breath, Luciano called on his ancient Roman heritage and stood up, fixing Man-Mountain with what he hoped was a flinty stare. To his astonishment, Luciano realized that what was needed here was intelligence, not brute strength.

'I only wish you'd given me a chance to warn you about that coffee,' he began, giving a rueful and faintly apologetic smile before continuing, 'But you were in such a hurry, you'd drunk it before I could explain. I wonder, do they have an isolation unit in this building? Infectious diseases unit? Barrier nursing, breathing apparatus, air scrubbing? Heavens, I do hope so. Wouldn't want to be responsible for wiping out the entire population of the west of Scotland—'

'WHAT?' Malky sat bolt upright. 'What're youse on about?'

'They arrested me at Glasgow Airport,' Luciano improvised. 'I'm a scientist. I synthesize tropical diseases. You know? Things for which there is no cure. Like bilharzia, dengue haemorrhagic fever, plague, hantavirus, Ebola, Lassa fever . . .'

Malky's complexion had bleached to light oak rather than sunbed-assisted mahogany. 'Whit's he sayin', Big Brian? Ah don't understaun'.'

'I imagine, since it's the enhanced laboratory version I'm carrying, it shouldn't take more than about an hour to kick in,' Luciano mused happily. 'Of course, with the antidote, you might stand a chan—'

'GUARD!' Malky was on his feet, crashing his tray against the bars of the cell. 'GUARD! AH'M GONNY DIE! GET ME OOTA HERE!'

Luciano risked a look at Big Brian, who was regarding him with a calculating eye, obviously weighing up his chances of exacting revenge for his colleague's condition.

'So damned infectious,' he muttered to himself, smiling sadly at Big Brainless and raising his voice in order to make himself heard over Malky's screams. 'Droplet, saliva, sneezes, even just being within, pfffff, say, twenty metres of an infected person is enough to—'

The bars shook with the impact of Big Braindead adding his weight to the plea for guards.

Luciano took a deep breath and sat down again on the bench, taking a huge bite of his curly sandwich. Suddenly he was *starving*.

S'tan on the Skids

Face down on a black leather massage table, S'tan, First Minister of the Hadean Executive, gave a roar of anguish as His masseur dug his fingertips into the back of His neck.

'GO EASY, SCUM,' He hissed, clenching His fists so hard that two of His fingernails snapped off and pinged across the room.

Seeing this, the masseur tutted reprovingly. '*Now* look what You've gone and done to Your Self. Silly boy. We'll have to give You a manicure next. Just lie still and we'll be all done in two shakes of a lamb's tail—'

'LAMB?'

'Ooops. Sorry. Forgot You're not too keen on

them. Two shakes of a goat's tail, then. Now relaaax. Chill—'

'CHILL?' S'tan's voice was menacing in the extreme. 'I DON'T DO CHILL, CRETIN. THIS IS HELL, AFTER ALL. ROAST, BRAISE, BOIL; ABSO*LUTELY*. FLAMBEZ, SEAR, TOAST IF YOU MUST — BUT *CHILL*? THAT IMPLIES A PROBLEM WITH ONE'S FURNACE.'

'Heck no. I . . . I . . . I never meant You had a problem with Your furnace, most Igneus One . . . um, er . . .' The masseur sensed that he was heading for permanent chilling unless he made good the damage he'd already done. He opened his mouth again and popped both his cloven feet straight in. 'Goodness me, no, o Pyretic Premier,' he squeaked, aware that beneath his fingers S'tan's muscle tone had turned from floppy flab to reinforced concrete. 'Oh Lordy, *never*, Your Imperial Inflammableness, long may Your chimneys smoke—'

'GOODNESS? LORDY?' Here S'tan sat up so abruptly that he knocked the hapless masseur to the floor. 'I DON'T *THINK* SO. GUARDS. ANOTHER ONE FOR INVOLUNTARY VOLUME DOWN-SIZING.'

'Pardon me?' squeaked the masseur.

'TOO LATE. NO PARDONS GIVEN.'

'B-b-b-but what do You *mean*?' squalled the masseur as two lumpen trolls entered the S'pa and began to drag him away. 'What's involuntary volume down-sizing? Your Maleficence?' His voice died away down the corridors, fading to silence immediately after uttering one tortured scream as,

_____ 81

presumably, one of S'tan's guards enlightened him as to the purpose of the tongue-secateurs carried by all members of the Executive Guard.

S'tan rolled Himself off the massage table and stood up, rubbing at the knot at the back of His neck and forcing Himself to unclench His jaw. How long had it been now? Ten days? Give or take a minute or two? Ten days since that idiot Isagoth had failed to make the deadline of the autumnal equinox. Ten days since that same dunderheaded demon Isagoth had vanished off the face of the planet, either because he'd failed to find the Chronostone by the due date or because he'd *found* the Chronostone and intended to hang onto it, thank You very much and with all due respect, Boss, now I've got the stone, You can go boil Your bottom in sump oil for all I care.

Ten days? Only *ten*?

S'tan nearly howled out loud. With each passing day that he was without the Chronostone, He found His evil powers ebbing away till He could barely work up a decent feral snarl, let alone feel even remotely maleficent. At this rate, He thought bleakly, I'm going to turn into a blooming cherub if I'm not careful. Staring morosely at His personal organizer, He wondered just how much longer He would get away with it before one of His underlings realized what was going on. When the Chronostone had first been mislaid two centuries ago, S'tan had been, well, even He had to admit, pretty peeved.

There had followed several decades of rages and cloven-footed-stamping sessions, then His anger had settled down to a volcanic simmer with occasional outbursts of pique. This was as nothing compared to what happened when the Chronostone fell into the hands of the Other Side and appeared to drop out of the space-time continuum. S'tan's spies informed Him that some interfering immortal had had the temerity to lodge the stone in the Etheric Library in an attempt to place it out of Hades' reach. That, truly, had been the absolute pits. S'tan had been so devastated, so *bereft*, He'd found himself with His head perpetually in His fridge, snacking, browsing, feeding, stuffing, cramming food down His neck till He fell asleep, stupefied with calories and enfeebled by jaw exhaustion. After He'd attained the same weight as an average blue whale, He began to experience some difficulty in sleeping, so He self-medicated with a variety of soporifics, hoping thus to knock Himself out and spare Himself the agony of missing the Chronostone. Overweight, sleep-deprived and drugged to the hilt, the S'tan of the twenty-first century was beginning to resemble a rock star on the skids more than the horned Satan of biblical mythology. Realizing that His credibility was slipping away He took Himself off to see a doctor, hoping if not for a cure, then at least for a temporary solution to His miseries until the Chronostone was returned to Him.

Initially, confronted with a bloated and weepy

devil, the doctor advised exercise, so dutifully S'tan installed a treadmill and weights in His office, next to the mini-bar. Every morning He'd wheeze and puff and sweat till He glowed. However, every night He'd lie awake with His thoughts spinning out of control. Miserable. That was the only word to describe how He felt. Miserable.

He'd gone back to the doctor to deliver the news that exercise simply wasn't cutting it. The doctor wisely didn't dare point out that His S'tainless S'teeliness had only been exercising for two days and couldn't expect to undo the bad habits of several thousand millennia in the space of forty-eight hours; the wise doctor knew better than to allow a breath of criticism to cross his lips. Accordingly, his next suggestion was that S'tan took a break. Book a holiday, he said. Just turn up at an airport. Be spontaneous. Try Torremolinos, the doctor improvised. Totally hellish. You'd feel right at home.

S'tan had lasted approximately two and a half hours in the clubby, noisy, three-in-the-morning-thumpa-thump-tsss-tsss, fish-'n'-chips-perfumed, thongs-and-lobster-flesh nightmare of Mediterranean resortland before rematerializing in Hades and turning the good doctor into a set of matching pink ostrich-skin luggage doomed to orbit a carousel in the bowels of Hades until such time as S'tan saw fit to release him.

However, S'tan's increase in weight was nothing

when set against the psychological impact of dis-covering that He was losing His S'tanic edge. When He discovered how feeble He was becoming, that was when His real problems began. The panic attacks had started: waking in the middle of the night, sweat-drenched, heart hammering in His chest, terror-stricken at the prospect of being found out; petrified that He'd be called upon to do some-thing really evilly vile in front of the assembled Hadean Executive; something that would soon be utterly beyond His rapidly diminishing powers. Something truly disgustingly, gruesomely, maliciously, vindictively foul. Something ... like pulling the wings off an angel .... 'OH MY GOD, NOOOOOO,' He squeaked. 'Not *that*.'

S'tan's eyes flew open. *What* had He just said? Surely not. God, no. Aaaargh. There it was again – that *name*. Blimey. Heck. And *blimey*? *Heck*? What had happened to the curses and foul, stomach-churning invective for which He was justly famed? What had happened to Him? It was far, far worse than He'd imagined. Without the Chronostone, He was nothing at all. The merest shadow of a bogey-man, invented to scare humans into behaving better. He had to get the stone back, He realized. His very survival depended upon it.

Titus Waxed

'What d'you mean, I have to be nice to him?' Titus stood poking the fitfully smoking library fire with a rusting pair of coal tongs. 'I can't *stand* him. As a matter of fact, I was waiting for a good time to boot him out.'

Baci gasped, her hands flying up to clutch at her hair. 'No. Titus, I *beg* you, please, don't. We need the best lawyer in Scotland to represent your father. Rand's father *is* the best one. I tried various criminal lawyers, but they all refused to touch your father's case with a barge-pole. I didn't even bother with old whatsisname – Ludo Grabbit down in the village. To be honest, I imagined that Slander, Defame and Grabbit would want to put as much distance as possible between us and them after that dreadful incident when Uncle Lucifer shot one of the partners. So Rand's father it was. I had no choice—'

'Yeah, you did. There's *millions* of lawyers in Scotland.' Titus stabbed the fire with the tongs, thus causing it to produce a sulky gout of yellow smoke. 'I bet Rand's father's hideously expensive as well. Dad'll have a fit when the bill comes in.'

'No, Titus. Dad won't have a fit. In fact, Rand's father has generously agreed to take your father's case on a *pro bono* basis.' Baci delivered this statement with understandable pride.

'What?'

'*Pro bono* – for nothing. For the common good. Out of the goodness of his heart.' She paused, then added, 'Well . . . sort of . . .'

Titus froze, the tongs dangling from his hand. 'Mu-uum? What d'you mean "sort of"?'

'Look, Titus' – Baci's tone was now business-like, brusque – 'sometimes we have to do things we don't care much for in order to achieve a desired goal—'

'*Mum?*'

Baci rolled on, unstoppable. 'You'll simply have to put up with it. Rand is going to be staying with us for a while. Munro – I mean, Mr MacAlister Hall – is in the middle of several big cases, including your dad's. That means he's away from home a lot and unfortunately his housekeeper's handed in her notice. Rand's not old enough to be left on his own and besides – Oh, Titus. It's very awkward to explain. It's . . . complicated. Rand's a very mixed-up young man—'

'Telling *me*,' muttered Titus, concentrating very hard on picking up a tiny lump of coal and transferring it from the coal scuttle to the fire.

'Well, without going into *too* much detail, Rand's mother died when he was nine, and ever since, he's been looked after by a series of *au pairs* and nannies. His father works very hard when he's involved in some big' – she shuddered, bit her lip and continued – 'murder trial.'

'Yeah, but so what?' Titus interrupted, still focusing on airlifting coal into the already over-fuelled fire. 'Like, what's that got to do with us?'

'Rand's father told me that he's involved with some big hush-hush case abroad.' Baci's eyes widened and she continued, her voice dropping dramatically to a whisper. 'He's worried that some of the – er – criminals he's trying to prosecute might try to kidnap his son. Apparently he's received anonymous phone calls in the middle of the night, and recently, death threats.'

Titus stared at Baci in horror, words for once failing him utterly.

'So, as you can imagine, until Rand's father can put these creeps behind bars, he'd rather his son didn't stay at Château MacAlister Hall. Yes, I *know*, Titus' – Baci held up a hand to forestall interruptions – 'it's a real mess, but who knows, perhaps we can help Rand feel a bit less . . . a bit more . . . slightly . . .' She tailed off, her fingers flexing and unflexing as if she could claw the desired word from the air.

Refusing to finish his mother's sentence for her, Titus dropped a fist-sized lump of coal into the grate from waist height and watched with bleak satisfaction as it landed directly on top of the solitary flickering flame. The coal wobbled, rattled and then extinguished the fire completely.

'Great,' he said, in a tone that implied the exact opposite. 'What room are you putting him in?'

'The one across from you. The one with its own bathroom. I know the carpet's a bit shabby and the light doesn't always come on when you flick the swi—'

'The mushroom,' Titus said, the faintest ghost of a smile appearing on his face. Noting his mother's puzzled expression, he explained, 'Pandora calls it that. It's not a bedroom, it's a mushroom. It's got mushrooms growing in the wardrobe or something. And under the bath. I imagine there'll be *monster* ones clinging behind the shutters. It's pretty damp.' The idea of Rand being forced to endure the mushroom had cheered Titus slightly. Baci, on the other hand, was sunk in gloom.

'Honestly, this *house*,' she groaned. 'It's riddled

with rots. Falling apart at the seams. No sooner do we fix one bit than another one falls off, sprouts spores or swells up and bursts. It's so *expensive* to keep up.'

Here we go, thought Titus, turning his attention to the dead fire. She's going to do the Must Economize Rant. How did it go again? More jumpers, fewer fires. Shallower baths. Closing doors to keep heat in. Less meat, more beans. Walk, don't drive. Darning socks – no, *that* was what Mrs McLachlan did. Talking of whom—

'But, Mum, aren't you saving money now that you're not paying for a nanny? I mean, since, um . . .' Titus tailed off into silence, cursing himself for straying into this conversational minefield. Like, what was he saying? *Hey, Mum, isn't it great we don't have to shell out for Mrs McLachlan's salary ever since she drowned? And*, his thoughts added, gleefully following this thread, *let's just bump off Latch, and that way we'll have so much spare money, we'll be able to heat this place for a change . . .*

Baci looked distinctly uncomfortable. The library was growing colder by the minute, due in part to Titus's earlier efforts to extinguish the fire, but also to the prevailing wind, which appeared to have blown straight in from Siberia. Baci shivered and crouched down beside Titus. Mother and son stared into the lukewarm cinders, both unwilling to return to the subject of their missing nanny. After what seemed to Titus like an eternity spent peering at inert lumps of carbon, they both broke the silence simultaneously.

'Mum—'

'Titus, I—'

'You go first.'

'No, darling, you. Oh. Why is this so *difficult*? Titus, I came to a decision today.'

Titus felt his stomach clench involuntarily. He *hated* it when adults prefaced sentences with this kind of thing. Still, 'I came to a decision' *had* to be better than 'Now, darling, you're going to have to be a brave boy.' He stared at his mother so hard, he could still see her imprint on his retinas when he blinked.

'Sweetheart, don't look at me like that,' Baci pleaded. 'I'm not about to say something awful. It's just . . . I, um . . . we – well, not "we", since your dad . . . er – for heaven's *sake*, I'm even beginning to *sound* like your father. Right, try again. Titus. I can't cope, I need help. I simply cannot look after all of you, do the cooking, maintain the house, temporarily adopt a deeply troubled teenager plus bring this baby to full term. I'm sorry. I'm doing my best, but I'm shattered. So. So that's why I've decided to employ another nanny' – again she held up her hand to show she hadn't finished yet – 'and, yes, I know that you probably think I'm betraying the memory of poor Mrs McLachlan by getting another nanny so soon, but you have to understand me when I say that I haven't got any choice—' She stopped, her gaze dropping to where Titus's nail-bitten hand was now patting her arm, and it suddenly dawned on her that his expression was so fixed and strange precisely because he was determined not to cry. She laid her hand on top of his and tactfully turned her attention to the complete lack of flames in the hearth.

'Let's hope that, whoever she is, the new nanny won't mind living in our old, cold house.'

Titus cleared his throat before daring to speak. Even so, his voice emerged as a strangled croak. 'Mum. Don't worry about the girls. I mean, telling them you're, er, we're getting a new . . . yeah. Um. I'll tell Pan and Damp. Save you having to go through all this again. And Mum? The cooking? Just *don't*, right? Between Pan, Latch and me, we can do it. Till you get another cook, or Dad comes back or – whatever. It's just . . .'

Baci shook her head sadly. 'I know, darling. Last night's dinner was . . . beyond vile.'

'The oven chips were OK,' Titus lied. 'Maybe you're just a bit out of practise. But the – the . . .' His stomach lurched at the memory and he blurted out, '*Please*. Don't ever make *that* again? Promise? I'll leave home if you do.'

Baci's forehead furrowed. 'What? My risotto? It wasn't *that* bad, was it? I mean, I know the peas were a bit on the hard side and the rice was a tiny bit crunchy but—'

Titus tried to banish the memory. What his

mother was glossing over was the fact that as well as bullet-hard frozen peas and undercooked rice, there had also been pallid goosefleshy bits of chicken skin floating on top of the risotto, the whole thing awash in a liquid that had been cheek-clenchingly sour. The risotto had been too salty and its cheesy aftertaste had lingered long after they'd consigned the remains to the slop-pail. It was right up there with the serial killers in the ranks of crimes against gastronomy. Even Knot had refused to eat it, and considering the culinary horrors the yeti had allowed to pass his lips, that was really saying something.

'Titus, I have a confession to make,' Baci began.

Titus winced. Here was *another* of those awful phrases that adults used prior to turning your life inside out.

'Mu-um.'

'It was late. I was tired. I wasn't thinking straight – your father had just been arrested – I'm so, so sorry. Oh, Titus—'

'*What?*' He was really worried now. What *was* she on about?

'I grated what I thought was parmesan into the risotto, but, but—' To Titus's alarm, his mother burst into tears. Through her sobs, he could make out about one word in every seven. 'Acanthoid wax . . . bought it online . . . looks *so* like cheese . . . not poisonous, thank heavens . . . I was waiting to see if . . . but it has already . . . fortunately the effects aren't permanent . . . two days to a week in some cases . . . rapid onset . . . secondary male characteristics . . . Oh God. *I'm* so *sorry*. Oh. My. God. Titus? Titus? Speak to me?'

Titus was stunned. Speechless, in fact. Very soon, if he wasn't mistaken, he was going to turn into a bloke? Tall, deep voiced, hair all over, all the *bits*? No *wonder* the risotto had tasted so awful— But hang on a minute, a rational part of his mind said, muscling past the remainder of his thoughts, which were running about in hysterically screaming circles. Just slow down and *think*, he instructed himself. Acanthoid wax was apparently harvested from 'the naturally occurring sebaceous oils responsible for keeping unicorn hooves supple'. Like, this *stuff* was the toe-jam of a mythical creature? Yeah, right. And his mother had paid good money for this rubbish? It was worse than he'd thought. Not only was his mum utterly gullible, but in all probability she was totally nuts as well. Titus had a brief but intense flash of longing for his father to come home, during which he experienced a profound urge to lie on the rug and sink his teeth into its unhoovered fibres, then he pulled himself together.

'OK, Mum. It's cool. No harm done.' And he managed a smile, just as his trousers burst along their seams.

The Diet of Dragons

Damp followed Pandora to the dungeons carrying a bag full of stale bread, a batch of burnt scones and a plastic tub full of Ffup's piebald low-carb, diet-approved bread dough; half carbonized, half raw; the whole still stubbornly unrisen. Pandora was similarly laden with the contents of the slop-pail; a bag of assorted mouldering vegetables from the back of the salad drawer; a perspex box of universally loathed nut-studded spherical chocolates that had done the rounds of house parties in Argyll before ending up, still unwanted and unopened, at StregaSchloss; a multipack of tins of baked beans; and a rapidly

defrosting brick of raspberry ripple ice-cream. One after the other, Pandora and Damp carefully negotiated the spiral stairs leading down to the beasts' dungeon apartments.

The mantle of beast-feeder had been one that Pandora had reluctantly assumed after Mrs McLachlan's disappearance. The nanny had been very conscientious about providing the beasts with a balanced diet; by complete contrast, Pandora callously reckoned that no matter what she fed them, the beasts would still outlive her. With this in mind, she decided not to waste a minute of her comparatively short human life in beastly food preparation. Fresh fruit and vegetables vanished entirely, replaced by out-of-date chocolates, ice-cream and tinned beans, with an occasional garnish of the contents of the slop-pail and compost bucket. Pandora knew that Mrs McLachlan wouldn't have approved, but with a lump in her throat she acknowledged that Mrs McLachlan wasn't there to pass judgement, or indeed to *see* how badly her family were faring without her.

Pandora reached the foot of the stairs and dropped her burden on the flagstones, turning round to help Damp down the last few steps. All the way downstairs the toddler had been experimenting with the echoing possibilities afforded by the vast spaces below StregaSchloss. In effect, she was practising some of the more arcane words from Vesper's vocabulary of technical terms for learner bats, but to Pandora it sounded like a continual high-pitched *EEE-ee-EE-eee* sound, each step producing an increase in pitch and volume until she itched to turn round and gag Damp with a furry courgette.

In his down-lined roost in the shadows, Ffup's baby son Nestor flapped his wings in greeting, causing a flurry of white feathers to spiral up into the air around his head. Damp's squeaks became ecstatic and, dropping her quota of beast-snacks beside Pandora's (*ee-EEE?*), she wobbled off unencumbered (*eeeeeeee-E!*) into the darkness (*e? e? e?*). Her piercing vowel sounds were swiftly muted by the immensity of StregaSchloss's subterranean caverns, and finally Damp's voice was completely swamped by the groans that accompanied the beasts' appraisal of their morning menu. They gathered round the little pile of offerings, nostrils flaring and upper lips doing a synchronized sneer.

'You *what*?' Sab's tone was incredulous, aghast at the prospect of eating such vile substances.

'Oh, puhleease.' Ffup emitted a massive sigh, which had the unfortunate effect of turning the raspberry ripple ice-cream into a steaming puddle of what looked like plasma with added bloodclots. 'How many times do I have to tell you?' she continued, stamping round Pandora in a little circular tantrum. 'How. Many. Times? I don't *do* carbohydrates. Look – scones equal carbohydrates: yuck.

_____ 97

Bread – ditto: yuck. Rancid ice-cream – ditto: yuck—'

'I disagree,' mumbled Knot, belching discreetly behind one matted paw. 'Both of those dittos were *not* yuck, they were delic—'

'Chocolates. I can't eat *them*,' Ffup moaned. 'Vegetables, assorted, mouldering from back of fridge – nope. Even if I could, I wouldn't. I mean, what are these *slops*? Are you out of your mind? Do you really expect me to desecrate the temple of my body with this leftover junk? What do you take me for? A waste-disposal unit? A wild beast?' The dragon broke off, poked Pandora in the chest with a knobbly talon, and then continued her rant. 'And *beans*? BEANS? Did you remember the tin-opener? I don't think so. So, great hunter-gatherer, just how are we supposed to open these tins? Hey, guys, hope you're not too famished. Breakfast may take a while. Especially since we have to *gnaw* our way through its metal packaging—'

'Calm down, Ffup.' Sab attempted to lay a restraining claw on his fellow-beast's shoulder, but Ffup had now gone past the point of no return.

'WHAT DO YOU TAKE ME FOR?' she shrieked, flames now popping coyly out of her vent, each eruption causing the dragon to wince, blush and then continue unabated. 'I'M A DRAGON, IN CASE THAT FACT HAD ESCAPED YOUR NOTICE. AND THE ONLY TINNED FOOD MY KIND HAVE EVER EATEN IS KNIGHTS-IN-ARMOUR—'

'That's not *strictly* true,' Sab interrupted, narrowing his eyes at Ffup, who stood, chest heaving, fanning herself with a cabbage leaf she'd plucked from the pile of beast rations. The gryphon padded across the dungeon and whispered in the dragon's ear, much to Pandora's annoyance. 'Pssspss the caravan, remember? It was a pssst *kind* of tin, wasn't it? And, boy, was it *packed* full of tasty morsels. Prsss? Those big, mean Glaswegians? Hsss, psss, whsspsss.'

'It's *rude* to whisper,' Pandora pointed out, picking up two tins of beans and marching across the dungeon to where Knot sat alone, idly examining his fur for edible content. The yeti gazed at her, peering through the tangled hairy clumps that fringed his eyes.

'Look, pet,' Pandora said. 'Self-opening snacks. Simply pull on this metal ring and, behold – dinner is served. Here, you try.'

Knot blinked, peered at the offered tin of beans and reached out to grasp it. He turned the tin over in his paws, shook it, sniffed deeply and then tipped it straight down his throat, regrettably still in its full metal jacket. Pandora stifled a wail and rolled her eyes in despair. As a teach-the-beasts self-sufficiency lesson, it had been a disaster. However, this had not been her only reason for visiting the dungeons.

'Look here. I have something really important to show you.' Pandora pulled an envelope from the waistband of her jeans and, realizing that she was being utterly ignored, raised her voice. 'Hello? Could you pay attention for a minute?' She removed a wallet of photographs from the envelope and began to pass them round. In such vast paws the photographs looked like postage stamps, and the beasts squinted at the tiny images like myopic great-aunts attempting to read the contraindications on an unfamiliar brand of laxative.

'Where *is* this?' Ffup hissed, bringing the photograph so close to her face that she was in danger of accidentally inhaling it. 'It looks like an island. And who's he? He's so . . . familiar. Why do I feel I've seen him before? Do we know him?' she demanded imperiously. 'And what's with that boat? It's a wreck – there're holes all over it—'

'*When* was this taken?' Sab demanded, his acute intelligence cutting straight to the heart of the matter. 'Ah, there. It's date-stamped in the corner – bother, the print seems blurred or something. I can't make out the numbers.'

'Mrs McLachlan's shoes are in this picture,' Knot mumbled, holding up another photo for group inspection. 'I used to love those shoes. They tasted delicious.'

Bizarrely, this comment made Pandora fling her arms around the yeti's unsanitary neck and hug him tight. 'Thank you, thank you, thank you,' she babbled, her voice muffled in yeti fur. 'I needed to check. I thought they were hers, but I wasn't one hundred per cent sure. Look at the date-stamp on *this* one, Sab.'

The gryphon peered at the photo in Knot's paw and inhaled sharply. 'Yesterday? ' he asked, visibly confused.

Pandora nodded and passed across another photograph. 'I wish I knew what was going on. I can't even *begin* to understand.' She watched as the beasts examined a picture of a pair of men's lace-up boots propped against a rock. At least, that's what Pandora thought they were, but admittedly it was hard to tell, since the photograph appeared to have been taken at night.

'No flash,' she muttered, passing over another one, this time taken in broad daylight. 'Date-stamped in two days' time,' she pointed out, trying to sound airily unconcerned. 'Perhaps it's a photo-premonition; perhaps my camera takes pictures of things that haven't happened yet . . .' She tailed off, waiting for the beasts to react to this new picture. This one was of a man sitting with his back to the camera, his head in his hands, like a charades player miming the word 'headache'. Diagonally opposite him, Damp was pointing upwards, her mouth curved in a smile, while beside her Mrs McLachlan was draping items of clothing over a rock.

'It's like a glimpse into the future, if such a thing were possible,' Pandora muttered.

'B-b-but l-look here.' Ffup's voice was growing

more shrill as the evidence piled up. 'Who . . . who . . . too-too-took—?'

'Have you turned into an *owl*?' Sab demanded peevishly. 'For Pete's sake, get a grip. You're a dragon, remember? Not some kind of wee, sleekit, cow'rin', tim'rous beastie.'

Ffup fixed Sab with a malevolent glare, took a deep shuddering breath, turned back to Pandora and tried again. 'Who took this photograph?' she whispered, her eyes as round and wide as soup plates. 'Who? You said it wasn't you, and you don't even know where it was taken – I mean, where it *will* be taken since it's in the future and hasn't happened yet . . . And it's got the same man in it – the same one as in the other photos, the man I'm sure I've seen before . . . And what's Damp doing, and . . . and . . .' Suddenly her self-control deserted her, and to everyone's acute embarrassment, Ffup Lost the Plot completely.

In the ensuing screams, smoke, flames and diarrhoeic eruptions, no-one could avoid hearing the diminishing echoes of dragon claws scrabbling up stone stairs, dragon footsteps thundering across the kitchen floor above, followed by a slam from the front door, and a diminishing dragon wail as Ffup fled down to the lochside to seek solace by the water. As silence fell once more in the dungeons, they heard Damp comforting the alarmed Nestor in a manner poignantly reminiscent of Mrs McLachlan.

'Don't worry, pet,' she said firmly. 'Mummy's prob'ly just got a wee bug in her tummy. She didn't mean to do a big poo in the middle of the room. It was a nax dident.'

Pandora retrieved her photographs from where Ffup had dropped them, and tucked them back in their envelope. Her mind was spinning with possibilities: some so exciting they took her breath away; others so freighted with menace, she had to force herself to dismiss them. She needed to take another look at the i-caramba and then she needed to speak to Titus. Alone.

'Damp? Let's go find Mum, shall we? And Nestor, isn't it your nap time?'

Beside her, Sab gave a disgusted snort. 'What alternative reality do *you* operate in, pray tell? Nestor doesn't *do* naps. Nestor barely does *sleeps*. A more undisciplined baby dragon I've yet to meet . . .' His voice tailed off as Pandora pointed at Damp, who was bending over to plant a kiss on Nestor's head. Nestor, whose little body was coiled into a spiny spiral, eyes shut, breathing evenly, stubby wings flopped on the flagstones, his front paws locked around a lovingly toasted teddy of Titus's.

'How did you *do* that?' the gryphon breathed.

'Magic,' said Damp, skipping across to tuck her hand into Pandora's. 'Magic word,' she added helpfully.

Sab sighed. 'Oh, very *well*. If you insist. *Please?*'

'Not *that* magic word.' Damp's tone was dismissive. 'Diffr'nt word. Secret. Only Damps speak it.'

'Only *Damps*? Well, that's helpful, isn't it?' Sab groaned. 'Just how many Damps are there in this world?'

'Seven,' stated Damp, somewhat surreally, but with a finality that indicated that this was as far as she was prepared to go. She let go of Pandora's hand, and with a dignity at odds with the fact that she still wore night-time nappies, Damp headed upstairs. Pandora pulled a face, shrugged and followed her little sister.

Tock on Top

The paperboy was new to the job. He bounced along the rutted track to StregaSchloss, hissing some unrecognizable tune through his front teeth and ill-advisedly stopping by the moat to dig out the Strega-Borgias' newspaper from his hoard. The sun slid behind a cloud, and the wind announced its Siberian origins.

'Naw. Not that yin,' the boy muttered, keeping up a running commentary as he sifted through his paper-bag. 'Folks in these big hooses dinnae buy square papers. They get big papers wi' big lang words in them.' The boy glanced up from his task, sure he'd heard something drop into the moat. Ripples spread out on the black surface of the water, and he shivered, suddenly aware of what an isolated place this was. His efforts to locate the right newspaper speeded up. At length he found the one he was looking for, and just as he was about to hurl it across the drive at the massive front door, his eye was caught by the newspaper's main headline. His mouth opened wide, exposing teeth that had seen too much action on the sugar front.

'Aw, nawww . . .' he whispered, his legs almost giving way with the realization that here he was, delivering a paper to the house of a suspected serial murdere—

'I'll take that,' a voice informed him, and he swivelled round, his bike crashing to the ground. Who had spoken?

There was nobody there. The rose-quartz drive was deserted, the door remained shut and there was no sign of life at any of the many windows of the house. The boy rotated slowly, his skin crawling with fear. Behind, the same story. No-one. The track he'd cycled in on, the trees, the faraway gate. Not a soul to be see—

'Coo-ee. Down here. At your feet.'

As Tock later explained to Latch, that was why the newspaper had ended up in the moat. The crocodile exposed a huge acreage of yellow teeth and added that he'd been *astonished* at the volume of the paperboy's shriek; after all, he'd only been a little chap, barely enough meat on him for a decent mouthful. What Tock *didn't* mention was that it had been he who'd hurled the paper into the moat after discovering that his beloved master Luciano's name and reputation were being bandied around the front page. By the time each sheet had absorbed its quota of greenish moat-water and had sunk to the bottom, the paperboy had probably made it to the Outer Hebrides in his haste to put as much distance between himself and the thankfully vegetarian Tock.

Latch stood kneading bread dough at the kitchen table, an old recipe book propped open against a bag of flour; the rhythmic press, turn and fold of the breadmaking process causing the table to rock and the tea in Tock's cup slop against the rim and splash into his saucer.

'How was your trip, anyway?' the butler enquired, stopping to scratch his chin with a floury finger. 'I imagine the river's in full spate. Did you catch anything?'

'A cold,' shivered Tock. 'Have you any idea how chilly the river Chrone is? Still, it was well worth the sneezes. I've found some gorgeous stones for my moat. Here, come outside and I'll show you—'

Latch was saved by the buzzer. The oven timer chose this moment to announce that his banana, almond and white chocolate muffins were ready, and for the next few minutes he was too pre-occupied with muffin allocations to pay Tock or his stones any attention. To the butler's amusement, Titus and Rand had miraculously appeared along with the muffins, possessing noses sensitive to even the faintest whiff of vanilla wafting up the many flights of stairs between the bedrooms and the kitchen.

Impatient to begin work on his moat, Tock waddled out of the kitchen, crossed the herb garden, skirted the side of the house and finally stopped beside the stone perimeter. Laid out like the hours on a clock were twelve perfect white quartz boulders. Tock sighed with pleasure. They were exquisite stones, he thought, his golden eyes caressing each one in turn. He intended them to provide bases for the dozen cairns he was hoping to build round the moat's edge. These towers would cast their shadows across the moat each morning, and as the sun swung round in the afternoon, the cairns would throw fingers of shade across the rose-quartz drive . . . Tock almost hugged himself with delight. It was a giant sundial, an artistic statement on a par with—

His lofty thoughts were interrupted by the sound of crunching rose quartz and he spun round as the vast serpentine coils of the Sleeper undulated into view.

'Haw, pal,' the beast roared in greeting. 'Seen ma wumman? She didn't appear wi' ma breakfast, an' ah wis wonderin' what's keepin' her. Like, it's nearly lunchtime, the noo.' There was a deep rumbling sound, like distant rolling thunder. The Sleeper blushed, the effect turning his normally dark blue face an interesting shade of purple. The rumble came again and he sighed mightily. 'Pardon me,' he mumbled. 'It's jist ah'm famished. Ah'm that hungry ah feel like ah'm fading awa'.'

Tock's eyes goggled. The Sleeper would have to starve himself for *millennia* to make any difference to his mountainous girth. Muscled like an eel on steroids, he could eat for Scotland, in direct contrast to his diet-obsessed fiancée Ffup, who would hardly swallow a mouthful of air without first weighing it, then looking it up in a hefty paperback manual to verify its fat-free status.

With his fiancée's fixation on diets and wedding plans, the Sleeper frequently felt sorely in need of the company of his own gender. Seeing a perfect male-bonding opportunity presenting itself, he clapped Tock on the back, sending the crocodile spinning across the rose-quartz drive like a reptilian frisbee.

'Anyway, how's it gawn, pal?' he yelled, peering at his reflection in the moat and scratching vigorously in an armpit. Tock picked himself up off the drive and spat out a couple of rose-quartz pebbles before staggering back to the moat-side, unfortunately too late to protect his precious stones. The Sleeper was turning his huge body round, his belly studded with rose quartz as he scraped a swathe across the drive, swept all twelve of Tock's precious boulders into the moat and accidentally dented the rear door of the family car with the end of his massive tail. Breathing heavily, he inched closer to Tock and demanded, 'Hey, pal. They wee pebbly things weren't dead important, eh no? Ah mean, like – youse weren't savin' them fir something special, were youse?'

Tock peered nervously up into the Sleeper's fish-scented face, profoundly relieved to have the colossal beast as a friend rather than a foe. 'Heck, no. Me? Those old stones?' he said, trying not to scream at the sight of the Sleeper's teeth bared in a monumental grin. 'Plenty more where they came from, up in the mountains.' He edged towards the moat, then remembered that there was no longer anything in its depths that he could gnaw. Ever since converting to vegetarianism two summers ago, he missed having an endless supply of bones nearby. Time was, he would dive to the bottom of the moat and trawl through the items in his larder, some of which, he was forced to admit, had been decidedly past their chew-by date. However, since he'd disposed of the decomposing ossuary that had dotted its muddy bottom, bones were decidedly off-menu. It was all part of the plan for moat-enhancement, along with quartz cairns. Tock sighed. The quartz cairns whose bases were now at the bottom of the moat . . .

Wondering if the Sleeper would mind fishing all twelve boulders back out for him, Tock smiled up at the big beast. But the Sleeper's attention was else-where, his eyes narrowed in concern as he stared at the distant road to Auchenlochtermuchty, along which came a file of police vans heading for StregaSchloss.

The League of Immortals

The island rose up out of the deep water, its hidden shoreline exposed by the retreating tides. Death's two oarsmen stood sentinel by their small dinghy, heads drooping with immeasurable exhaustion as they held their oars upright like spears. Hours had passed since they'd ferried their VIP passenger to the island; hours during which the figures had stood motionless, the hems of their long robes slowly drying out as the tide stole away into the darkness, leaving a rime of salt behind. Smoke unravelled from a driftwood fire; an unbroken thread which linked the island below with the hook of the crescent moon above, as if something below the waters was fishing the night sky for stars.

The three figures sitting round the fire appeared to have taken root. Sparks flew up into the darkness as a resinous log spat and fizzled in the flames. The demon Isagoth yawned widely, not bothering to cover his mouth and thus affording the others an unwelcome view of his tonsils.

'I'm pooped,' he declared, unlacing first one boot and then the other as he prepared to turn in for the night. 'Thanks for, er, dinner, by the way. Even though it was the same as the night before – and the night before that. *Not* that I'm complaining. Heck no. I love fish, me. Delicious. I'll be sure to get the stone-mason to make a particular point of mentioning that when he carves out your headstone.'

'I *beg* your pardon?' Mrs McLachlan's head jerked upwards. She'd been daydreaming, staring intently at Isagoth's boots but not really seeing them, lost in a world of her own; a world she was struggling to recall. Oh, what *were* their names? If she could only remember . . .

'Oh, come *on*,' Isagoth insisted. 'You know what I mean. *Here lies the mortal remains of Flora McLachlan* kind of thing? *Died saving mankind. Lost at sea. Beloved wife of—? Maker of possibly the best chocolate meringue cake in the known universe, and pretty nifty with the old steamed mussels. There.* Whadd'ya say, Flora? Did I leave anything out?'

On the other side of the fire shadows stirred. A languid hand fanned the air as if trying to bat away the demon's words like a cloud of insects.

'You left yourself out, my dear chap,' Death murmured. 'You're frightfully *chatty* when it comes to planning Flora's headstone, but what about your own? What should we get the stonemason to write on *that*? one wonders. Maybe there's nothing to say about your life? How about, *Here lies Isagoth. He smoked a lot of cigars, and propped up a lot of bars. It was a cough that carried him off. It was a coffin they carried him offin.*'

'But . . . but . . . You're joking, right?' the demon blustered, staring at Death, whose expression remained impassive. 'Aw, come *on*. You're kidding. This is a morbid wind-up. You're pulling my cloven-footed leg. I don't need a tombstone. *You* know that. I won't *ever* need a tombstone. I'm an immortal.'

As if to underline his point, a peal of thunder rumbled far out across the loch, and a sheet of lightning backlit the silent figures of Death's ferrymen.

'So are we *all*,' Death snapped. 'Do keep up.'

'Uhhh.' Isagoth slapped himself on his forehead. 'Of *course*. I'd forgotten about her. She doesn't *act* like an immortal though.'

'Rrrrreally?' drawled Death, skewering Isagoth with a glare. 'And, pray tell, just how *are* immortals supposed to behave? Like you, Mr Isagoth? I think *not*. You and your kind give the League of Immortals a bad name.'

'My *kind*? What are you on about?'

'Bottom-feeders, Mr Isagoth. Demons, imps,

succubi, gremlins, djinnis and other such lower orders,' Death continued serenely, ignoring the spluttering sounds coming from Isagoth. 'Your inclusion in the League of Immortals merely indicates the presence of a divine sense of humour.' Seeing the demon's face scrunch up into a frown of incomprehension, Death explained, 'You're a cosmic joke, Mr Isagoth. You provide some much-needed light entertainment for the angels. Think how *tedious* immortality would be if it weren't for the antics of your chap S'tan and his legions. At best, you entertain us; at worst . . . you irritate. And as any oyster could tell you, it's the bit of gritty irritation that makes the pearl. Every time. And so, Mr Isagoth, just as the oyster will always overcome the grit, good will always overcome evil and love will conquer all. Don't you agree, Flora?'

Mrs McLachlan's thoughts were miles away. She'd remembered that she *hadn't* made a birthday cake for the girl. Oh, what *was* her name? Pamela? Anne? Dora? She could see the child in front of her, eyes bright with tears, willing her to remember. 'Please,' she was pleading, 'you *have* to remember. Hold on. Don't lose the thread.'

But there wasn't time. That was the problem. The longer she stayed here on the island, the further away she drifted from everything that had gone before. Concentrate, Flora, she told herself. Think about cakes. Chocolate meringue cake. Eggs, butter, cream. In the fridge. Walk to the fridge. What do you see?

She feels the cool flagstones underfoot, the cracks between them faintly gritty. The floor needs sweeping again, the brushes standing bristle up in the broom cupboard. There is someone sitting at the kitchen table. Sitting with his face half-hidden in his hands. His face – what little she can see of it – is wet with tears. She longs to reach out and comfort him. Longs to. Cannot. Her hands are mist and air. He is beyond her reach. Looking down, she sees her feet have brought her to the other side of the kitchen. To the white wall of the refrigerator. There she finds a note held fast to the door with several fridge magnets. She reads the note in disbelief:

Latch

Luciano's 1st hearing today.
I've gone to court with lawyer,
then I'm going on to ante-natal
clinic check-up thingy. I'll stay
over in town, so back tomorrow.
Forgot new nanny is coming by
taxi @ three. I've put her in the
Lilac Room — can you show her
around? I'll see her when I get back.

Many thanks

B

New nanny? New nanny? Her mind keeps returning to this, sticks on this. Impaled on the stark words. Even qualified with 'Forgot' it still hurts dreadfully. How can she be replaced so quickly? For alongside the pain of reading Baci's note to Latch comes a tidal race of returning memory. She is Flora McLachlan, she is the old nanny to Baci and Luciano's children. She is going to make a birthday cake for Pandora – not Pamela, Anne or even Dora. The man weeping at the kitchen table is Latch. She has promised to marry him. He believes her to be dead. She must comfort him. Without touch or speech she must reach him. Show him that love will never die. Will conquer all.

Now Baci's note flutters as the magnetic letters holding it in place move so fast they blur. First they form names: Latch; Damp; Pandora; Titus. Then words: will; love; all. And then, spinning in a spiral, they melt and fuse into new forms. New letters appear, and now the fridge magnets say: 'Love will conquer all'.

and Flora's eyes open on Death and the demon staring at her across a dimming mound of embers.

Love on a Cold Climate

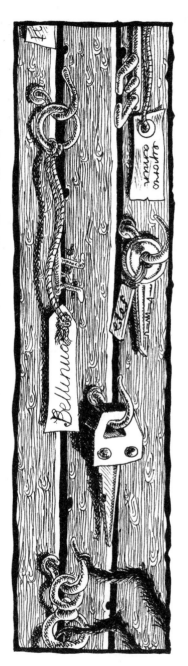

Taking great pains to protect the still-tender stump of her missing leg, Tarantella squeezed herself into the key cupboard and gazed at her daughters in despair. The seven girl-tarantulas peered back blearily through eye-watering encrustations of mascara and attempted to speak through mouth-gumming layers of lipstick smeared across their mouthparts.

'M m m m - m m m m ,' Novella the first-born managed and then, with a supreme effort, unglued her lips and uttered a desperate, 'Mmm-UM!'

'Give me strength,' groaned Tarantella, reaching for the tiny vial of make-up remover which she always carried with her when visiting her children's nursery. One by one, she scrubbed her daughters clean. First Novella, then her sisters Epistolia, Anecdota, Trilogia, Epicsaga, Emailia and finally the unfortunately named Diarya. Stripped of layers of paint and powder, the spider babies looked rather sweet, if a touch bedraggled. Aware that yet again they'd somehow managed to disgrace themselves, they prepared themselves for a long lecture from their Ageing Parent.

Tarantella took a deep breath. 'Didn't I tell you not to babble bibble yibber yibble?' she began.

'Yeah, Mum,' the spider babies sighed in unison.

'Blah blah de dum one coat of lippy only mutter mumble drone drone.'

'Whatever,' they groaned, rolling their multiple eyeballs to startling effect.

'Yada yada mascara bad nasty blah witter.'

'Uh-huh,' they grunted, their arachnid minds elsewhere entirely. Then, suddenly, they snapped back to attention. Ageing Parent was actually saying something interesting for once. Much to her amazement, Tarantella found she had her daughters' undivided attention. They were actually *listening* to her, their many eyeballs keenly focused on *her* instead of the middle distance. Tarantella rose to the occasion.

'New nanny, blah hiss, just arrived in a taxi, shock, blah hiss.'

Respectful silence from the baby spiders, whose

earliest memories included seeing the *previous* nanny, Mrs McLachlan, hurling herself into Lochnagargoyle, never to return.

'The missus gone to visit hubby in hiss prison hiss, lawyer blah.'

Sound of several baby spider jaws dropping in amazement.

'Spider-phobic Titus biped hiss, hiss, mutter, mutter, ate acanthoid wax—'

Percussive patter of seven spider baby mouths snapping shut simultaneously, followed by the shuffling sound of their little bodies heaving with barely suppressed laughter. Tiny tears of hysteria began to trickle down tiny furry faces as the spiders whooped and squeaked and snorted at the prospect of a biped with legs hairier than theirs. Helpless with laughter, they clung to the rows of ancient keys which had been quietly rusting in the gloom of the cupboard for hundreds of years. The spiderlings were having far too much fun to notice their mother's throat-cutting mime, or to hear her hissed entreaties to shut up, or even to realize that after commanding them to run for cover, she herself had vanished from sight.

Suddenly light spilt into the key cupboard and Latch's voice boomed all around. 'I wouldn't begin to know where to look, Constable...' Then a massive hand rummaged in the mess of rusting metal lying at the bottom of the cupboard, pulling out tangles of keys fringed with yellowing labels written in a faded copperplate hand.

Garden Room, Parlour, Scullery and *Maid's Room*, they read, all referring to rooms that had long since ceased to be known by these names. Latch's voice continued, 'Of course, Officer. One *could* just force the lock. However, the wardrobe in question is early Flemish Van Hausfarben, possibly from the hand of the master carpenter Ikey Yarr himself, from around seventeen hundred, and is probably the only example left in existence. While one appreciates the need to gather any evidence relating to the disappearance of Flor— Mrs McLachlan, one is nonetheless reluctant to author-ize the senseless destruction of such an inestimably precious antique treasure just because you can't be bothered to wait while I find the— Ah. *There* it is.'

Whereupon Latch's hand brushed the quivering Diarya to one side, closed around a tiny tarnished brass key and removed it from the cupboard. Outside, the sound of footsteps faded into silence, leaving just the faintest hiss of breathing some-where nearby. The spider babies listened as first their mother, then Latch, spoke together in whispers.

'Ikey *Yarr* indeed. I thought he'd spot that straight away. And what's all that nonsense about Mrs McLachlan's "disappearance"? I thought she'd committed suicide. Thrown herself in the lo— wa— I can't *bring* myself to say it.'

'Shhhhhh. Hush, spider. That's what she *wanted*

most people to think. Or at least I *think* that's what she wanted people to think. But not us. Nor the children. Especially *not* the children. Oh, it's so hard to explain.'

'Try,' came Tarantella's languid drawl. 'After all, what else do I have to do all day? Toil and spin? I don't *think* so. Come on, butler-biped, I know you're not telling me the whole story because my daughters *witnessed* what happened to Mrs McLachlan. They were *there*, remember? They *saw* her hurl herself in the company of a demon into the lo— lo— wa— Nope, can't say it, but you know what I mean. They waited in the boat for her to come back; they— Oh, for heaven's sake, you're *leaking*.'

Whereupon Latch's tear-sodden voice choked out, 'What do you *expect*? I *loved* that woman. I was so sure she hadn't drowned. For all these weeks I've been hoping she'd somehow swum to safety, was alive, hiding, waiting for the right time to return, my wee lassie, my Flora. And – and now you – *you* have stolen my hope away—'

After a short silence the spider babies could all hear the voice of Multitudina, the Illiterat, unaware that she was muscling in at an inopportune moment.

'Honestly. Why is this so *hard*? I really don't feel I've got the hang of this reading stuff at all, Tarantella. Look – what's this s'posed to mean? Love will con – love will conger – love will conger eel? *What?* Tarantella? Help!'

Embarrassed to be found weeping in front of a rat, Latch turned away and blew his nose. Tarantella scuttled across the kitchen to assist Multitudina, who was peering at the fridge, where someone had laboriously spelled out a message in nursery alphabet magnets.

'Love weel conger ill? Lav wool clanger ell? Live wall clingon all?' Multitudina squeaked with frustration and slapped herself on her head as if trying to beat understanding into her brain. 'Ohhhh, why am I so *dumb*?'

Tarantella closed her eyes briefly, took several deep breaths, then gathering her mouthparts into an approximation of a smile said, '*If* you'd paid more attention to my earlier seminars on correct vowel usage, you'd be reading by now. Sigh. However, I refuse to give up on you, no matter how dumb you appear to be. Rrrrright. From the top. How do we pronounce the one like a nose without whiskers?'

'A,' muttered Multitudina.

'And the one like a sideways fork?'

'E,' the rat sighed.

'And a single twiglet?'

'I.'

'And the inedible bit of a doughnut?'

'O.'

'And finally, an empty cup?'

'Uh.'

'*Now* read the message on the fridge,' the spider instructed.

'Love will conquer all,' Multitudina pronounced slowly, then muttered to herself, 'I *still* don't understand.'

Latch, meanwhile, was staring at the fridge as if it had addressed him personally. 'Tarantella,' he whispered, 'did you write that? *Love will conquer all?*'

The spider rolled her eyes in disgust. 'Hardly. I didn't write it and I don't believe it either. Romantic nonsense. Love doesn't conquer anything, it's just something you bipeds have invented to sweeten the bitter truth: life is nasty, brutish and sho—'

The kitchen door opened to reveal a weasel-faced detective holding an item of women's underwear at arm's length as if he expected it to launch itself at his throat and attempt to throttle him in its lacy folds. Colour flooded Latch's face: he realized that he was probably looking at a garment only intended for the eyes of its missing owner.

'Would you say that this item belonged to Mrs Flora McLachlan . . . sir?

'I . . . um,' Latch began, his face aflame. 'I, er . . . can't say, Officer. Never having seen Flo— Mrs McLachlan . . . in her underwear . . . not part of one's official uniform . . . Oh, for heaven's *sake*, man. If that was in her chest of drawers or wherever women keep such . . . items, then I imagine it must be safe to assume that it was hers, don't you think?'

The policeman's eyes narrowed, making him look even more like a weasel. 'Oh, no, sir. In murder cases there's no such thing as a safe assumption. We in the CID only deal in hard facts and traceable evidence. I must ask you to accompany me to Mrs McLachlan's bedroom in order to assist me in finding some item that you can positively identify as having belonged to her. For the DNA, sir. A hairbrush would be perfect. We've found traces of human blood inside the boat that you keep down by the loch and we'd like to see if there's a match.' Noticing Latch's expression, the detective added, 'I appreciate that this is very distressing for you, sir, but we won't take up more of your time than necessary. Now, if you wouldn't mind, the sooner we do this, the sooner we'll be on our way.' And striding towards the kitchen door, the policeman stood to one side to allow Latch to precede him into the hall.

Freshly Minty

The doorbell rang in the great hall for the third time. Pandora almost collided with one of the younger plainclothes officers as they reached the door at the same time. Catching sight of his horrified face, she realized her mistake.

'Titus?' she gasped, as the door opened to reveal a complete stranger standing smiling uncertainly on the front step.

There was an awkward pause; just long enough to bring colour to the stranger's face; plenty of time for Pandora to wish herself elsewhere; and aeons for Titus to discover that the young woman on the doorstep had eyes the exact shade of blue of the bowl of lavender flowers on the table in the great hall. He took a deep and shaky breath.

'Signor Strega-Borgia?' the stranger guessed, extending a hand.

'Not *exactly*.' Titus's voice had altered, along with his appearance. He risked a look at his sister, then wished he hadn't. She really ought to close her mouth, he decided. Total strangers simply don't need to see that kind of acreage of tonsil tissue.

The stranger faltered, blushed and turned to the gaping Pandora. 'Pavlova?' she enquired hopefully in a cut-glass accent. 'Um. I'm looking for Mrs Baci Borgia. I'm the temporary, the, er, the replacement— Oh, gosh, this is all a bit awkward. Your mummy told me about poor Mrs McGloughlin—'

'McLachlan,' Pandora snapped, wondering what on earth this young woman was doing here.

Titus suddenly remembered that he had promised his mother that he would tell Pandora about the new nanny.

'Sorry,' the stranger continued. 'Gosh, I am *so* sorry. Mrs McLachlan. Well, er, your mummy – I mean your *mother* asked me to stand in for – to, er, just for a while until, um. Yes . . .' She tailed off, blushing deeply, gazed at her feet for a second, took a deep breath and tried again.

'Pavlova. I'm delighted to meet you. Your mum— mother's told me so much about you. About you both. About all of you. I'm your temporary, replacement, stand-in new nanny, Minty.'

Pandora stared, aghast, then looked across at Titus, who was looking guilty and somewhat embarrassed. She summoned all her reserves of politeness and managed to say, 'Do come inside. I'm sorry but our mother has had to go to co— out for a while.'

Minty's smile wobbled as they all simultaneously became aware of a reek of ripe decay rolling in the front door. Titus gagged, Pandora coughed, Minty's nose wrinkled and she pointed her face into the air like a well-trained golden retriever scenting spoor. Upwind from where they stood was the moat, now in the process of being drained. Several policemen in full uniform were watching while a large yellow truck sucked up moat water with a shuddering pink hose, before disgorging it into the nearby shrubbery. The smell was indescribably foul and to add to everyone's discomfort, the vibrations of the hose made it look like a giant length of throbbing intestine. It pulsed and spluttered and stank as Pandora and Titus hauled Minty's vast collection of luggage into StregaSchloss, while the owner of all seventeen suitcases, trunks and rucksacks apologized profusely, got in the way, talked non-stop and took sneaky peeks at her reflection in the burnished metal of the suit of armour in the hall.

'There,' growled Titus. For the first time since the onset of his acanthoid-accelerated manhood he was delighted to have the extra muscle-power that it had bestowed upon him. No *way*, he decided, could he have hauled that lot into the house yesterday. But, more importantly, what on earth did the new nanny need all those cases *for*? Pandora's thoughts were running along similar lines. She was remembering the day Mrs McLachlan first came to StregaSchloss to be their nanny. *She'd* arrived in the clothes she stood up in, carrying nothing more than a battered plastic handbag . . . And now Pandora's nose was prickling and her eyes were filling up – bother, bother, bother—

'Oh, *look*.' Minty gasped. 'This must be Dump.'

Hurling herself downstairs under Vesper's guidance, Damp was too absorbed in trying to achieve lift-off to notice the presence of a stranger in the hall. Vesper, however, had spotted Minty, and decided to make himself scarce, incorrectly putting her down as the type who'd throw a hissy-fit followed by anything else within reach upon sighting a bat. Unaware that her tutor had vanished, Damp came to a halt on the bottom step of the main staircase, folded her arms against her chest in the manner Vesper had shown her and was about to demonstrate her newfound talent for hanging upside down from the banisters when she caught sight of Minty.

Minty beamed and clapped both her hands together in a display of barely contained enthusiasm. Pandora groaned. She'd always loathed anything that smacked of organized 'fun', and here was the new nanny acting like a bouncy combination of gym mistress, nursery nurse and children's TV presenter. Oh, sigh, she thought, watching in dismay as Minty breezed onwards.

'Hello, Dump,' she said softly, walking towards the child. 'I'm Minty. Gosh, I *do* hope we're going to become the best of friends—'

Gosh, thought Damp. I don't think so; not if you can't say my name prop'ly.

'I'm *so* looking forward to playing lots and lots of games with you – and meeting *all* your lovely toys and dollies and teddies.'

Don't let me hold you back, Damp decided, wondering why it was that strange grown-ups always spoke to her as if she were slightly dim and profoundly deaf.

'And do you know what, Dump? Ever since your mummy asked me to come and be your nanny, I've just been *so* exci—'

'Nanny?' Damp's brows plunged.

Oh *heck*, thought Titus. I was supposed to tell Damp too. And I forgot. Something to do with hiding in my room and hoping I could stay hidden until the acanthoid wax wore off. Oh triple heck, he amended, catching sight of Damp's expression.

'*Not* nanny,' Damp stated. 'Got nanny. Don't want 'nother one. Thank you. Go 'way. *Go 'way. Not want nanny.*'

'Oh, sweetheart, don't worry . . .' Minty breathed, aghast at having unwittingly caused such distress, and trying to draw Damp into her arms for a consoling hug.

'GO 'WAY. GO 'WAY. GO 'WAY!' Damp sobbed, flapping her arms like a demented windmill. 'OUT, OUT. GO 'WAY. NOT WANT YOU, LADY.'

Pandora looked down at the floor and observed that Damp's feet were hovering several centimetres *above* the bottom step. Suspecting that the new nanny would pass out in terror if she saw that her youngest client was able to levitate, she wrapped her arms round her little sister and hauled her off towards the kitchen.

'Damp, come *on*. It's OK. Let's go and make some pudding for supper. I'll look after you till Mum gets back.' Smiling insincerely at Minty, Pandora turned to her brother. 'Titus? Why don't you introduce Mini— Oh *sorry*, Ninny to the beasts? Or vice versa. I'm sure they'll be *far* more scared of her than she'll be of them.' She left this veiled threat a-dangle, and bore Damp off.

Seeing Minty's eyes widen as several possible meanings of Pandora's words occurred to her, Titus attempted to be hospitable. 'Let me take your stuff upstairs,' he suggested, hauling a rucksack onto his back and hefting a suitcase in each hand. 'Follow me,' he gasped, and praying he wouldn't fall to his knees under the combined weight of all three items of luggage, Titus made a run for the stairs. Halfway to the first landing he knew he had to stop before his arms fell off. Pretending he was merely stopping to brush a stray hair from his eyes, he turned round to see that the new nanny hadn't even made it to the first step. Indeed, she was standing in the middle of the hall, exactly where he'd left her, transfixed with terror as Ffup came lumbering along the corridor towards her. The dragon carried her baby son Nestor under one arm, her voice raised in loud dismay.

'I *told* you to let me know when you *need* a poo. Not after you've *done* one. *Then* it's too late. *Then* poor Mummy has to go and find the shovel, the scrubbing brush, the disinfectant, the rubber gloves, three rolls of toilet paper *and* a clothes peg for Mummy's no—' Ffup came to an abrupt halt in front of Minty. Her vast yellow eyes widened in alarm. 'Oh *dear*,' she quavered, clutching Nestor tightly and pointing at the new nanny with a vibrating talon. 'Look, pet. It's a *golden-hair*. Our horoscope said to beware of them. Specially ones with tinned boyfriends called George. Let's not panic, will we?' The pitch of Ffup's voice was creeping upwards as the dragon began to hyperventilate. 'We'll just tiptoe past it, pretending it's not there – try not to attract its attention. Slowly, that's it – oh no. It's – it's – it's staring straight *at* us. *Aaaaaaaargh* – RUN FOR YOUR LIFE!'

And dropping Nestor on the floor, Ffup leapt for the front door and struggled hysterically with the latch, little jets of flame escaping from her nostrils and vent in her haste to put as much distance as possible between herself and the unspecified threat of Minty the golden-hair.

Titus rushed back downstairs just in time to witness the new nanny's eyes roll backwards in her head as she crumpled to the floor in a faint.

'Oh *no!*' Titus roared in dismay. '*No. No. NO!* Not all the suitcases and *her* too. Pandora! *Pan!* Help! HELP!'

'You . . . still . . . haven't . . . explained . . . what's *happened* to you.' Pandora's words were punctuated by gasps of effort as together she and Titus dragged the final cabin trunk upstairs to Minty's room.

'Phew – what a *beast.* What on earth was *in* that one? Bricks? Weights? Maybe she's a secret body builder – talking of which, come *on,* Titus, what's happened to you? Yesterday you looked like a scrawny twig and today . . .' Pandora blushed. Suddenly she'd run out of words.

'Today?' Titus raised his eyebrows. 'Oh – you know. Mum's been on at us for years to eat our greens, and I guess finally the broccoli worked and made me grow up stron— Ow! *Don't.* That *hurt.*'

'Well, you deserve it, you lying toad. Come *on,* Titus. Those muscles aren't due to eating broccoli. And your voice has gone all growly . . .' Pandora tailed off: she didn't think she could mention Titus's incipient five-o'clock shadow or his six-pack or the gruesome fact that even his toes appeared to have sprouted little puffs of fur. She could see all these changes, but she knew she'd spontaneously self-combust if she had to voice them. Fortunately Titus had no such qualms.

'You mean the fact I've turned into a grown-up?' he muttered, heaving Minty's biggest cabin trunk across the floor and dropping it with a crash beside the bed. 'I guess I'd hoped you wouldn't notice. Or something. You know. Like, because I'm your brother I'm sort of invisible kind of thing. Oh, *God*, Pandora, can't you tell? This is another one of Mum's dodgy spells. Some stupid stuff she calls acanthoid wax. She put it in our dinner by mistake—'

'WHAAAAAT?' Pandora yelped. 'You mean I ate it too? I'm going to go all hairy? Oh, *no*. No! Tell me it's not—'

'You didn't eat it, remember?' Titus sighed. 'None of us did. Not even Mum, and *she* cooked it. I ate one mouthful, but you took one sniff and dumped the lot into Knot's bowl when Mum's back was turned. So don't worry. You're safe. Even Knot didn't eat it – though he's a bloke already and he couldn't *get* any hairier. Now come on and help me drag Minty onto a sofa or something.'

'She sounds like a toothpaste,' Pandora grumbled, following Titus out into the corridor. 'How long will it last then, Titus? Your – er . . . furriness?'

'Two days to a week, Mum said.' Titus tried to

smile, but failed utterly. 'I tried to use Dad's electric razor this morning, and it *bit* me. *And* I don't fit my own clothes, either. I'm wearing Dad's stuff, which feels seriously weird, not to mention deeply sad. I mean, Dad's clothes are just so . . . boring. Shirts and trousers. Not a single pair of jeans. No T-shirts. God. I feel like an accountant or something. Stop laughing, Pan. It's *not* funny.' And turning his back on her, he fled downstairs feeling more like a toddler having a tantrum than the grown man reflected back at him in the hall mirror.

Gagged with a Spoon

Damp stood on a chair at the kitchen table, counting frozen raspberries into a bowl under Latch's supervision.

'Eleventy, twelveteen, sixty, a *hundered*.'

'Who on earth is this *now*?' Latch muttered to himself, hearing a vehicle approaching outside.

'Twelveteen, seventyleven, a *thousand*.'

Wiping his hands on a dishcloth, Latch hurried into the hall. He saw a black Range Rover crawling along the track to StregaSchloss. Blacked-out windows too, he observed, wondering if Baci had decided to come home early. He'd found her note half-hidden under the fridge, but by then the new

nanny had not only arrived, she'd been introduced to the children, the beasts *and* the rats – with predictable results. Plus she'd been given the Ancestors' Room, not the Lilac Room, which was *always* a mistake, even for the psychically lumpen guest – which, he suspected, Miss Minty was not.

'Six thousand million squillion and *one*,' Damp said loudly, trying to impress Latch with her precocious grasp of numbers. She poked the mound of frozen raspberries in the bowl in front of her and sighed. Latch was busy, Mummy had gone to see Daddy, Pandora and Titus were looking after the not-nanny, and of Vesper there was no sign save for a little offering of bat-poo on top of a wizened apple in the fruit bowl. Damp prodded the raspberries again and then paused, her attention caught by something in amongst the frosty berries. She could see a thread buried under the top layer of raspberries. A silver thread. Had Latch found it in the freezer along with the fruit? Damp reached out to touch it just as the doorbell rang three times.

Luciano sat handcuffed to a bench in the rear of a windowless police van, miserably contemplating the miles now dividing him from his beloved family back at StregaSchloss. He was stunned by the day's events, unable to grasp just how desperate a position he now found himself in. It was un-bearable. He was going to die – he couldn't—

Beside him, a youth who appeared to have been

marinaded in essence of rancid ashtray stirred himself and gave a series of fruity bubbling coughs while gasping out, 'Was. That. Hack, cough, wheeze. Your. Missus?'

'I beg your pardon?'

'Back there. In court? The one all in black? Hair, hat, dress. Nice legs, if you don't mind my saying—'

'I do, actually,' Luciano muttered. 'I mind a lot. That lady is my wife. I'd be very grateful if you refrained from making personal remar—'

'Hold it, hold it. Calm *down*, Jimmy.' The wheezing youth held up his hands in surrender. 'No offence meant, pal. I'm sure she's very ladylike. Very. That is when your fancy lawyer isn't patting her on the bu—'

'Listen,' Luciano hissed, 'one more remark like that, signore, and I'll find a way to ram these handcuffs right down your insolent lying throat. Shut *up. Capisce?*' Had he really just said that? His eyes were hot and dry, his jaw rigid, teeth clenched; he was horribly aware that he had just been consumed by a red tide of rage.

'Jeeez – no need for that,' whined the wheezy one. 'Don't get your knickers in a twist, Jimmy. Aw right?' He moved away, rattling his chains till his handcuffs brought him to an abrupt halt. Coughing revoltingly, he subsided into a sullen silence.

Luciano stared at him, trying to drag his thoughts away from the memory of Baci. Baci in deepest black. Baci in mourning. For him? For their marriage? He felt sick. The deathly reek of stale cigarettes coming from his fellow prisoner coupled with the police van's reek of industrial-strength disinfectant were conspiring to make him feel horribly nauseous. He tried to think of something else; his eyes roamed desperately over the graffitied metal walls surrounding him. Regrettably, these were decorated with words which alone would have made his gorge rise. Luciano closed his eyes. He was in hell, he decided. He'd been in hell for approximately three hours now, ever since the judge had peered down at him with an expression of utter disgust, spitting out the words as if he grudged even the tiny effort required in pronouncing them.

'Trial is fixed for December the twenty-first. Take the prisoner down.'

That was when Luciano had howled out loud. Like a dog. He hadn't realized he was capable of producing such a noise, but he was incapable of stopping himself.

'AowwwwwwwwOOOOOOOOOOOOOOO.'

The judge glared and banged his gavel, but Luciano didn't or wouldn't or couldn't hear. He was staring transfixed at Baci. Poor Baci, crying as they led him away from her; back to those filthy cells; back to Malky and Man-Mountain; back to that unspeakable coffee-drek. And as he turned round to gaze at her one last time before they hauled him off, he saw his fancy new lawyer was leading her away, one proprietorial arm around her shoulders, smirking at Luciano with an expression on his face that clearly said, *This one's* mine, *and there's not a thing you can do about it.*

And he was right, Luciano thought wretchedly. There was nothing he could do about it. Not only had he lost his liberty, and appeared to be in danger of losing his wife; if the signals now coming from his stomach were to be believed, he was about to lose his lunch as well (one ham sandwich with scant acquaintance with pigs or, indeed, wheat, followed by one carton of fruits of the forest drink, about which the best one could say was that it was wet).

Oh dear, thought Luciano as his stomach hurtled upwards. Oh dear, oh dear, oh dear.

Hours later, showered and changed into an elegant après-vomit number in brown sacking with repeating arrow details, Luciano was dropped straight into the main prison population at Her Majesty's concrete hotel for bad blokes in Glasgow. By then he was past caring. If a demon had appeared, impaled Luciano on the business end of a toasting fork and slung him onto a barbecue, he couldn't have felt any worse. Holding a plastic tray in both hands, he sleepwalked forwards in a queue whose destination was a row of aluminium food vats of the kind popular in schools, hospitals and other such institutions the world over. A dank miasma of massacred vegetables curled around the line of men, all of whom appeared to have experienced DIY plastic surgery to their faces. Edging closer to Luciano than was strictly necessary was a particularly fine example: a shrunken man, his mouth twisted out of shape by a fearsome pink scar which snaked down from his nose, bisected his upper lip, dimpled his chin and vanished from sight below his Adam's apple. Luciano blinked. Dear God, mustn't *stare*. Mustn't. Look into the middle distance, he commanded himself. Do *not*, repeat *not*, make eye contact.

The edge of the man's dinner tray pressed insistently into Luciano's ribs, and to his horror he heard himself addressed thus:

'Hey. Psssst. You. Yeah, *you*. Borgia, yeah.'

With a supreme effort of will, Luciano forced himself not to react. He transformed his neck into a pillar of concrete laced with steel girders and his mouth clamped shut on a squeak of terror. Unfortunately, his stomach wasn't quite so reticent. Recently evacuated, it let rip with an echoing, twanging arpeggio of digestive complaint which sounded as if it was being broadcast live from Coventry Cathedral. This appeared to mollify his tormentor.

'Hungry, huh? I'll let you eat, then,' and the dinner tray was removed from Luciano's ribs as a meaty hand descended on his shoulder. *'Buon giorno*, signore.' The man's voice was hoarse and urgent, as if he was talking against a ticking clock.

'No, thassa right. Don't turn round. Just keep looking straight ahead. Thassa good, *capisce*?'

Luciano grunted assent, amazed at how manly his grunt sounded.

'I justa have to pass on my congratulations,' the voice continued, kneading Luciano's shoulder with quite unnecessary enthusiasm. 'Your brother Lucifer – what a guy. What an incredible guy. A giant amongst pygmies. You know, signore, your brother is my hero. *Si*. You musta be so *proud* to be related to him. And only lasta week – that bank? The aeroplane? All those dumb cops? What bravado. Sucha brilliance. He's one in a million, don'tcha think?'

Luciano assessed this. What on earth was the man on about? His brother Lucifer was bad news. He was scum. *Last* time he'd seen his wonderful brother, Lucifer had just shot Luciano's lawyer and had been threatening to kill Baci – oh my God, Baci.

Luciano's shoulder went another three rounds with the meat-grinder as his fellow-prisoner continued with his sycophantic ravings.

'Those cops – puh. He blew them away, huh? Bam bam bam BAM! They hada no idea what kind of man they were dealing with.'

Luciano drifted away inside his head. He had no wish to hear what kind of man his brother was. He knew *exactly* what kind of man Lucifer was. To his cost, he knew that Lucifer was the kind of man who grew out of a child whose mission statement appeared to have been to cause pain. Luciano shuddered. Thanks to his brother, he had no finger-prints left on either of his hands from the day when Lucifer had embedded Frosty, his pet mouse, inside a vast ball of dry ice. Although Luciano knew that his mouse was beyond saving, he had still tried to rescue it and had to be hospitalized afterwards. Thanks to his brother, Luciano had a bald spot behind his left ear where Lucifer had branded him with a white-hot poker ('Let's play cattle ranchers, Luce – I'll be the rancher branding my herd, you'll be the herd'). Thanks to his vile, corrupt, vicious brother, even now, thirty years later, he couldn't eat anything with pastry around it, not since the awful time when Lucifer had told him exactly what kind of meat had been in the pie he'd so keenly devoured – Luciano had never kept a dog again, either . . .

Trying to drag his mind away from such horrors, Luciano turned to thoughts of his real family; the family he'd *made*, as opposed to the one he'd inherited. He corrected himself. The family he and *Baci* had made. He missed her so much. Right now he needed her more than he'd ever done before. She alone could push the nightmares away. When would he ever see her again? It's so *unfair*, he thought. Here am I, an innocent man, stuck in this filthy prison which by rights is where that evil swine of a brother of mine ought to be. And where is my brother?

A voice hissed in his ear, 'Is it true, signore, that

your brother still keeps a suite at the Bagliadi in Bologna, one of the most expensive hotels in Italy? And that he has the local police chiefs over to dinner once a month? Pfffff. What a guy. *What* an incredible g-g-g-gug-g—'

Luciano spun round. The queue behind him had scattered, as if they'd discovered a plague victim in their midst. Luciano's garrulous colleague had fallen to his knees, his sightless eyes fixed on Luciano's navel as he slowly toppled towards the floor, the sharpened handle of a spoon embedded in his neck, his silenced tongue proving once and for all that dead men don't tell tales.

Letting Go

Hearing her husband howl like a wolf had shocked Baci out of her assumption that justice would prevail. He is *innocent*, she wanted to scream. Can't you *see*? The Luciano she knew and loved would never, *could* never harm another living being. Her heart hammered in her chest and she felt as if she were about to faint. Inside her, the unborn baby uncurled from its furled slumbers, its limbs twitching frantically. *What?* it wailed silently. *What fresh hell is this?*

As Luciano's howls echoed round the courtroom, the repulsive Munro MacAlister Hall wrapped a heavy arm around Baci's shoulders and she felt the

first stirrings of real fear. She was no lawyer, but even with a layman's understanding of what had occurred in court, it looked as if the fabled Munro MacAlister Hall had just ensured that Luciano was indeed sent to prison. But *why*? He was supposed to be keeping Luciano *out* of prison. Something was seriously wrong. MacAlister Hall was acting like the prosecution, not the defence. And if he didn't stop patting her like – like *that*, she was going to take a swing at him with her handbag. Something of this must have shown in her expression because he suddenly backed off, swept his papers into a brief-case and gave her a cursory nod.

'I must run, signora. Time is money. I'll be in touch in due course.' And without offering a single word of comfort regarding Luciano's plight, Munro MacAlister Hall left the building.

Thankfully, the ghastly slurping mud-sucking sounds had stopped and the moat was now officially drained. A band of yellow and black crime-scene tape fluttered forlornly in the chilly breeze, cordoning off the area from everyone except the Serious Crimes Unit. The rose-quartz drive was smeared with decaying lily pads and, in the absence of master, mistress and now moat, Tock had decamped to the guest bathroom on the first floor of StregaSchloss. The blank windows of the house reflected two figures standing on the rose quartz, the smaller one hunched and shivering, hands jammed in pockets, the larger one waving its arms around while taking a meagre rucksack out of the back of its car and dropping it onto the drive. Drawing the collar of his cashmere coat up against the cold, Munro MacAlister Hall slammed the back door of the Range Rover and turned to his scowling son.

'Right. I'm off. Have you got everything?' he barked, aware that he was going to miss his flight if he didn't get a move on. The client had been very specific. There was to be no face-to-face meeting. The money would be in a suitcase in the south-facing changing room of the Armani boutique on Via Fiscale-Castrato . . .

'Dad—'

'*What?* I'm in a hurry, you know. D'you need more money?'

'Dad. Is Titus's dad really a – you know, a murderer?'

Munro looked longingly at the driver's seat of his car. Having spent approximately two precious minutes of his afternoon explaining to the Borgia children why Daddy wasn't likely to be walking in through the front door at any point in the near future, Munro had just about exhausted his year's allowance of tact and sensitivity.

'Who *cares*?' he snapped. 'Now. Out of my way. I've got business to attend to.' And seeing Rand's stricken expression – 'Oh, for crying out loud, don't *look* at me like that, you pathetic excuse for a son' –

he strode round to the driver's door, hauled it open and climbed inside.

Rand flinched as the big engine roared into life, his look of pure hatred glancing off the armoured panels of his father's car. Moments later the Range Rover had gone, leaving behind a cloud of dust and fumes in which stood a boy with a ghost-white face and fists clenching and unclenching with impotent rage.

As the bloated Range Rover disappeared down the track in a cloud of dust, Latch took charge. Armed with a pen, a notepad and the telephone, the butler had spent the next hour on the phone in Luciano's study, trying to find out what had gone so disastrously wrong in court. Waiting in the kitchen for news of their father, Titus and Pandora had chewed their fingernails down to the quick by the time they heard Latch finish on the phone. Damp was in the garden being unamused by Minty and the beasts were huddled round the kitchen range in a most uncharacteristic silence. The atmosphere of impending doom was so intense, Titus felt he was being buried alive.

When Latch reappeared in the kitchen, he seemed to bring air, light and sunshine in with him. Against all odds he made them believe that everything would come right in the end. He hugged Pandora and patted Titus on the shoulder in a man-to-man fashion; he poured large cups of tea and suggested that with Luciano temporarily 'detained', Titus was now the man of the house. Then, spotting Titus's expression of terror at this prospect, the butler added swiftly that because he'd been employed at StregaSchloss long before any of the children had been born, it might be a good idea if *he* were to take charge of the running of the house, instead of his young master or mistress being burdened with such matters. Not in charge of anything important, he had said, twinkling reassuringly at the children; just taking care of incidentals like – oh, all the cooking, shopping, driving, laundry and bill paying. Also he could take care of supervising other members of staff, which with Marie Bain gone and Flo— Mrs McLachlan missing, really only consisted of Miss Araminta.

At this point Titus had to restrain himself from flinging his arms round Latch's neck and weeping with relief.

In the humming, ticking darkness of the freezer lay Strega-Nonna, oldest surviving Strega-Borgia, great-great-great-great-great-great-grandmother of Titus, Pandora and Damp, deep-frozen at her own request till a cure was found for old age. Beneath her foil-wrapped body a bag of frozen peas shifted, this in turn causing a plastic box full of tiny deep-frozen clones to dream of an invasion by green asteroids. Strega-Nonna's lips moved imperceptibly, forming one syllable of denial.

No . . .

Her hands now scrabbled frantically, breaking free of the layers of protective tinfoil, scraping against the lid of the freezer; her nails removing the rime of frost covering the helpful tips printed there: **MEAT**, 3 MONTHS; **FISH**, I MONTH; **BREAD**, I MONTH; **ANCESTORS**, 600 YEARS.

Again her lips moved, this time twice.

Flora. Flooooraaaaaaaa.

Since her voice was no louder than the beat of moth wings on a lampshade, it was hardly surprising that no-one heard her cries.

Helllllllp, she breathed. *I've gone and lost Flora's thread.*

Many frozen moments of ticking darkness passed while Strega-Nonna regretted the loss of spontaneity that comes from being packed in permafrost. Not for the first time, she wished that medical science would speed up the work she hoped they were doing to find a cure for old age. Though for once, she comforted herself, it wasn't extreme decrepitude to blame for losing Flora's magic thread. Someone has been in my freezer, disturbing my slumbers, she decided. Some hungry family member, no doubt, in too much of a hurry to notice that they'd pulled Flora's thread from my grasp along with their fish fungus and coven chips. The *thread*, she mourned. Oh confound it. I'm going to *have* to defreeze myself. Exfrost? Unchill? It would take about seventy-two hours in a warm kitchen before she could safely be said to have defrosted, and only then could she begin to search for her lost thread. Bother. Bother, drat, blast and a pox on it. A plague on its houses, a blight on its policies.

Again Strega-Nonna's fingers scrabbled in the darkness, and again they found nothing save for the remote control, which, when pressed, began the lengthy defrosting process. The ancient bones beneath her skin gleamed white as her fingers clamped down on the keypad and cut the power supply to the freezer. Right, she thought. Get me out of here. The remote fell from her hand, sliding over a bag of oven chips and coming to rest beside a box of fish fingers. Strega-Nonna forced her heart to slow down once more while she waited in the dark for movement to return to her limbs, her thoughts spinning freely in circles. Where was that thread? Was it lost for ever? How would Flora ever return without it?

The thread was the magical equivalent of Hansel and Gretel's breadcrumbs; without it Strega-Nonna feared that Flora would be doomed to wander in the dark forest for ever. *If* that was where she was. Strega-Nonna never asked, and Flora never told. There had been many times over the centuries when she'd reeled her friend back to safety on the end of that thread, like an angler landing a fish. Sometimes, Flora had fairly flown back, the thread spiralling in silver coils, spinning through Strega-Nonna's fingers; other times, she had been a dead weight, drained by some unspoken event, barely able to assist in her own return. But *never* before had the thread been lost, or broken.

Entombed in ice, Strega-Nonna nearly wept with frustration at her own powerlessness. She'd hoped to cheat death by choosing the half-life of the cryogenically preserved, but as the centuries had rolled past, she realized that the only person she was cheating was herself. Friends, lovers, husbands and children had grown old and died as Strega-Nonna passed through cycles of freezing and defrosting like a human ice floe. Time upon time she would find herself burying a loved one and swearing that this time she would allow death to claim her; but over and over a little voice in her head would say, *Not yet. Just a little more time, Amelia. Who knows, maybe a day might come when humans won't have to die. Let's not go just yet, Amelia.*

It had been very persuasive, that little voice. Strega-Nonna had listened to its seductive whisper for over six hundred years and had built a life of sorts around staying alive, even if most of that life was no life at all, but merely a state of suspended animation. But now . . . she was tired of waiting. Human beings were never going to be immortal, no matter how much they might strive to be. The bittersweet knowledge of their own mortality was the very thing that made them human. Take that away, she decided, and they had as much heart as – as an ice floe. So. It was time, she thought. Time to go. Find the thread, reel Flora back in and allow herself to become part of the earth that had nourished her for all these long years. Let her great-great-great-great-great-great-grandchildren plant a tree above her, so that one day some tiny particle of her, some atom of herself would rejoice in the feel of the wind and the sun and the welcome rain once more. With luck, she would get to hold the newest little Strega-Borgia before—

In the distance the phone rang several times, then stopped. The normal sounds of StregaSchloss wove their soporific spell around Strega-Nonna and she drifted off once more, her fingers reflexively clutching a thread that wasn't there, her walnut-wrinkly face gathered into a puzzled frown.

One of Us

The raspberries had defrosted and dissolved into a magenta puddle by the time Damp remembered that she'd been supposed to be counting them out to bolster the apple crumble Latch had intended to serve at supper time. Now, it was debatable whether anyone would have any appetite left after the grumpy man had driven away in his big black car. Supper lay in its component parts across the kitchen table, Latch had gone to find Minty, Titus was making headache-inducing sounds upstairs with Rand and Pandora had retreated with a book to her bedroom. Left alone in the kitchen, Damp wondered why everyone was pretending not to know when Mummy and Daddy would come home. Why did Mummy have to go to hostiple and see Auntie Naytil. Who *was* Auntie Naytil anyway? Why was Daddy unable to get away from work? Daddy always used to go into the library and say he was going to work. Why did everyone think Damp wasn't clever enough to spot all the big fat lies that were piling up, one on top of the other, like a badly made Lego tower?

Perched on the rim of a teapot high up on the china dresser, Tarantella was knitting a tiny vest for one of her daughters out of a surplus length of spider silk and was disinclined to answer questions.

'Haven't you anything better to do?' she enquired peevishly as Damp stirred the raspberries into pink sludge with her index finger. 'In the absence of *both* your parents you really ought to consider leaving home and getting a job. *I* left home when I was three weeks old. Still, at least you've finally perfected toilet training. For the supposed master race, you lot are surprisingly slow to work out what those big white porcelain things with flush mechanisms are for.' Sighing mightily, Tarantella peered at her knitting and mumbled to herself, 'Knit one, purl two, transfer next three stitches to cable needle and drop down back of work, purl two, knit one—' She broke off, staring at the silver thread Damp was wrapping round her thumb. With a gasp, the tarantula scampered down from her vantage point and swung onto the kitchen table.

'Did you spin that yourself?' she gasped in awed tones, reaching out to stroke the thread with one leg. 'It's remarkably fine work – all the more so considering you're an absolute beginner.' Tarantella bestowed on Damp her toothiest and most encouraging smile, her mouthparts agape.

Damp gazed at the silver thread wound round her thumb, then peered at the grinning tarantula. Feeling mystified as to what Tarantella was talking about, she popped her thumb into her mouth while she considered what to do next.

'Auuuuuk,' squawked Tarantella, her seven legs giving way beneath her. 'Oh, the horror, the horror – don't *do* that.'

Damp's mouth opened and she hauled her thumb back out again, remembering that in common with this bossy tarantula, Mrs McLachlan had also commanded her to remove her thumb from her mouth when the occasion demanded. She looked at her thumb in confusion, wondering just what it was about *this* digit in particular that roused such passionate antipathy in grown-ups. Suddenly she noticed that the silvery thread was not only wrapped several times around her thumb; it also snaked across the kitchen table and disappeared out of the door to the herb garden. Climbing down from her seat, Damp tugged on the thread to see if it would stretch or snap. Instead, it gave a distant deep *twonggg*, as if a giant cello string had been plucked on the other side of the world. Intrigued, she tugged again, and once more the same far-off bass note sounded.

From the kitchen table, Tarantella coughed pointedly. 'When you've *quite* finished,' she began. '*As* I was saying, I think it's high time you began your proper education. You're a baby witch, in case you've forgotten. Now that you've finished your flying lessons with that vulgar bat, I think I ought to teach you some basic web design, hmmm?'

Damp looked with longing at her silver thread, desperate to discover what lay at its other end. However, she was aware that Tarantella was making her a most generous and unrepeatable offer and would be mortally offended if she declined. Swallowing her impatience to follow the thread to its conclusion, Damp stuffed it under the cushion of her chair, climbed on top of it and smiled at Tarantella with affection.

'Tan'tella, show me. Please, thank you.'

'Rrrrright.' Tarantella extruded a long length of perfect silk and held it up for Damp to admire. '*Don't* touch. Today I shall demonstrate how to wrap your dinner, your enemies, your larder and anything else that takes your fancy.'

'Hurry up, please,' Damp demanded abruptly. 'Not-nanny Toothpaste coming soon.'

'I *beg* your pardon?' Tarantella frowned. 'Hurry *up*? Do you think these kinds of skills can be learnt in one easy lesson? These are arcane secrets I am about to divulge to you; arachnid lore passed down from mother to daughter in an unbroken thread of wisdom which has flowed from generation to gen—'

'Tan'tella?' Damp whispered. 'You're like me, aren't you?'

Surprisingly the tarantula didn't snort in derision or fall about laughing at such human presumption. Instead, she blinked several times in rapid succession and then said, 'I'm impressed, human-child. I wouldn't have expected you to put that one together for years yet. Yes. We're the same. I'm one of you, you're one of us. I chose a spider form, and you chose to be human. Pfffff. Poor you. No matter. You can always change your mind next time round. Now, enough. Don't interrupt. You have a lot of catching up to do. Today, we're going to learn wrapping. Watch verrrry closely – here we go . . .'

The Moral Munros

Rand glared at Titus across the expanse of balding rug that graced the floor of his guest bedroom.

'What's your problem?' he sneered, raising the drumsticks above the hi-hat prior to bringing them down so fast and hard that further conversation proved to be impossible until the after-echo of clashing cymbals had faded to a dull hiss.

By which time Rand was beating out a measured *thudda, thud, thud, thudda, thud* on the bass drum, over which he laid a vaguely familiar rhythm on snare and bells. He looked up at Titus and gave a twisted grin, closed his eyes and surrendered himself to the beat.

'*Rand*' – Titus tried to keep his voice level – 'those are *my* drums. They live in *my* room, not yours.'

This remark was obviously having no effect whatsoever, judging by Rand's continued drumming which, if anything, grew louder and more insistent.

Titus tried again. 'Look. I mean, it's cool if you want to use them, but I'd rather you asked me first' – *thudda, thud, thud, thudda, thud* – 'and it's really *not* a good idea to take them out of my bedroom. Your room's way too damp—' Titus stopped, aware that he'd put his foot in it.

'Yeah,' Rand said, 'you're telling *me*. A frog would feel right at home here.' He narrowed his eyes and stared at Titus, then stood up from behind the sprawling drum kit. 'Talking of frogs, what happened to you, anyway? You've, er . . .'

Titus willed his face to remain pale. No rosy cheeks for this chap, right? Got that? Don't blush, don't blush, don't— Oh, never mind.

'*And* you've got taller. Have you been working out? Sneaking off to the gym? Sprinkling steroids on your Cheerios?'

'Miserablios,' Titus corrected automatically. 'And no. No drugs, no weights, nothing. Just . . . er . . . some of Mum's wax.'

'Wax?' Rand's expression radiated confusion. 'What? Like hair wax? Candle wax? Modelling wax like – er, Madame Tussauds?'

'If I told you, you wouldn't believe me.' Titus picked up his bass drum and nodded towards the bedroom door. 'C'mon. Give me a hand to put this lot back in my room, then I'll find you a different bedroom. OK?'

'No,' Rand muttered. 'It's *not* OK. You haven't answered my question. What wax? Where can I get some? I want to look older too.' His voice was rising in pitch and his punctured face was pink with effort and embarrassment. 'I want to sound like a bloke, not like a squeaky freak – that's what my dad's always calling me . . .'

Titus stared. Judging by his voice, Rand was on the point of losing it completely. He'd no idea Rand's father called him *names*. The very notion appalled Titus, coming as he did from a family where affection underpinned every word and deed; where he knew himself to be loved extravagantly, embarrassingly and totally without restraint; loved no matter what he looked like or, indeed, how he spoke. Remembering how vile Rand's dad had been when he delivered the news about Luciano, Titus decided that Munro MacAlister Hall had been about as warm and reassuring as an iceberg. His parting shot had been, 'Of course, the house will have to be sold. Your mother patently can't manage this mausoleum on her own, and with a new baby on the way she can hardly be expected to go out to work. So you'd all better prepare yourselves to tighten your belts considerably . . .'

Titus shuddered at the memory. What a horrible, unfeeling scumbag he'd turned out to be. Imagine *him* being your dad? No wonder Rand was so . . . awful. God. What a *mess*. He tried not to notice that Rand's nose was running. Copiously.

'Yeah. OK,' he muttered. 'Don't panic. First the drums, then a nicer room and *then* the wax. But don't get your hopes up. I don't know if there's any left. Mum might have used the last on me.' Titus jerked his head in the direction of the door once again. 'Let's get a move on, shall we?' He tried desperately to take Rand's mind off whatever dark thoughts had threatened to consume him. 'What was that riff you were playing back there? On the snare, with the bells? It sounded so – like some tune I know really well, but I can't place it.'

'That thing?' Rand sniffed, rubbed his eyes and gave a small watery smile. 'Ah. Don't you know anything? That was Mozart's first ever composition. He wrote it for the klavier when he was only *three*. Pretty amazing, actually. I've kind of, yeah, chopped it up a bit and reassembled it, added in a be-bop beat with a smattering of jazz-type syncopation in the backing, but, um, basically it's *Twinkle, Twinkle, Little Star* with menaces.'

At this, Titus burst out laughing and nearly dropped the bass drum. Maybe Rand staying wasn't going to be a total nightmare after all. Perhaps there was a sense of humour buried under all that attitude.

Plucking the hi-hat cymbals off their stand, Rand opened the door for Titus and followed him out.

'Problem is,' he continued, his thin voice echoing down the corridor, 'I need to come up with some lyrics that're slightly more cutting-edge than *Twinkle-twinkle*.'

Up ahead, Titus kicked his bedroom door open and turned back to him. 'Don't be too quick to dismiss those original lyrics. You know, *Twinkle-twinkle*'s got a lot going for it.' He paused and ad-libbed, 'We *could* turn it into something, er, like a ballad about the destructive nature of fame. You know. Like, *Twinkle, twinkle, superstar, Pickled in a whisky jar—*'

'*Drinking, smoking, getting high, Thinking you're too cool to die,*' Rand improvised, laying the cymbals down on the floor outside Titus's bedroom and turning back to fetch another armload of drumming paraphernalia.

Titus stopped on the threshold of his room and stared, open-mouthed, at something inside. 'Ex*cuse* me?' he managed, at length. 'Just *what* are you doing on my computer?'

Pandora didn't bother to turn round. Flapping her right hand in the air as if to indicate that she was too busy to be disturbed, she continued tapping something on the keyboard with the other. Titus suppressed a scream. He'd crossed his bedroom in five strides before remembering that he was hefting a bass drum above his head as if he intended to brain his sister with it. On reflection, that didn't seem like such a bad idea . . .

'I *said*, what are you doing—?' Then he caught sight of what Pandora had on the screen. 'Is that me? When did—? God. I look like a wee kid. Pandora?'

Pandora gave an exaggerated sigh, turned round and raked Titus with a sisterly stare before turning back to the screen and muttering, 'Did you know your head has sprouted a big drum? The mind boggles as to what's next. A piano tucked between your teeth? Flutes up your nose? Bagpipes in your pits? Castanets between your legs? Er – perhaps not. Anyway. Look, check this out. Who d'you think this *is*?'

Pandora moved the cursor over the image and double clicked on it. Immediately, the figures on the screen quadrupled in size, and Titus found himself gazing at a vastly enlarged nostril, complete with an enhanced thicket of hair sprouting out of it.

'Ooops.' Pandora moved the cursor to the toolbar and clicked on a little mountain glyph. After a chitter of protest from somewhere inside the computer, the nostril was replaced by the face it originally came from.

'Him?' Titus squinched up his eyes in an effort to recall who he was looking at. 'No. Don't tell me. I know who that is – I *know* I know who that is – I know I'm going to kick myself when you *tell* me who that is . . . Give in. Who is it?'

'Watch,' Pandora said, clicking on an open-hand glyph and dragging it until it was on top of the almost-recognizable face. She clicked, and the hand became a fist, grabbing the image and hauling it across the screen until Titus could see who else was in the picture.

'When did you take—? How did this get—? That's Damp, *and* Mrs McLach— What's going *on*, Pan?'

She ignored him, keying in commands and manipulating picture files with an apparent ease that Titus was beginning to find, well, maddening. Since when had Pandora become such an expert? Last time he'd looked, she'd been claiming that any-one who was computer-literate was a lower life-form, several evolutionary stages behind tape-worms. He was on the point of reaching out and spinning her round to face him when an image appeared on the screen that sucked the breath out of his lungs completely.

'Oh, *hell*,' he groaned, 'I know who that is now. It's *him*. That photographer who turned up on the night Mrs McLachlan van— die— disap— yeah.'

Pandora turned round slowly to face him. 'You know, Titus, for a lower life-form, you do manage some incredible intuitive leaps. I'm impressed. Now pay attention. This is a photograph from a film I took last week. I ran off thirty-six shots of trees and clouds and—'

'Girly stuff. Yeah, I know. I've seen you—' Catching sight of Pandora's expression, Titus imme-diately backtracked. 'Um, what I mean to say is, yeah, artistic compositions – er, painterly cloud-scapes and— Oh, help, you know I haven't the first idea about photography – I'm a digital man myself—'

'I'd say binary, not digital,' Pandora muttered. 'You've only got two settings: "Off" and "Totally off". Anyway' – she heaved a huge sigh – '*if* you'd let me finish – thirty-six photos. I posted the film off to the developers, and a few days later back came my prints together with a free CD. At first I thought I'd been sent someone else's prints by mistake, so I loaded the CD into the computer—'

'*My* computer, actually.'

'Whatever. And anyway, the pictures were the same. What you see here is what I got. All of them. Not a single one of which I recognize. Not one. I didn't take these pictures, Titus. And look, check out the date in the corner of the prints.'

What little blood there was left in Titus's face flooded south. 'Today?' he whispered. 'They're dated today? How? Wh-what's—? I don't like this one little bit.'

'Really.' Pandora smiled grimly. 'Guess what, I don't much like it either. Especially not seeing that creep of a photographer again. D'you remember how *bad* he smelt? Like rotten eggs.'

'Sulphur,' Titus said, remembering something else that turned his blood to ice, and wondering if he should share this sudden knowledge with his sister.

Pandora got there before him: 'It's the smell of demons,' she said in a very small voice. 'Like that one from Mum's witchcraft class – Fiamma Whatsername...' She tailed off, biting her lip. 'D'you know what, Titus? I think Mrs McLachlan threw herself in the loch as – as bait.'

Titus reeled visibly. Something about the word 'bait' made him want to howl. It implied being bitten. Bait got itself devoured by vast things, blindly predatory things, things which were drawn to the bait by its smell – or taste.

'I think she was protecting us from ... *it*,' Pandora whispered, and her eyes widened as the logic of Mrs McLachlan's sacrifice began to dawn on her. 'I think these photos are – oh, it sounds crazy, but I'm sure the photos are from her—' She broke off, stared meaningfully at Titus and gave an exaggerated sigh.

Rand had appeared in the corridor outside Titus's room, and was looking at Pandora with an expression of such intense longing that Titus wanted to slap him. Stop it, stop it, he thought. Not *now*. We're busy, can't you see?

But it was too late. Rolling her eyes, Pandora turned back to the computer and ejected the disk of photos, dropped it into its case and stood up to go.

'Thanks for the loan of your computer,' she said, bowing slightly towards Titus. 'While I was waiting, I downloaded an upgrade to your virus protection software, de-fragmented your hard disk and tidied up your inbox—' She held up a hand as if to forestall any interruptions. 'No. Don't thank me. It was my pleasure. You'll find I've changed your screensaver, too.' Squeezing past her brother, she stopped in front of Rand and turned back, as if struck by a sudden thought. 'I've left copies of all the photos on your computer. Have a look. I put them in your picture file inside your maths/physics homework folder on the hard disk.'

Titus immediately turned a luminous shade of pink. *How* had she known to go *there*? Oh, bloody *hell*, he thought bitterly, mortified beyond measure. Of all the files he hadn't *ever* wanted anyone to find ever, ever . . . Oh, please let the ground swallow me, he begged. I want to die—

'Don't—' he managed to say, before realizing that Pandora had the upper hand. As usual.

'Don't worry,' she snapped back, turning the CD over in her hands. 'Unlike you guys, I haven't got the *least* interest in looking at half-dressed blondes on a computer screen. Why ever would I?' And with this parting shot she sidestepped Rand and stalked off down the corridor, her head angled back as she breathed in the rarefied air of the moral high ground.

The Baleful Bain

'**I**nterview with Marie Bain, one-time chef de partie at StregaSchloss House, Auchenlochtermuchty, Argyll and Bute. Two p.m., second of October, attending officers DS Bill Waters and DCI Finbar McIntosh— Something I said amused you, *Sergeant* Waters?'

'No, sir. Just never heard your name before, sir.'

'Indeed.' The weasel-faced Detective Inspector from the Serious Crimes Unit fixed his colleague with a look so sharp it required its own scabbard. '*As* I was saying: *Interview with Marie Bain, two-oh-two p.m., second October, also attending, officers Detective Sergeant Waters and interrogating officer, myself, Detective Chief Inspector*

McIntosh of the SCU Caledonian Division. The witness was present at the SoC at StregaSchloss House on the evening of August fifth when she saw the accused acting in a suspicious fashion. In your own words, Ms Bain, what caused you to become alarmed?'

Sitting across a pockmarked table, Marie Bain twisted her hands in her lap and hunched her shoulders. Observing this, the DS made a note to book a shoulder massage at the police gym; just looking at the witness made his neck ache as if he'd been doing bench-presses with a couple of rhinocerii. Marie Bain batted her eyelids at the DCI in a forlorn attempt to make herself alluring; combined with continual hand-wringing and hunched shoulders, this gave her the appearance of a neurotic vulture badly in need of a laxative.

DCI Finbar McIntosh groaned inwardly. It was going to be a long day, and it had barely begun. Come *on*, woman, he thought. Get on with it. Marie Bain's bottom lip trembled with emotion and her hands abruptly disengaged, flying off on separate search missions for a handkerchief to stem the flow of tears beginning to well up in her pale eyes.

And *this* is our star witness for the prosecution, the DCI thought bleakly. Oh dear, oh dear. Wish I was anywhere but here. He looked away, trying to appear fascinated by the pattern of cigarette burn-marks on the linoleum floor beneath his feet. Beside him, the police tape recorder stopped, standing by automatically until activated by the sound of voices.

Time passed, measured out by silent dabbings of a grey handkerchief at Marie Bain's nose, then Marie Bain's eyes.

At length Marie Bain composed herself sufficiently to blurt out, 'Eeet was so horreeble . . .' And then they were off, the tape recorder whirring away in a corner, a veritable floodtide of disinformation pouring forth from the vengeful cook; her grey handkerchief growing wetter and wetter until the nauseated DS vowed to buy a box of tissues for the interview room against the possibility of future repeats of Marie Bain's snurking, blowing, honking, nose-dabbing and endless unfolding and searching for a mucus-free zone on that vile and disgustingly germ-laden linen square that more than qualified for the name snot-rag.

Finally, she stopped, a strangely triumphant smile on her face, a shiny patina of nasal effluent still visible around the general area of her nostrils. 'Therrrrre,' she pronounced with evident satisfaction. 'Zat ought to nail the murrrderrrous crrreep, *n'est-ce pas*?'

Something wasn't right, the DS decided, trying and failing to catch his superior officer's eye. It wasn't that Marie Bain's story didn't add up; it did, spectacularly, putting that pathetic Italianate landowner slap-bang in the frame for just about every single murder committed in Argyll over the previous decade. This was good news for the crime-solving rate, and the DCI was obviously delighted with Miss Bain's account, judging by the way he was now praising her powers of observation, but – the DS shook his head – it was *too* good. Real life and real crime didn't work like that. Crime was messy; the majority of murders were committed by extremely stupid people in order to get their point of view across when reasoned debate and intellectual argument had failed. In the DS's opinion, Luciano Strega-Borgia was far too intelligent. He also had too much going for him: beautiful wife, great kids, huge house, new baby on the way . . . Why on earth would he risk all that by bumping off the nanny? Even if, as Miss Bain had implied, the nanny had witnessed Luciano fatally shooting a lawyer the previous summer – a lawyer who, again according to Miss Bain, was blackmailing Luciano over the matter of a multiple murder Luciano had purportedly also committed the winter before that; this mass murder apparently being a further cover-up attempt after Luciano had fed four of his half-brother's bodyguards to his pet alligator – or was it a crocodile?

His head throbbed, just trying to straighten out the witness's tangled account. Rubbing his temples, the DS tried to concentrate on what his colleague was saying. To his annoyance he found that the plan was now for both policemen to escort Marie Bain back to StregaSchloss the next day. The purpose of this trip was to refresh the witness's memory regarding the exact times and locations of the events

172 ——

leading up to the abduction and murder of Mrs Flora McLachlan.

'Tomorrow?' the DS squeaked. 'But – but, sir, it's my day off, sir. I've got an appointment with my chiropodist at ten. I can't accompany you to Streg...' He tailed off, aware that he'd need an appointment with a cosmetic surgeon if the Chief Inspector kept spearing him with more of those barbed glances. Clearing his throat, he tried again. 'Of *course*, sir. Right away, sir. Say ... nine? Sir?'

The DCI stood up and gallantly helped Marie Bain to her feet, steering her out of the interview room with a guiding hand clasped around her elbow. Halfway through the door, he turned round as if suddenly remembering that the DS was still there, waiting for further instructions.

'Bring the car round at nine forty, Sergeant Waters. That means twenty minutes to ten. Don't be late. I'm a busy man, as I'm sure you're well aware. And' – he narrowed his eyes in warning – 'a word to the wise, DS Waters. If you are ever to have any chance of promotion beyond detective *sergeant*, you'd better sharpen up your act.' To the humiliated DS's horror, the DCI adopted a squeaky falsetto and minced out of the door chirruping, '*Ooooh, sorry, sir, can't come with you to the SoC because my feet hurt something wicked, sir* ...'

His voice faded away, leaving the DS staring aghast at the door. Waiting till the red mist cleared from his vision, he counted to ten, cleared his throat, and muttered, 'Sorry, sir. Not me, sir. Me, I'm keen as mustard, sir. In fact, sir, I'll bring the car round now, sir. Won't bother going home at all, sir. Anything for you, sir. Slurp, slurp, grovel, grovel, lick your boots, sir. Hate your guts, sir; same goes for your voice, sir— Oh, hell's *teeth*.' This last remark was occasioned by his discovery that the tape machine was still running quietly in the corner, recording everything he'd just said onto two identical cassettes. For legal reasons, these had been locked into the machine by the duty sergeant; under express orders to unlock and retrieve them only in the presence of his commanding officer, the universally loathed DCI Finbar McIntosh.

For the Love of Lucre

Damp was beginning to feel as if, while her attention was elsewhere, some unseen hand had laid a vanishing cloak around her shoulders. It is quite astonishing how invisible a small person can become if everyone around her is preoccupied with matters of consequence. Latch was lighting the fire in the library, Mama was still in hostiple, Titus and his friend were asleep upstairs, Pandora was curled up in bed reading and Toothpaste . . . Damp's eyebrows plunged towards her nose with a nearly audible *thud*.

Minty was in the kitchen, surrounded by piles of cookery books and assorted mixing bowls, all of which she had unpacked from her luggage and ferried downstairs in a manner indicating that she intended to stay at StregaSchloss for a while. Now she was trying to find a suitable place to plug in her massive stainless steel food mixer – an alarmingly industrial machine which looked as if it could whip up an airy batch of concrete along with whatever else Minty cared to hurl into its gaping bowl.

Puzzled, Damp watched as Minty wrapped her arms around the huge machine, heaved it aloft, staggered across the kitchen and placed it tenderly on top of a cupboard before standing back to admire the effect. She repeated this procedure several times before finally dumping the mixer in the middle of the kitchen table and, in rapid succession, whipping up a three-tier chocolate hazelnut meringue ice-cream cake, kneading a batch of honey and cinnamon bagels and, getting into her stride, rolling out pastry and effortlessly blind-baking two dozen tiny tartlets. Moments after she had plucked these golden pastry cases from the oven, she filled them with sweet vanilla cream onto which she grated some dark chocolate.

At which point Damp's traitorous stomach had roared its approval, and she decided that Something Had To Be Done. Minty was employing guerrilla tactics to win the family's approval, filling first the kitchen, then the house, and finally all their hearts with the deeply evocative scents of home baking: vanilla, cinnamon and dark melted chocolate. Soon it would be time for elevenses, when the calorific seduction of the Strega-Borgias would commence, and Damp knew that, with Mummy and Daddy missing, none of them would be able to resist. Furthermore she suspected that when their resistance crumbled, the past would rapidly become a fading memory and Mrs McLachlan would vanish for ever. Scowling like Beethoven, Damp retrieved the silver thread from under her seat cushion and blinked, her fists squeezed so tight that her knuckles ached. She didn't want to forget Mrs McLachlan, ever. She didn't want to bury memories of her old nanny under a lava flow of sugar; nor did she want to seek solace in the soft and gently perfumed embrace of this new not-nanny.

Feeling Damp's hot and furious gaze upon her, Minty turned from the table and squatted down so that her eyes were on the same level as the child's. She smiled at the poor little thing and held out her hands in an unmistakable gesture of friendship. Damp regarded her balefully and suppressed a deep desire to be enfolded in those outstretched arms. The seconds ticked by, Minty holding the pose, Damp likewise, hands now jammed in pockets, her eyes prickling as she bit down hard on her bottom lip.

Then the thread wrapped round Damp's fingers twitched, tightened and gave two distinct movements. *Tug. Tug.* Damp's heart clenched and her eyes widened. Sensing that something was wrong, Minty broke the silence.

'Oh, poppet – what's the *matter*? You look terrified. I won't bite, really – I promise . . .'

But it was too late. Like an animal breaking cover, Damp bolted out of the door to the garden at the same moment as the oven timer reminded Minty that a cherry cake needed her immediate attention. When the nanny finally looked up from her culinary labours, Damp had vanished entirely.

Marie Bain peered out of the windows of the police car, her fishy eyes glittering with malice. All those years of slaving over dinner for the Borgias and for what?

Certainly not the money. The pay was pitiful, insulting even. Low wages had forced her to seek other means of earning an income while she wasted her life cooking for the Strega-Borgias. Pressing her thin lips together so tightly that they turned white, Marie Bain recalled all those dishes she had created. Exquisite morsel after exquisite morsel, picked over, sneered at and ultimately discarded. Day after day of her life wasted in service to a family who'd made plain their preference for greasy Italian muck over the finest French cuisine. In vain had she simmered, strained, moulied, pared, reduced, grated, whipped, folded and zested. Countless vegetables and fruits had been boiled to mush; the finest fish, fowl and game had been roasted to carbon; she had transformed the firm flesh of assorted farmyard beasts into grey string in the quest for a dish to please her employer's fickle palate.

At the thought of her now *ex*-employer, Marie Bain's eyes glittered and her mouth curved upwards into a rictal smile. Luciano. Luciano Strega-Borgia, probably now dressed in prison suiting – shapeless, itchy and undoubtedly blood-stained to boot. Her smile turned into a smirk as she considered her future. Waiting for her, glittering with the promise of fabulous wealth, were thirteen uncut diamonds, their street value more than enough to ensure that she never had to overboil a Brussels sprout ever again. Thirteen rough gems – payment to make sure Luciano Strega-Borgia spent the remainder of his life behind bars.

And her vindictive benefactor? None other than Luciano's half-brother Lucifer; Lucifer di S'Embowelli Borgia, Mafioso, murderer and, recently, multimillionaire. Lucifer, whose wealth was courtesy of the Borgia Inheritance, which made him richer than Croesus but simultaneously ensnared him in a centuries-old pact with the Devil. Lucifer, who, thanks to the money, plus a bungled episode of plastic surgery, was now as ugly on the outside as he was undoubtedly on the inside. Lucifer, who, post-surgery, could only communicate in mangled squeaks, most of which concerned his avowed mission to destroy his half-brother. It is a fact that money can't buy you love, but money certainly had helped Lucifer buy most other things he desired, including the fanatical loyalty of a vengeful employee.

And now, speeding towards StregaSchloss, Marie Bain blessed the fate that had brought Lucifer and his diamonds into her life. For the first time ever she felt important. Lucifer had *told* her how essential her evidence was to Luciano's trial and eventual imprisonment; so too had the policemen, impressing upon her that she, and no other, was the key witness for the prosecution.

'*Moi*,' she whispered. '*Moi*, Madame Bain. The twenty-first century's answer to Madame Lafarge. Perrrrhaps I too shall sit by the guillotine and work on my *embonpoint*.'

'I *beg* your pardon?' Sitting rigid with embarrassment beside her on the back seat, DCI McIntosh took a deep, shuddering breath. This witness was a total flake. Her head must button up the back or something, because there they were, nearly at the SoC, and she was rapidly unravelling before his very eyes, talking about guillotines. Beam me up, Scotty, he begged silently as he closed his eyes. Full warp speed for home and fazers on stun.

Just as the police car's tyres met the rose-quartz drive, DS Waters swung the steering wheel sharply to the right and slammed on the brakes just in time to avoid hitting a small girl who'd run out in front of the car with no warning whatsoever. Before he could sound his horn or roll down his window to roar at her, the most extraordinary thing happened. The kid was still running, legging it away from the house towards the open countryside, but her feet were no longer touching the ground. Impossible as it sounded, she was rising up into the air, arms flapping, legs tucked up against her chest. DS Waters's mouth fell open. There was a ragged black shape flying alongside the child, swooping and circling around her, almost as if it were offering . . . encouragement.

The policeman shook his head. Stress, he decided. They'd been taught at police academy how to recognize the signs, except it was well-nigh impossible to separate stress-related symptoms from the ailments that had come bundled along with his fiftieth birthday wrinkles. Sleeplessness, irritability, indigestion – he ticked them off – and then added visual hallucinations to the list as, overhead, Damp made a final orbit of the chimneys of StregaSchloss and, clasping Vesper firmly in her arms, went supersonic.

There was a boom, then a popping sound as all the displaced air rushed back in to fill the space they'd just vacated, but Damp was blissfully unaware. She was paying rapt attention to the silver thread that spun through her fingers, reeling her closer to something – someone she dared not yet name. Together, she and her familiar flew high over Lochnagargoyle – so fast that they began to turn time backwards. Battling the slipstream, wings flapping, Vesper muttered something under his breath that sounded like, 'Cabin crew, doors to manual and crosscheck.'

Then he turned his attention to Damp. 'We'd like to extend a warm welcome to you on board this flight today. For your comfort and safety, the cabin crew will now take you through the safety demonstration. Although you may have flown before, we would appreciate it if you give this demonstration your fullest attention. Please ensure your back is in the upright position and that your legs are stowed away for take-off. Place all bags in the overhead lockers or below the seat in front of you. Please take a moment to locate the nearest exit to you . . . seatbelts are fastened . . . and adjusted, so . . . masks will drop . . . place over nose and mouth and breathe normally . . . inflate by pulling on the red . . . top up by means of . . . a light and whistle for attracting attention—'

'Vesper?'

The little bat's mouth snapped shut and he sighed deeply. 'I know, I know. I'm talking nonsense. There *are* no seatbelts, lifejackets, oxygen masks or emergency exits. I just made them up to take my mind off the blue, blue sky and big white clouds and that unforgivingly hard thing called planet Earth. We're undoubtedly flying too high. We're definitely going too fast. We're probably going to die. In fact, we may be dead already. Whoooh, we're flying by the seat of our pants today, ma'am. Where are we going? *Terra incognita.* How many miles? Lordy, how I do babble on. Three score miles and ten. Will I get there by candlelight—?'

'*Vesper*,' Damp groaned. 'Shoosh. Nearly there.'

Following the silver thread to wherever it led, Damp and Vesper clung together, hardly daring to look down. Miles below, a grey and misty abyss reached up towards the blue heaven. A blink later they were in the fog; cold, wet and without radar, blinded.

Desert Island Risks

The demon Isagoth paced back and forth along the shoreline, head down, hands clasped behind his back, his boots viciously splintering shells and stamping a pattern of ridges into the wet sand as he tried to buy a one-way ticket home to Hades. Ignoring him, Death's two boatmen stood knee-deep in the incoming tide and held their bladeless oars aloft.

'Ssssso, let me get this straight,' Isagoth hissed. 'I should assume from your silence that you guys are immune to bribery? That no matter what, I can't buy a safe passage off this island? You mean to say you *don't* want gold, jewels, camels,

oil wells, palaces or peerages? You're telling me that you don't have a burning desire for unlimited business-class air travel, vast wealth salted away in a secret Swiss bank account, get-out-of-jail-free cards and the unspoken loyalty of several senior politicians who owe you big?'

Isagoth massaged the bridge of his nose, where the faintest prickle of an incoming migraine signalled its arrival. Next his temples would begin to beat out a rhythm, followed closely by his stomach announcing its intention to eject all contents, after which the only thing he'd be fit for was lying down in the heather and wishing he was dead. This, Isagoth decided, was one of the true horrors of being immortal. You just *knew* a headache couldn't kill you, no matter how much you might desire it to. Rolling his eyes he turned his attention back to the silent oarsmen.

'Right. I get it. You'd rather stand there like twin rocks, like pillars of lumpen flesh, too dumb to realize their hems are getting wet. Again.'

Dumba-dumba-thud came the herald of the headache, and realizing that he had approximately five minutes left before the migraine claimed him utterly, Isagoth lost his temper.

'You two are – are – *stupid*, *stupid*, and *stupid*. What's *wrong* with everybody? Like, how *hard* does this have to be? I'm more than happy to pay whatever it takes to get me out of here. Like – are you there? Hello? Anybody home? Why doesn't anybody listen to me? I WANT TO LEAVE!'

In the ensuing silence Isagoth almost wept with frustration. He'd wasted *hours* trying to persuade these morons, these spectres with Swiss cheese for brains, that all he wanted was a means of escape from his imprisonment on the island – in vain did he promise wealth, knighthoods, vast chunks of real estate – anything: you name it, Izzy will provide. But *no*. Nothing worked. He was trapped. His imprisonment here was like the ultimate island-holiday-from-hell scenario. Nightmare fellow-castaways, ghastly food, uncomfortable beds and no hot water . . .

'DAMN YOU ALL!' Isagoth shrieked. 'GET ME OUT OF HERE.'

Dumba-dumba-thud, insisted the migraine, and Isagoth stamped on a mussel so hard its shell splintered under his boot and splattered him with vivid orange pulp. Trying to rise above a wave of nausea, the demon focused on his frustration at having no-one to vent his spleen upon. He longed to wrap his fingers round a pale white neck and squeeze; if that was off-menu, he'd settle for dishing out a monster of a Chinese burn. It was insufferable. He would go insane if he had to stay here any longer. Knowing that somewhere out there S'tan would be waiting to rip him limb from limb didn't exactly help his mental health either. He'd promised to deliver the Chronostone to the Boss by the autumnal equinox, the twenty-second of September, but here he was, in the first week of October, still stoneless and likely to remain so, unless . . .

Unless he could escape. Somehow he had to get away from this island, muster help and return for the stone. *Then* he could face S'tan's wrath. With the stone on board, he could face anything. Yes, Isagoth thought, I need to assemble a task force of mindless demons; mindless *and* obedient. Get them to the island and put them to work sifting through the stones and rocks for the Chronostone. After all, he reminded himself, he was far too important a minister in the Hadean Executive to spend months trawling through the millions of pebbles fringing the shore in search of S'tan's precious bauble. Let the lower echelons of demons sieve the pebbles and destroy *their* manicures in the process. He, Isagoth, one-time Defence Minister of Hades, had had enough. As if to underline this decision, the demon leant forward and was copiously sick all over his black boots, and thus was last to witness the arrival of two more castaways.

Unlike Isagoth, Mrs McLachlan had no intention of trying to bribe her way off the island. She had spent the previous night, while Isagoth slept, making a passionate appeal to Death; beseeching him to help her remember where she'd hidden the Chronostone and take both it and her with him when he returned to his realm of shadows. Death had heard her out, nodding from time to time, his long narrow fingers steepled under his chin, his grey eyes impassive. When Flora's words ran down like an unwound clock spring, Death did not rush to fill the silence. Instead, he sat utterly still as the tide washed in and out and the temperature began to fall. In the deepening chill Flora was forced to jam her hands into the pockets of her cardigan, and that was when her fingers rediscovered the forgotten thread.

Across from her, Death took a deep breath and shook his head. 'I do apologize, Flora,' he began, 'but I'm not going to be able to give you the answer you seek.'

Hardly aware of she was doing, Flora wound the thread round and round her fingers in a one-handed cat's cradle as a wave of exhaustion swept over her. So ... did this mean that her sacrifice was for nothing? Had she effectively drowned herself in order to bring the stone into Death's realm; to defuse its power; to ensure that S'tan and his kind could never again use it to further their foul schemes – all for nothing?

Death leant forward and spoke urgently, his words scarcely audible as if he was afraid of being overheard. 'Flora ... Flora, Flora. Come now, my dear. *You* of all people. You know the *rules*. My realm is not some kind of dumping ground for unwanted magical artefacts. You came here, to the island, to hide the stone from the Lord of Darkness. He cannot see it now, nor can he feel its power, nor feed from its energies. Even though the stone had been mislaid by the Dark Lord for two centuries, it was still on the Earth, and thus its power could still be used by demons and angels alike. Seeking to insulate the stone from the Dark Lord, you hid it in the Etheric Library, with catastrophic results for the Librarian. Now you have brought it here and summoned me, Death, to your aid. I understand why you want me to take the stone back with me: you correctly reason that I alone am beyond the reach of Heaven or Hades, and thus would be a neutral, unbiased curator for the Chronostone. And yes, in this you are quite correct. Once the stone was with me, so would it remain for all eternity.'

Oh please, Flora begged silently, please bend the rules. Just once? And then, suddenly, all thoughts of stones and rules were driven from her mind. In her pocket the thread which bound her fingers gave a determined quiver. Just as the thought, *Did that really happen?* flashed across her mind, the impossible occurred:

Tug, went the thread, and then again, twice: *Tug, tug*.

'Flora – you seem miles away. Listen, there is one way, and one way only. Do I really need to spell out how it has to be done?'

Flora stared at Death in some confusion and then forced her thoughts into order. 'No. I understand,' she whispered. 'Someone has to bring the stone to your realm.'

Death nodded and then slowly raised his eyebrows, indicating that he was waiting for her to finish. In a tone awash with sadness, Flora said, 'Someone not like me. Someone . . . mortal.'

Death had left shortly afterwards, and Flora had lain awake for hours, her eyes fixed on the starry canopy overhead. All night long the thread had kicked and twitched, calling to her, tugging at her, trying to pull her back. But whoever was at the other end lacked the strength to reel her in. Whoever held the thread, it certainly wasn't Strega-Nonna. As night turned to morning a faint suspicion was beginning to form at the back of Mrs McLachlan's mind; a faint suspicion that grew stronger with each passing minute; a faint suspicion coupled now with a feeling of acute dread. For, if her hunch was correct, the person on the other end wasn't reeling her in, wasn't providing her with the only means to escape the island. No, Mrs McLachlan decided, the person on the other end was following the thread *towards* her; was using it exactly like the trail of breadcrumbs in *Hansel and Gretel*; was unwittingly ruining any hope of escape for both herself and Mrs McLachlan. Flora's mind shrieked to a standstill. '*Herself?*' she demanded. Oh yes, her mind replied. Herself. As in—

Just then, their shadows cast across the sand by the watery sunlight, Damp and Vesper floated into view.

Just Desserts

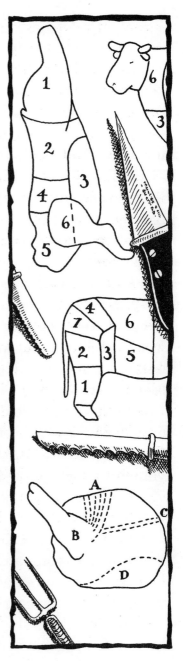

Drawn by the smell of vanilla, Titus found himself standing in the kitchen before his brain had woken up properly. A vast stainless steel mixer sat at his accustomed place at the table, gobbets of cake mix dotted between it and the sink. Someone appeared to have made an attempt to wash dishes and then given up halfway through. The door to the garden stood wide open, and judging by the kitchen temperature, had stood open for some time. Apart from the tantalizing smells wafting across from a freshly baked cherry cake cooling on a rack by the range, the room seemed to have been abandoned for some time. Shivering, Titus crossed the kitchen, closed the garden door and rewarded himself with a thin sliver of cherry cake for his efforts. Instantly, his brain booted up. There. *That* was better. Food was all that was required. Yum, he thought, nibbling a second slice – well, perhaps more of a *slab* than a slice, he amended, but hey, I no longer have the modest appetite of a boy. Pleased with this thought, Titus paused to admire his reflection in the side of a copper pan hanging over the range.

Yup. Coming along nicely, he decided, rubbing a hand over his rough chin. Not sure I can cope with Dad's electric razor, though – it's way too vicious. Shivering slightly, he comforted himself with a third wedge of cake. He needed to talk to Pandora. In fact he would have done so, followed up on the whole chilling photos-of-demons scenario last night except . . .

Except last night he'd been too embarrassed to go anywhere *near* his sister, hadn't he? Pandora stumbling across his computer file of beautiful women was as bad as having her barge in on him while he was in the shower. Hmmm. More cake required, he decided, cramming a fourth slice into his mouth. So lost in thought was he that he didn't realize he had company until Ffup slapped him on the back and burst out laughing as he choked, gagged and spat a cherry across the kitchen.

'Don't *do* that!' he roared at the unabashed dragon. 'You *moron* – you could've *killed* me.'

Unimpressed, Ffup rolled her eyes and leant over to breathe fishy fumes into Titus's face.

'And go brush your teeth, why don't you?' he snapped, then immediately regretted his outburst.

The dragon gazed at him with a wounded expression. Her golden eyes pooled with tears and her wings drooped dejectedly. 'Thought *I* was supposed to be the beastly one around here,' she mumbled, turning her attention to the fridge and its contents. Clanking sounds came from its interior as she hunted in vain for something edible within. Keen to make amends, Titus carved another slab of cake and held it out to Ffup. She turned round and peered down her nostrils at the peace offering. Locking eyes with Titus and emitting a warning puff of flame, she demanded shrilly, '*When* will you get it through your fat head? I. Don't. Do. Carbs. Ever. I want to fit into my size double D wedding gown, remember? Even if I do happen to be "with egg".'

'*With egg?*' Titus stared at Ffup in some confusion.

'Oh puhlease,' she groaned. 'With *egg*, as in "with bun in oven". In the pudding club? Gravid? Expectantly expecting? Parous? And I'm not talking foreign capitals, either.'

'You're *pregnant*? Again?'

'Yurrrrgh.' Ffup slapped a paw against her forehead. 'Dear boy – I *was* trying to avoid *that* word. Such an ugly term for such an exalted state. And yes. Since you mention it. Yes. *Again*. Have you got a problem with that?'

Titus was spared the embarrassment of replying by a trio of rings from the doorbell followed immediately by a loud pounding on the front door. As he went to answer the summons, the sound of footsteps approaching from the kitchen garden made him spin round just as Minty ran into the kitchen in a state of alarm. Catching sight of the nanny, Ffup stifled a shriek of terror and bolted for the dungeons via the wine cellar, splashing noisily through the freezer-melt from Strega-Nonna's slow thaw.

'Oh thank *God* you're here,' Minty gasped. 'I simply didn't know what to *do*. I can't find Damp anywhere.' She clutched Titus's arm. 'There's a police car parked outside – what's going *on?*' Suddenly they both became aware of the sound of raised voices.

'Do you really have to go around *hammering* on people's doors? Officer?' Latch's voice was clipped and decidedly unfriendly. To the reddening ears of Detective Sergeant Waters, it was the kind of voice that held no promise of a cup of tea in the offing; which was a great pity since the wind-chill factor here on the shores of Lochnagargoyle, coupled with the fact that it was almost time for elevenses, meant that a cup of tea would have been just the thing to make a policeman's life slightly more bearable.

Suppressing a shiver, the policeman tried to inch forwards into the shelter of StregaSchloss, only to find his way firmly barred by the arm of the

Borgias' officious employee, old whatsisname. Lock? Launch? Snitch? Whatever. Right, DS Waters decided, time to take the gloves off. 'I have to caution you, sir,' he began, encouraged by a nod from DCI McIntosh who, along with the witness, was still enjoying the warmth inside the police car. 'We are presently in possession of a search warrant and I must inform you that any persons obstructing officers of the law in the course of their enquiries relating to a murder investig—'

'Oh, for heaven's sake,' Latch interrupted, catching sight of the passenger huddled in the rear of the police car. 'Marie *Bain*. I should have known. Like a dog returning to its vomit. You'd better come in, Officer. All of you. No point in standing freezing on the doorstep.' And turning his back on the policeman, the butler stalked away down the corridor, heading for the kitchen.

'It's – it's as if she just vanished into thin air,' Minty wailed, her hands clinging to the cup of tea Titus had placed in front of her. This hospitality had not been extended to the two policemen, nor to Marie Bain, who was walking round the kitchen in the hope of jogging her memory regarding the night of Mrs McLachlan's disappearance.

'Knives, Ms Bain?' the weasel-faced DCI suggested, ignoring Minty completely and opening a cutlery drawer to rattle its contents with unnecessary vigour. 'Just have a wee squint and tell me if you're aware of any that might be missing.'

'*Knives?*' Minty's voice was strained with the effort of not screaming out loud. 'You're carefully counting the silver while right under your noses a tiny child has gone *missing*? How can you think of cutlery at a time like this? Who *cares* what items of silver have gone awol—?'

Latch crossed the kitchen. Bending over close to her ear and speaking very quietly, he placed a hand on her shoulder and another under her elbow, drawing her gently to her feet. '*If* you'll excuse us for a moment,' he said in a manner indicating that this wasn't a request but a statement of fact, and clasping Minty's arm, he propelled her out of the kitchen.

Marie Bain stood in the centre of the room, her expression radiating malice and her eyes darting around the kitchen until finally they alighted on the racks of baking cooling by the range. 'Ptui,' she spat, prodding Minty's half-devoured cherry cake with an outstretched finger. 'Eet ees like falling off ze lurg, zis. I could do zees with my eyes shut.'

To Titus's horror, she excavated a fingerful of the warm centre of the cake, sniffed it, and with a grimace of disgust, flung it into the sink.

'Too soft,' she decided. 'Ees not cooked prrroperly, zat. I show you how eet ees done, *moi*. Last year, before I go on my *vacances*, I make ze perrrfect Christmas cake for zees ungrrrateful people. Of course, zey not eat *my* cake. Zey preferrr to eat Meesis Macacklong's Dundee cake instead. So mine languish in ze cupboard . . .' Her voice now came from the pantry, accompanied by thumps and clunks as she hunted through the Kilner jars and cake tins piled high on the shelves.

'Could we stick to the point, Miss, er . . . Ban?' DS Waters tried and failed to catch the eye of his colleague, who was examining his fingernails with every evidence of utter fascination.

'Here eet ees,' Marie Bain pronounced, emerging once more clutching a small rusting cake tin which she prised apart, dumping its contents onto the table in front of Titus. Like a macabre version of pass-the-parcel, the object she'd decanted from the cake tin was wrapped in several stained layers of tin-foil; underneath lay drifts of greaseproof paper which had not only failed to live up to their name, but also neglected to ward off bacterial and fungal invasions of the cake itself. This, once fully unwrapped, revealed itself to be a sunken green disc of spectacular unwholesomeness. It emitted a reek of rotting fruit, which Marie Bain inhaled ecstatically before lurching towards the knife drawer to rake through its contents.

'At last,' muttered DCI McIntosh, distracted from the examination of his manicure by the prospect of progress on the knife-as-murder-weapon front.

However, Marie Bain was not to be thwarted by anything as trivial as evidence-gathering. She spun back to the table, her eyes a-glitter, an eerie smile hovering across her lips and a vast chopping knife clutched in both her trembling hands. Titus sprang back from the table just in time, as Marie Bain brought the knife thudding down into her antique cake.

As DS Waters was later to confirm, at this stage the cake was giving every indication that the correct thing to do now was to transfer it straight from the table into the compost bucket. A brownish-green ooze leaked out from the site of the knife wound, and the detective was sure that he saw a bubble appear on the surface of the cake – some vapour or gas trapped deep within. Slowly, the cake slumped towards its centre, as if Marie Bain had delivered it a death blow. With a stubbornness that was ultimately to prove fatal, the cook stabbed her cake once more and thus succeeded in cutting herself a sliver studded with what looked like sections of tar-stained eyeballs.

'Eees golden cherrries,' she explained, disappointed that there appeared to be no takers for this culinary delight. Like a determined salesperson, she began to extol the virtues of her cake, pausing only to pick mould off its sunken surface before cramming gobbets of it into her mouth. 'Ahhh . . . ees *délicieux*, zis. And so mature, *non*? All ze best things in zis worrrld are mature, are zey not?'

To DCI McIntosh's acute consternation, Marie Bain sidled in his direction, batted her eyelashes and leered at him. Poking a final morsel between her lips, she spun in a little circle before catching her heel in a crack between the flagstones. She stumbled, coughed and clutched at the DCI for support. Gagging and choking, she flung her arms around the policeman's neck, gazing beseechingly up into his face as she tried and failed to draw air past the golden cherry lodged tightly in her throat. Each attempt only drew the little sphere deeper, until it was wedged so tightly in her airway that only an emergency tracheotomy could possibly have saved her life. Repeated and increasingly desperate endeavours by DCI McIntosh to perform the Heimlich manoeuvre resulted only in the post-mortem discovery that he'd managed to break two of Marie Bain's ribs in his efforts to stop her suffocating.

Throughout it all, Titus sat statue-still, frozen with horror and oblivious to the twin tracks of tears that rolled down his ashen face. After what felt like several lifetimes, DCI McIntosh lowered Marie Bain's lifeless body to the floor and stood up. The policeman was holding his hands out as if uncertain what to do next; his mouth opening and closing, words spilling forth, words that refused to form the syllables and phrases of police procedure. Only then did Titus stand up and walk shakily round to where Marie Bain lay on the stone floor. Taking a deep breath, he rushed across the kitchen and was violently sick out of the back door.

A Made Man

Luciano lay on his bunk in the darkness before dawn, struggling to expunge the memory of the previous day's events. Try as he might, he could not erase the vision of the prisoner in the dinner queue who'd been fatally gagged with a spoon. As this unfortunate man had lain there, drowning in his own blood, all hell had broken loose. Voices had roared orders over the tannoy system; what had seemed like hundreds of prison guards had descended on the dining hall, their truncheons raised, their boots lashing out – and for a short while, in the noise and pandemonium, Luciano had been convinced that he was next in line to be murdered. Jostled and shoved in a mass of sweating prisoners, herded along a corridor, bawled at by purple-faced brutes and pressure-hosed into the showers for the second time in an hour, Luciano felt himself turn numb and mute with fear. Naked and shivering he stood in line to be strip-searched and nearly kissed his captors out of sheer gratitude when he was finally reissued with grey prison clothes three sizes too large.

After what seemed like an age he had been frog-marched to a cell and instructed to lie down on the topmost of one of the two bunk beds. Lights went out at ten o'clock and in the pale glow of the moon shining in through his barred window, Luciano saw the lumpen shadows of his cell-mates moving down below. It proved to be impossible not to overhear their muttered conversation, but mercifully ninety per cent of this was beyond understanding, mainly because it was conducted in the broadest of Glaswegian accents. Luciano tried to sleep; to stop up his ears against the voices; to count sheep; to walk round the perimeter of StregaSchloss in his imagination; and finally to compose a letter to his beloved wife inside his head – all to no avail.

From below came the scratch of a match being struck, a hiss and then the unmistakable smell of burning tobacco. Luciano's eyes sprang open. Honestly – this was *insufferable*. His head pounded, his heartbeat raced and he sat upright, on the point of demanding that the smoker extinguish his cigarette immediately, when he caught sight of who it was smiling up at him, a little burning ember dangling from his lips.

I'm going to die, he decided as his bunk shuddered and tipped to one side. Big Brian's head appeared beside Luciano's pillow, an expression of glee just visible in the moonlight.

'It's the wee man,' Malky observed from the bunk opposite, reclining like a shrunken emperor. He released a trickle of smoke from both nostrils and curled his lips upwards, thus exposing his pointy teeth to maximum effect. 'You didnae even say thanks for shutting up yon pesky wee clipe, eh no? After a' they hours youse spent, Big Brian, sharpening yon spoon youse nicked frae the kitchens.' Malky tutted, took a deep drag from his cigarette and shrugged. 'Here's tae us,' he intoned cheerily, producing a plastic water bottle from under his pillow. 'Wha's like us?' he demanded, tilting the bottle to one side and holding it up to the light before adding, 'Gie few and they're a' deid.' Taking a healthy swig, he stood up and passed the bottle to Big Brian as he came across to join in the fun at Luciano's bedside.

'Aye, Wee Man. You're a bit of a joker, eh no?' he demanded, his breath rank with the smell of some close cousin to paint stripper. 'Youse really had us gawn there wi' all yer talk aboot furrin diseases. Fir a wee while, Big Brian here thought he wis dee'n.' Beside him, Big Brian swilled a large mouthful from the bottle, gargled repulsively, swallowed and then let rip with a belch that made the bars on the window rattle. 'Hing oan, Big Brian,' Malky commanded, snatching the bottle back and, to Luciano's stunned amazement, passing it up to him. 'Leave a wee swally for ma friend here, eh? Aye. See we didnae ken youse were a made man, eh no?' Malky's smile was ingratiating, his entire body language radiating submission to a bigger threat than himself. 'See no-one telt me that youse were that well-connected. 'F I'd kent, ah'd've no gied you a hard time back in they cells under the High Court, eh no?'

'Er, no. I mean, yes. I mean, aye,' Luciano managed to bleat, his mind racing ahead of his vocal cords. *What on earth?* And, more importantly, what was he supposed to *do* with this bottle of raw alcohol? The answer to both questions was immediate.

'G'wan, Don Borgia. Tek a wee dram. Let's have a wee drink and pit the past behint us. No harm done, eh no?'

Don Borgia? *Don Lucifer di S'Embowelli Borgia?* Luciano's eyes watered. Aghast as he was to be mistaken for his vile half-brother, he wasn't suicidally minded enough to point out to Malky the error of his ways.

At least, not yet.

Fixing what he fervently hoped was an inscrutable expression on his face, Luciano tipped his head back, took a deep pull on the bottle and by sheer will-power forced himself to swallow without choking.

'Nhhho,' he wheezed, throat aflame, vision blurring while what felt like an atomic bomb detonated behind his eyes. 'Nhhho. Harm. Done.' And, praying that this was indeed true, he passed the bottle back to Malky as consciousness fled and he fell backwards into deep and drunken slumber.

Sitting in the rear of a taxi parked on the rain-drenched Via Fiscale-Castrato in Bologna, Munro MacAlister Hall cursed the weather. Torrential rain had delayed the departure of the Glasgow-to-London shuttle, and after a heroic sprint along Heathrow's escalators, tunnels and moving walk-ways; followed by mowing down several slow-moving Americans trundling their outsize luggage; then sending a gaggle of Asiatic toddlers crashing to the concourse floor like unbalanced Weebles; and finally, despite offering the British Airways ground crew substantial bribes, Munro MacAlister Hall had not been allowed to board the gate-closed, now-departing flight for Bologna. That flight was the last that would have got him to the Armani boutique in time to pick up the promised item of baggage. As previously arranged, this was to be a locked silver suitcase stuffed full of cash in used and untraceable notes. This, Munro MacAlister

Hall understood, was to be his payment for services rendered in making sure Mr Luciano Borgia remained in prison for a very long time indeed.

Staring at the shaved neck of the taxi driver in front of him, the lawyer bleakly scrolled through the remaining options left open to him. Although the client had specified that there was to be no face-to-face meeting, Munro MacAlister Hall was pretty certain that *someone* would have had to check that the suitcase was going to the right lawyer. Therefore, he reasoned, either that someone would have had to lurk in the changing rooms in the Armani boutique, or, more likely, one of the members of staff would have had to be involved. Looking at his watch, the lawyer reckoned that the boutique's employees would be emerging from the building any time now.

However, there remained an insurmountable problem. How on earth was he meant to assess which one of them was bent? It wasn't as if they'd be wearing an impeccably tailored shirt proclaiming: I ♡ THE MAFIA. Nor, he decided, would they be carrying a violin case or wearing shades and a fedora with bullet holes puncturing its brim. And how many of them were likely to emerge? As the shutters barring the front door twitched and began to rise, Munro MacAlister Hall's heart sank. A large group of exceptionally well-dressed young women teetered out into the rain, loudly discussing the various shortcomings of their footwear, their salaries and their menfolk. None of them stood out as being particularly villainous or in any way different to her colleagues.

The lawyer slumped back against his seat. This was hopeless. He'd simply have to try again tomorrow in the remote chance that no-one had noticed an immensely valuable suitcase propped against the mirror in the south-facing changing roo—

'Signore?' The taxi driver turned round, one arm slung casually over the back of his seat. 'We have beena sitting in the rain for twenty minutes. The Armani boutique, it is closed. Tomorrow, it will be open again – this I promise, signore. But for now it is time for me to go home, *si*? And therefore, signore, you have to tell me where you want me to take you. Do you want to go back to the *aeroporto*, or would you prefer me to take you to a hotel?'

'A hotel,' Munro MacAlister Hall muttered, watching the rain turn the windows of the taxi into a watery blur. 'A good hotel, mind you. What would you recommend?'

'Ah . . .' The taxi driver recalled the lawyer's monogrammed luggage and correctly assessed that Signor MMH's cashmere coat would have cost more than he could make in a year of non-stop ferrying fares around the city. 'I think, signore, for a gentleman such as you, I would recommend the Grand Hotel Bagliadi on Indipendenza. Not simply because it is the most beautiful hotel in all of

Bologna, but also because yesterday many senior policemen from all over Italy come to Bologna to stay in the Bagliadi. With so many officers of the law under its roof, I can promise you that you will be staying in the safest hotel in Emilia-Romagna.'

A little while later he dropped him in front of the Grand Hotel Bagliadi; the chosen location for the monthly meeting of the Cosa Nostra, otherwise known as the Mafia.

Lavender's Blue

Dawn leached blood-red into the darkness, lighting bruised clouds from beneath and cutting the night with a horizon vivid as a knife wound. Somewhere in the fiery distance a factory hooter screamed a summons to the sleeping citizens of Hades. Tiptoeing out of His chambers into His five-car garage, S'tan regarded the vehicles at His disposal. *Not* the Aston Martin, He decided regretfully, all too aware that His recent weight gain meant the Porsche and the Lamborghini were out too. He'd never be able to squeeze His vast bottom into anything remotely sporty until He lost some of His blubber . . .

'Oh, *God*,' He groaned, then gave a tiny squeak of dismay. There He went *again*. That was the *third* time He'd invoked the Other Side since His alarm clock had woken Him out of a dreamless sleep. Rummaging in the pocket of His XXXL grey sweatpants, S'tan found an overlooked shard of peanut brittle and stuffed it into His mouth, sucking frantically while He concentrated on the matter of transport. What was it to be? The white van or the black Range Rover? Deciding on the latter only because He recalled leaving a half-full bag of pork scratchings on the passenger seat, S'tan waddled across to His SUV, almost drooling with anticipation.

Two hours later He pulled up outside a pair of white-gold gates which, He dimly recalled, had in a bygone time before acid rain been studded with pearls. Overhead, the sky had changed from a suffocating bloody dawn into a cool baby-blue morning. As His car's electric window slid down, S'tan smelled the rarefied air that permeated the Other Side.

'I'm expected for breakfast,' He muttered to the gatekeeper, and pulling on a pair of dark sunglasses against the bright glare of Heaven, waited to gain admittance.

'Name?' the cherub demanded in an insolent tone. This was completely unnecessary since S'tan was instantly identifiable, despite the layers of fat swaddling His body. He was red, wasn't He?

Horns? Pointy tail? It didn't require a degree in theology to work out who He was, after all. Again the cherub demanded identification, but this time it added something that sounded suspiciously like *lard-for-brains* under its breath, and at this, an ember of S'tan's old fire was rekindled.

Moments later S'tan plucked a stray feather from between His teeth and checked again in His rear-view mirror for incriminating evidence. Devouring that disrespectful gatekeeper had been a spur-of-the-moment thing, with no premeditation involved. Guiltily, S'tan considered the calorific value of one plump cherub and wondered if He should atone by avoiding the breakfast entirely. That would be utterly *hellish*. Breakfast in Heaven was His monthly treat. He couldn't miss it. It was too good. The Chef was the nearest thing to a domestic goddess that He'd ever encountered. He was assailed by an almost Proustian memory of bacon, sausages, hash browns . . . And then, wafting across the celestial car park, came the evidence that someone was cooking *pancakes*. The temptation was more than He could stand.

Swallowing in anticipation, S'tan barrelled through the revolving front door, skidded across a marble hallway and bounced into one of the lifts just as the doors were closing. As he rapidly ascended to the revolving restaurant on Heaven's topmost floor, it suddenly occurred to S'tan exactly why He'd completely cut cherubs out of His diet the previous year. How *could* He have forgotten? *So indigestible*, He recalled, assailed by a griping pain around His midriff. All those ghastly feathers. Oh God, He thought, unable to stop Himself – this was the *fourth* time He'd invoked the Other Side. Hot, bothered and awash in Self-loathing, He found Himself unable to suppress a gaseous eruption of such spectacular redolence and resonance that He felt obliged to turn round and apologize to His fellow lift-users.

Rotating with some difficulty, He slowly became aware that the lift was crammed full of living versions of His indigestible pre-breakfast snack. Hundreds of tiny cherubs clustered round His knees, their green faces and pained expressions bearing witness to their inability to avoid inhaling the gassy by-product of their fellow cherub's final transformation into the fabled Fart of the Arch-Fiend; the Gas of His Gruesomeness; the Wind of Ur-Wicca.

Thank Heavens this only happens once a month, the Chef thought, watching as S'tan helped Himself to a fourth croissant from the bread basket. Tearing the pastry in half, the demon squashed it into the yolk of His eleventh egg Benedict, raised the dripping handful to His mouth and poked it inside.

'Mffrg,' S'tan mumbled, waving His hands by way of punctuation and adding, 'Arffl duph shlumtle.'

'Absolutely,' agreed the Chef. 'How perceptive of you. The eggs *were* organic. Now, what can I tempt you with? More coffee? Toast? Bagels? Bacon? Sausages? Hash browns?'

'Yeshh,' S'tan groaned. 'All of thosh. Phwooof. Lordy, that was *divine*.'

Across the table, the Chef felt the breath stop in his throat. *Lordy? Divine?* How remarkable, he thought. Imagine *that*. After all these aeons. Around the room, conversations had stopped, stuttered and tried to carry on as if nothing untoward had happened. An angel at his table choked on a mouthful of fat-free natural yoghurt and tried to disguise her outburst by turning it into a cough. S'tan's expression grew slightly pained, and rooting through the pockets of His vast grey sweatpants, He produced a small cough-sweet, partly covered in grey fluff but still emitting a faint whiff of menthol. He passed this across to the coughing angel, holding up His hands to forestall her thanks.

'No, no, no. Not at all,' He murmured modestly. 'Least I could do. Thank Heavens I had the means at hand to assist. God forbid you should choke to death while I sit back doing nothing.'

The Chef had to look away. *Modesty? Thank Heavens? God forbid?* Random acts of kindness? Something was definitely Up, and this suspicion was confirmed by S'tan's next utterance.

'Well, what's it to be, hmmm? Shall I clear the tables and wash up, or d'you want me to dry?' The bloated Devil climbed to His feet, slapped His belly and began to stack plates and bowls, humming under His breath as He moved from table to table. Suppressing a strong desire to scream out loud, the Chef realized that the Devil was humming a *Christmas* carol as He waddled virtuously off towards Heaven's kitchen.

A waitress slid a trayful of rubbery fried eggs under a heat lamp and stood back to admire the effect. Around the dining room, conversation was subdued as the hotel guests chewed doggedly through breakfast. Choosing to avoid all eggs, sausages, bacon, haggis, black pudding and hash browns, Baci spooned muesli into a bowl, topped it with poached apricots and yoghurt and returned to her seat, glowing with dietary virtue. The waitress poked morosely at the skin forming on top of a mound of scrambled eggs and sighed as the swing door to the kitchens opened. The breakfast chef emerged bearing a bowl of yesterday's re-microwaved porridge and sidled up to the waitress.

'I'm gonny have to take another part-time job,' he complained. 'This hotel's no payin' me enough. I spent all last month's wages on ma car, and there's only seventy-one shopping days till Christmas – ma kids all want computers this year; last year it was roller blades, year before . . .'

Baci flinched. Christmas? Already? She hadn't given it a thought recently, what with . . . She laid down her spoon and gazed sadly at her untouched breakfast. Overcome by a wave of sadness, she bowed her head and tried not to drip tears into her muesli. Christmas. What a hollow travesty *that* would be without Luciano by her side. My poor, poor Luciano, she thought, pushing her chair back from the table and standing up. The vision of him locked up, cold and frightened, surrounded by real murderers, made Baci's legs shake so much she feared she would collapse with sheer terror. Teetering along the deeply carpeted hotel corridors, she fled for the sanctuary of her bedroom, fumbling her key card in the slot and rushing into the tiny bathroom, only to dissolve in floods of tears. She'd just been struck by an even more hideous thought. With Luciano in prison, she would have to go through childbirth *alone*. It was most unlikely that he would be released before Christmas, especially since Munro MacAlister Hall had made such a hash of his defence.

Or *was* it a hash? Wasn't it a deliberate campaign of misinformation coupled with several glaringly obvious omissions on the alibi front? After all, Baci reasoned, Latch, herself *and* the children had all been witness to Luciano's presence in StregaSchloss on the night Mrs McLachlan had gone miss— gone for ev— A sob welled up in Baci's throat as she remembered how everything had started to go wrong after Flora had vanished. Hardly able to breathe, she thought how completely lost they now were without Mrs McLachlan in their lives.

They'd *all* loved her so much, not just Damp. Sunk in mourning, the Strega-Borgias had never imagined that *they* might be suspected of doing away with their beloved nanny. In the confusion of the days immediately following her disappearance the family had hardly even been aware of the police and forensic scientists crawling over the house, the moat and the lochside. They were in too deep a state of shock to take any notice of anything. Despite repeated questioning by the police, none of them had any idea what could have happened to Flora. Between them, they had pieced together an account of that fateful evening, but nothing gave any indication of why, or how, or where the nanny might have gone. One minute she'd been dishing out supper; putting Damp to bed as usual; finding a plaster for Ffup's talon . . .

Under pressure to recall each and every event, no matter how insignificant it might seem, they all vaguely remembered that this had been the day a photographer had turned up at StregaSchloss to take engagement photos of Ffup, but, as they all agreed, Mrs McLachlan hadn't been part of the group posing on the front steps.

A distant alarm bell sounded in Baci's mind. What had happened to those photos? Did they ever turn up? She had a sudden sharp recollection of how uncomfortable she had felt under the gaze of the photographer. As if – she shuddered, sitting down abruptly on the edge of the bath – as if he were peeling her apart layer by layer until he found the unborn baby curled deep inside her. Breathing deeply, Baci tried to banish such thoughts from her mind. Focus on what you *know*, she ordered herself. There's quite enough going on right now to scare you witless without conjuring demons out of your memory. The bald facts of the matter remained: Mrs McLachlan was, in all probability, dead; Luciano was in prison; and she, Baci, had to get herself well enough to return home to her children. At the thought of spending the foreseeable future as a single parent, she began to cry again. She simply couldn't seem to pull herself together.

Outside, in the anonymous blandness of the hotel corridors, she heard a vacuum cleaner start up; over its approaching drone a woman's voice was raised in song. Baci grabbed a length of toilet paper, blew her nose, sniffed, blinked – and sniffed again. What was that fragrance? Was it the hotel's complimentary soap? The shower gel? She inhaled deeply, trying to identify the perfume. Lavender? Yes. It had to be lavender. Then came a discreet tap on the bathroom door and a voice said, 'Are you all right, dear?'

Baci's head snapped upright, her eyes immediately flooding with more tears.

'Don't say a word,' the voice whispered, as if its owner had pressed her mouth up against the door. Baci's gaze fell to the gap beneath the door, but there was nothing there: no shadows, no feet in sensible shoes, no—

'We need you to come home,' continued the impossible voice. 'You know the wee baby's fine and as long as you don't panic, *dear* . . .'

Baci forced herself to breathe. For a split second she'd been convinced she was about to faint – but after all, being addressed by one's possibly dead ex-nanny does tend to have that effect—

'Signora' – Mrs McLachlan's voice was strained with the effort – 'go home. Go home to StregaSchloss. Everyone is coming home. *All* of those you love. Love will . . . conquer . . . all . . .' Her voice was so faint now, drowned by the din of the vacuum cleaner outside the door. 'Storms . . . Amelia's thread . . . we're safe . . . don't worry . . . for now it is . . . time.'

The vacuum cleaner was turned off and Baci could clearly hear the singer's voice: *'Lavender's blue, dilly dilly, Lavender's green . . .'*

'Flo— Flora? FLORAAAAAAA!'

Baci's self-control deserted her as, flinging open her bathroom door, she found herself face to face with one of the hotel maids, who dropped a curtsy and said, with unintentional accuracy, 'Are youse a'right, hen? Youse look like youse've seen a ghost. Awfy sorry, hen – ah thought youse had checked oot.'

The Stinger Stung

An icy drizzle had begun to fall as DS Waters parked outside the police station in Auchenlochtermuchty. In the passenger seat beside him, DCI McIntosh exhaled noisily. DC Waters braced himself. What had he done wrong *now*? He was aware that he'd managed to cover their entire car in a thin scrim of mud driving back along that dreadful track from StregaSchloss, but that was hardly *his* fault. Was it the fact that he'd set off a speed camera on the straight bit before the roundabout that had caused the Chief Inspector to look so monumentally hacked off? Or was it the fact that he'd reversed into a wheelie bin trying to

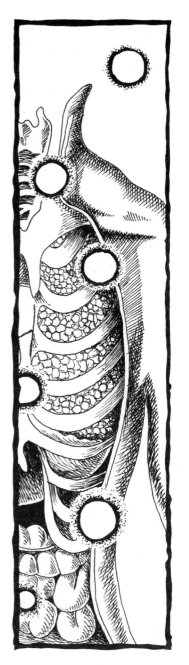

squeeze into this squitty wee parking space? Whatever it was, DS Waters reckoned he was about to find out.

'Can I, er, offer you a cup of coffee, sir?' he said, furious with himself for sounding so boot-lickingly ingratiating. 'Or tea, perhaps? I've got some nice chocolate biscuits, sir.' At this rate he'd be face-down on the pavement next, offering to act as a human boot-scraper. Gritting his teeth, he pressed on. 'I'm sure we've even got some fruit teas if you're off caffeine, sir. Mint, blackcurrant, cherry—' Ooops, he thought, skidding to a verbal standstill. Perhaps *not* the cherry, huh?

The Chief Inspector turned round to face him, his expression inscrutable. 'Detective Sergeant Waters,' he managed at length, 'I don't want any peely-wally namby-pamby fruit *tea*. After what I've just been through, tea's the *last* thing I need. That bloody woman was our only witness. There's nobody else prepared to stand up in court and swear that Lucy, Lukey, Lootch – oh, what*ever* he's called bumped off all those people. Don't you realize that our entire case against that weedy, murdering Italian aristocrat has just gone down the *pan*?' During this rant the DCI's voice had risen steadily, and was now loud enough to cause passers-by to stop and stare into the mud-encrusted police car in an attempt to see what was going on. Any minute now, DS Waters thought, the windows are going to blow out.

'WE'RE GOING TO HAVE TO LET HIM GO!' roared the

DCI. 'EAT HUMBLE PIE. APOLOGIZE. WRITE A MILLION REPORTS.' Scowling at several pedestrians, who immediately tried to pretend they weren't listening as they hurried past, he continued hoarsely, 'Fill out forms in triplicate, attend disciplinary meetings, grovel to the press—'

'Sir' – the DS tugged at his collar, which suddenly seemed too tight for comfort – 'there's also the matter of the – er, oh, Lord. The moat, sir. Their moat. At the house. We, er, accidentally demolished it with one of the diggers. Will we have to . . . er . . . ?'

'YES!' bawled the DCI. 'We'll have to rebuild the damn thing. Put it back. Bring the diggers back, send in the marine architects, technical engineers, stonemasons . . . It's going to cost an absolute *fortune*. In fact, you can just forget the tea,' he said, patting his briefcase meaningfully. 'I've got a bottle of Scotch right here. Shall we just take a wee drive somewhere quiet and discuss this over a wee dram?'

DS Waters's brow furrowed in some confusion. 'Are you suggesting that we should consume alcoholic beverages while on duty? Sir?'

'No, Sergeant,' DCI McIntosh snapped. 'That's not a suggestion. It's an order.'

Munro MacAlister Hall sat in the Hotel Bagliadi cocktail bar, his face hidden behind an English newspaper. On the table in front of him lay a dish of black olives, a whisky and soda and his mobile phone. On the opposite side of the room a large party of noisy Italians were draining their glasses before going in to dinner. Munro observed them from behind his paper, his curiosity piqued as one of their number slipped away in order to make a phone call in private. The Italian removed a mobile (Lord, Munro thought, that's one of those *hideously* expensive Swedish jobbies, isn't it?) from the breast pocket of his suit (*And* an Armani suit if I'm not mistaken) and leant casually against a pillar, his eyes raking the perimeter of the bar-room. Munro hid behind his newspaper for a few seconds, and then resumed his surveillance. The Italian had lit a cigarette (Golly, is that *allowed*?) and was keying a number into his phone. (Obviously *not* one he used frequently, otherwise he'd have speed-dialled, Munro deduced.)

The remainder of the smoking Italian's party trickled out of the bar, the diminishing clamour of their voices replaced by the sound of muted opera trickling from the Bagliadi's state-of-the-art sound system. On the table in front of Munro his mobile lit up and launched loudly into a squeakily computer-generated travesty of *The Ride of the Valkyries*. With a roar, Munro snatched his phone off the table, cursing his son through gritted teeth, and consigning him to the outer darkness for secretly changing the phone's ringtone.

'This simply isn't *on*, Rand,' Munro hissed under his breath. 'Not bloody funny. Leave my stuff alone or I'll halve your allowance, understood?'

Across the room the Italian removed his cigarette from his mouth, dropped it to the floor and frowned, holding the phone away from his head before replacing it and resuming his telephone conversation. Munro frowned too, unable to understand one single word of what was being said to him.

'I say. Sorry,' he managed, at length. 'I seem to have my wires crossed. Thought you were my son, actually. Now, about the pick-up—'

A rapid burst of Italian peppered his ear, loud enough to make him wince. The voice on the other end did not belong to a happy chappie – that much was obvious from both the tone and the volume of what was now pouring into Munro MacAlister Hall's ear. Peeved at being thus addressed by someone who was, when all was said and done, little more than a hired *thug*, the lawyer held the phone away from his ear and summoned a waiter to refill his glass.

From his mobile came the ranting of a tiny voice, its volume diminished to that of a psychotic elf. Across the room Munro saw Armani Man, hand waving, barking something incomprehensible down his mobile, then pausing for a moment to light another cigarette, his eyes flicking in his direction. Smiling conspiratorially (mobile phones – *such* a nuisance) the lawyer noticed that as the Italian resumed his tirade, so too did his anonymous caller. Odd, he thought, as two more instances of synchronicity occurred, his phone falling silent each time Armani Man paused to draw deeply on his cigarette. Then, just as the waiter tonged two ice cubes into Munro's drink, he put two and two together and arrived at a sum that made him grab his whisky and soda and drain it instantly.

'Signore?' The waiter raised his eyebrows. 'Is there something the matter?'

On the other side of the room the Italian was staring straight at him, a twisted smile on his lips. Oh, Lord, Munro MacAlister Hall thought. I'm in trouble now. This *wasn't* supposed to happen. No face-to-face contact. Ever. What bloody awful luck . . .

Walking through the door of the cocktail bar came proof that luck had nothing whatsoever to do with it. Considerably better dressed than he had been earlier that evening, the taxi driver sauntered across to whisper something in Armani Man's ear. Both men now turned to stare at Munro, both wearing identically chilling smiles. From the speaker over Munro's head the plaintive arias of grand opera swelled and grew, drowning out his attempts to call for help. Over at the bar, a man with a ruined face stirred his drink with a finger and stared into the middle distance, studiously ignoring the scuffle now taking place on the other side of the room. The bartender, polishing glasses with a linen cloth, was deaf to MacAlister Hall's muffled screams; his mouth was set in a pale, thin line. The lawyer's body was dragged out of the bar, but the waiter carried on scrubbing the table where he'd sat without looking up; removing every shred of evidence that he had ever set foot in the same hotel as his final, fatal client – the man with the ruined face: the notorious Don Lucifer di S'Embowelli Borgia.

Meet the Relatives

Unaware that a death had recently taken place in the StregaSchloss kitchen, Rand was conducting a thorough search for signs of Mrs Borgia's fabled acanthoid wax. Sitting on a shelf, level with his horrified gaze, was a stained glass jar with what appeared to be a human brain floating inside, suspended in a sulphurous yellow fluid. Closer examination of a brown label stuck to the jar revealed the contents to be a cauliflower in saffron broth, which, judging by the date of its bottling, was a vegetable with a similar vintage to Rand's father. Snorting down his metal-studded nostrils, Rand continued his hunt.

Problem was, Mrs Borgia had no clear filing system in place, he decided. Eyeballs of newts rubbed shoulders with larks' tongues in calves' foot jelly. Except, he reminded himself, eyeballs and tongues don't *have* shoulders . . . And really, half this collection of rancid old parts had to be well past their spell-by date. God. This pantry was a bacteriological minefield.

Rand shuddered, dragging his gaze away from a Kilner jar with what *had* to be a human heart in a gruesome state of decomposition floating inside it. His eyes skittered across dark jeroboams festooned with cobwebs, vaulted over rusty tins sitting in puddles of ooze and finally scanned a high shelf which bore witness to having recently been disturbed. There was a clearly discernible gouge dug through the dust and spider webs; could this possibly be a furrow made by dragging a jar of acanthoid wax across to the edge of the shelf before removing it from the pantry?

Seconds later Rand was balancing precariously on top of a flour bin, one hand outstretched, his fingers seeking purchase on a tiny stoppered jar which slid out of reach a couple of times before finally rolling effortlessly into his grasp – and just as effortlessly sliding away to shatter on the floor below. Cursing under his breath, Rand leapt off his perch and gathered up the jagged shards of the little jar, some of which still bore the tattered remains of a label stuck to them, their reverse side coated with a thick waxy paste which, judging by its smell alone, contained something very powerful indeed. Try as he might, Rand was unable to piece the tiny jar back together, so he laid all the fragments out on a lower shelf, label side up, and shuffled them around until he was reasonably happy with the result. There was an 'A', something that looked a bit like 'ca', an exceedingly hard-to-read 'th' and a clearly legible 'oid'. Eureka! He managed, with some difficulty, to restrain himself from pulling his T-shirt up over his head and running round in circles like a victorious footballer, mainly because he heard the sound of heavy footsteps climbing up from the dungeons. Hastily, he scraped the waxy residue off the back of each pot shard with a finger that was almost quivering with excitement.

Taking a deep breath, Rand braced himself for acanthoid-accelerated manhood.

Seconds later his entire body was a-quiver – this time with disgust and with the sheer effort required to stop himself gobbing the entire mouthful of acanthoid wax straight back out. The *taste* . . . it was gross beyond belief, greasy like – like lard, with a pronounced flavour of what he imagined rotting meat must be like, overlaid with something cloying, sickly sweet, closely related – twinned in fact, maybe even the soul-brother of – er, an over-ripe sock. Closing his eyes, Rand forced himself to swallow, just as the Borgias' pet dragon waddled into the pantry. Despite the horrors taking place inside his mouth, he couldn't help but notice that Ffup wore a furtive expression and was trying to conceal the loaf of bread she was clutching between her paws.

'AAAARGHH!' she shrieked, then, 'Phwoof. What a *fright*. Er . . . do I know you?'

Opening his mouth would surely make him throw up immediately, so Rand smiled apologetically and waved his hands in front of his face to mime that he was eating, and thus unable to speak. Ffup peered at him in some confusion, enlightenment gradually dawning as Rand's hand signals became more frenzied.

'Ooooooh,' the dragon squealed. 'Charades. I *love* charades. What *fun*. Let me see now. Fan mouth? Flap lips? Wave hands? Burping wave hands? Belch and hush mouth? Puff cheeks and roll eyes? Gosh, this *is* a difficult one.' She babbled on happily for several minutes as Rand clutched his stomach, groaned and staggered towards a stone sink in a corner of the pantry, stuck his mouth under the tap and drank hugely.

'Golly,' Ffup muttered. 'This is far harder than it looks. Um . . . choking? Drowning? Cough and splutter? Drink up? Cold water? Cool down? Water? Water water . . . ah. Er. Oh, *dear*. Are you all right? Gosh, you poor thing. And *all* down your T-shirt too. What a *pity*. Still – judging by the smell, it's better out than in, hmmmm?'

Edging towards the door and breathing through

her mouth, Ffup realized she was still holding the incriminating loaf of bread between her paws. Eyes swivelling from side to side, she dumped it in a dark corner behind a flour bin (the same place where she'd hidden its five predecessors) and headed for the dungeon with her appetite temporarily put on hold.

Minty sat on the edge of her bed, her thoughts in turmoil after Latch had gone. This had not been part of the job description, she decided. Life at StregaSchloss was nothing like she'd been led to believe. No-one had mentioned that her workplace would be crawling with policemen, nor that it would be populated with the entire cast from some B-movie fantasy epic, nor pointed out the sheer impossibility of communicating with that poor, poor, lost, little Damp . . .

Abruptly, Minty stood up, commanding herself *not* to think about how small and vulnerable the lost child was; *not* to consider just how many physical hazards and potential toddler-traps lay both inside and outside StregaSchloss. Latch had said not to worry, but what did *he* know? He was a butler, not a nanny, Minty reminded herself. If the domestic fires went unlit and the silverware was tarnished, then the butler was held responsible; but if the children were unwashed, unfed or, perish the thought, *missing*, then the entire household would unite in pointing a finger at the nanny. Don't worry,

Latch had said, before heading down to the lake.

Loch.

Minty frowned. Had she corrected herself? For a moment there . . . But no. It *had* sounded remarkably like another voice, somewhere in the bedroom . . . Shaking her head, she walked across to her dressing table and sat down in front of it. Behind her pale-faced reflection hung some of the family's large collection of portraits commemorating Borgias long buried. Dating back to the thirteenth century, this assembly of dark-eyed forebears had frowned down upon successions of wet-nurses, ladies-in-waiting, nursemaids, governesses and nannies; the combined weight of their masculine disapproval probably driving some of the more sensitive members of the domestic staff to plead for quarters in rooms with less of an atmosphere of manly gloom. As part of a stately home, the Ancestors' Room was spectacular, but as a bedroom it was downright spooky.

In the conversational style employed by stately home tour guides the world over, a voice informed Minty, 'Due to the constancy of the northern light falling upon it, this room was favoured by Apollonius "the Greek" Borgia; mapmaker, draughtsman, lutenist and cartographical adviser to His Majesty King James the Thirteenth, the monarch known to his detractors as "Frozen Buns the Baker's Dozen" . . .'

Reflected in the mirror, Minty caught a glimpse of

movement inside the frame of one of the portraits on the far wall. Unable to believe what she was seeing, she turned round, hoping that by confronting the reality rather than the reflection, she would restore normality. This was not to be. Staring brazenly out of the gilt frame housing Apollonius 'the Greek' was a man for whom the word 'hero' might have been invented. His smile dazzled, his eyes shone and he breathed and moved as if *he* were the golden, living being, and Minty, by some reverse alchemy, had turned into an inanimate, leaden painting. Moreover, she now saw that he was not alone. In their assorted gilded frames the dead Borgias had come to life. Ruddy-cheeked, raucous – some with lace jabots at their throats, others resplendent in ruby-rich velvets and brocades – the heads nodded, the mouths smiled and the heavy eyelids blinked away the sleep of centuries. Here, framed beside the fireplace, his face stained brown with wood smoke, was the first of the Borgias to shelter under the roof of StregaSchloss, Malvolio di S'Enchantedino Borgia, beloved grandson of Strega-Nonna, dead for hundreds of years – yet here he was, calling his assembled descendants to order, chiming a wicked-looking notched dagger against the bowl of his pewter goblet.

'Gentlemen, gentlemen, I beg you. Pray, silence please. Order, if you will. I wish to bring your attention to the fact that there has been a breach of the barrier between the worlds of the quick and the dead. A breach, gentlemen, a rip in the fabric of Time itself, allowing the past foreknowledge of the future, and the dead to find shelter among the living. I would caution you all to beware, to avoid temptation, to ignore the siren song of the Other Side. Stop up your ears, cover your eyes and resist at all costs. There will be signs and portents, the dead will dance on the cradles of newborns and the living will seek the solace of the crypt. Whole oceans will drain away to wastes of salt, islands will rise out of waters where no islands existed before and Evil will walk the Earth.'

Malvolio took a deep breath, looked down at his dagger and lifted his pewter goblet to his lips, draining its contents. In the ensuing silence Minty saw the portraits dim and darken one by one across the room. Bizarrely, this was even more frightening than when they had all sprung to life. This felt far more sinister; as if each ancestor was falling under the shadow of a malign eclipse.

One portrait remained vivid and animated: Apollonius's, his head nodding slowly, his hand beckoning her forward. Aghast, Minty found herself obediently standing up and walking towards the wall, one hand in front of herself as if she would bump into an invisible membrane separating her world from his. Up close, she saw his eyes were flecked with gold. Though a chill wind blew through the picture frame, making her hair swirl around her head, blowing strands against her mouth and eyes, Apollonius's breath felt warm against her face. Still she pressed forwards as if spellbound, entranced, her mind tearing itself softly apart, its rational part offering all the resistance of wet tissue paper. Underfoot, the floor creaked and lurched and she would have lost her balance, fallen . . .

. . . had it not been for a hand which clasped hers above the wrist and hauled her upright. The wind howled, deafening her; it was hard to make out what Apollonius was trying to say. Minty became aware of her surroundings, numbly accepting the reality of her situation even as the logical part of her brain curled itself into a ball in a corner of her skull and howled in denial. She clutched at the tarry ropes holding the wicker gondola below the silk panels of Apollonius's balloon and forced herself to look over the edge and down . . .

. . . down below, hundreds of dizzying, stomach-lurching metres, down to where vast cascading waterfalls were reduced to thin white lines like scars on the mountains; down to where clouds lay far below her feet, lying in wisps and strands, trapped in coires and wrapped around high lochans; down to where no juniper or heather could cling; down to high plateaux where only lichen could live; down to the haunt of hawk and ptarmigan, the territory of the black grouse and mountain hare; all fleeing from the skimming shadow their balloon sent scudding across the quartz-strewn rocks below . . .

'The Devils' Retort,' Apollonius said, his ink-stained fingers indicating a nearby peak wreathed in mist, its twin horned tops breaking through the veil and grazing the sky above. Now the balloon swung out, way beyond the mountain tops, the view opening out beneath them like an abyss. Thousands of vertical metres of nothingness lay between them and the turning Earth, but this, Minty realized with mounting horror, this was only a temporary state of affairs. Apollonius hauled on a rope, and with a roar, hot air rushed out of the balloon and they began to plunge towards the ground. Minty's ears popped, her eyes streamed and she clung to Apollonius in terror.

'Stop,' she wailed, barely able to force the words past her frozen lips. 'Make it s-s-stop!'

Apollonius affected not to hear; he tied off ropes, checked knots, stowed away maps and charts and tended his charcoal brazier, ignoring Minty's entreaties. Frozen to the marrow and scared witless, the nanny could only watch as they swung dizzyingly across the landscape, heading for the vast blue sea that fringed the lands below. As they drew closer, it was as if the view suddenly swam into focus; as if some internal compass behind Minty's eyes had swung round to point its quivering needle at true north. Rising out of the atmospheric cloak of sea mist was StregaSchloss and, if she wasn't mistaken, there was Lochnagargoyle, unchanged save for a small island floating in its centre like a pebble artfully placed in a suburban garden's water feature. As they drew closer, the balloonist's skill and the prevailing northerly wind brought them within sight of the island and Minty's breath caught in her throat. A gust of wind stripped away the mist and she saw three figures moving on the land below. It was hard to be certain from this distance, but they looked like a man with his head in his hands, a woman of middle years and a familiar tiny child . . .

. . . all of whom saw her, stopped, waved their arms and ran towards where the balloon hung above the shore . . .

The child waved cheerily, tugging at the hand of the woman at her side.

'DAMP!' Minty yelled, her voice betraying the maelstrom of emotions churning inside her: relief that the little girl was alive; confusion as to what she was doing here in this – this hallucination; fear that she was in real danger and that this was some kind of premonition; and finally, utter helplessness. What could she do?

'Damp,' she repeated, her voice cracking with the effort. 'Please, darling. Come back home.'

Below, the little girl smiled and turned to her companion. 'That's Toothpaste,' she explained helpfully. 'She's s'posed to be a nanny too.'

Minty was temporarily distracted from wondering who Damp was talking to by the sight of the thin man loping along the shore, coming closer with every passing second. As the gondola lurched and bumped, caught in cross-winds which buffeted it back and forth, Minty could now see that he was making straight for the balloon, his face contorted with the effort of running and his chest visibly heaving as he tried to drag air into his lungs.

'There's no point in killing yourself, dear,' she heard Damp's companion say. 'You'll only make your migraine worse, not better.'

To Minty's horror, an expression so black and foul flashed across the man's face that she couldn't stop herself uttering a sob of fright. What manner of creature was he? And what was he doing on this island? And for that matter, was any of this real? Had her fevered imagination conjured up this whole thing like a hastily erected film set; all picture-perfect on the face that showed to a camera, but behind, a series of painted canvases and rough wooden pallets? In her panic had she invented an island to place Damp safely out of harm's way? And if so, why had she populated it with this limited cast of one grandmother figure and this – this vile and devilish thing? Damp's next words drove a bulldozer straight through Minty's tottering theory.

'Tell Mama I'm coming home soon. Not worry. Tell Mama I'm bringing the best surprise. And Toothpaste—'

Minty leant over the side, hardly able to hear the little girl, aghast at how fast the devil-thing was gaining on the balloon, his outstretched hands nearly touching a trailing rope which had unspooled from a coil tied to the gondola.

'– you're not deeming. Go home and make raspy muffins for Titus. Flora says your cherry cake looks brilliant, but Titus really likes muffins best . . .'

Minty saw the woman bend over the child to say something in her ear, and Damp smiled. 'Flora says muffin respy is in the drawer under the blackbid. Ba-bye, Toothpaste . . . see soon.'

As her words were swallowed up by the mist, Minty felt the entire gondola lurch to one side. To her dismay, she saw the demon had managed to grasp the dangling rope and was now swinging below them, his breath hissing up towards her in gouts of foulness, his hands clawing at the hempen rope. Then, with another sickening lurch from the gondola and a ghastly shriek from the demon, he was gone and by Minty's side stood Apollonius, white-knuckled, his fist gripping a familiar notched dagger. Seeing her eyes widen at the sight of this weapon, he shrugged.

'Malvolio – pffff. Such a worrywart. Too busy seeking signs and portents to see what goes on under his nose. The seasons will turn before he notices that I borrowed this.' Apollonius peered over the edge of the gondola to make sure that he really had succeeded in cutting off the demon in mid-flight. Far beneath, mist rolled and coiled, swallowing the figures, the island and the entire loch in a churning cauldron of white. Apollonius heaped charcoal on his brazier, fanned the flames with ox-hide bellows and made good haste to put the island behind them.

'What . . .? Where are we . . .?' Minty began, falling silent when she became aware of what he was holding out to her. She saw a vast gilded frame and, through it, her bedroom, its familiar furnishings made utterly surreal by having materialized in the middle of the gondola under a hot-air balloon.

'It is time,' Apollonius murmured, stepping closer until Minty could feel the warmth of the sunshine pouring through the windows of her bedroom. 'Great art *outlives the brief span of our human lives,' he whispered, gallantly taking Minty's hand to help her climb through the frame. Behind her she heard cawing gulls and creaking wicker; ahead, a distant chime as, somewhere in StregaSchloss, a clock sounded the hour.*

As Minty turned back to thank him, his image was already diminished. The hero had become no more than oil on canvas, turning into a painted memorial to himself; the shrieking gulls now silenced and the wind-tossed balloon frozen in time. Of the miracle that had just occurred nothing remained save for a newly painted dagger held in the hand of Apollonius 'the Greek', and a tiny rip in the portrait of the dagger's original owner, Malvolio di S'Enchantedino Borgia, one-time guardian of the Chronostone. Malvolio, grandson of Strega-Nonna and the ancestor whose bright idea it had been to hide the Chronostone in the chandelier hanging in the great hall of his country house, thus turning StregaSchloss into an irresistible demon-magnet.

Ladybird, Ladybird

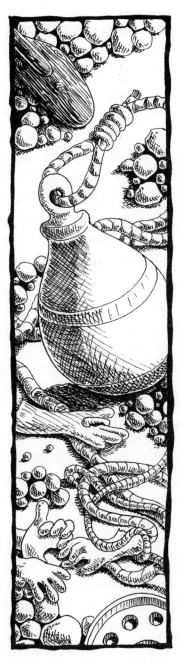

Latch walked swiftly across the pebbles, calling Damp's name with little hope of an answer. His hunt along the shores of Lochnagargoyle had been fruitless: thick mist descended as the butler walked further than he imagined even the most determined toddler would have dared venture. High tides had dumped drifts of seaweed on the pebbly shore, vast stranded embankments of greeny-brown bladderwrack, its fronds entangled with the sea-borne trash of several continents. Latch had lost track of the numbers of blue rubber gloves he'd counted on these shores, the forests of waterlogged hands washed off fishing boats hundreds of miles out at sea. Ropes and buoys too, single oars, snapped-off rowlocks; as if someone at StregaSchloss had wished for a boat and the loch had obliged, obediently delivering it in instalments, one plank at a time. The same serendipity applied to car parts: the loch spat out one bald tyre or rusty wheel with each high tide, as if in some sunken place fathoms deep lay a vast car transporter, its cargo of rusting hulks giving up its secrets one by one. Most of what arrived on these shores was worthless, an eyesore; the seemingly endless flow of rubbish proving that certain sectors of humanity were ill-qualified to be planetary custodians. Despite this, Latch paid close attention to the flotsam: he retraced his steps along the shore, head bent, eyes carefully scanning the tangled mats of seaweed in case they held any clues to Damp's disappearance.

For reasons he couldn't explain, either to Miss Araminta or to himself, Latch wasn't in the least worried about Damp. Ever since he'd caught sight of the magnetic fridge letters spelling out their message to him – to remind him, as if he needed reminding, that love would indeed triumph, would conquer all – since that moment he'd felt like a child waiting for his birthday to roll around again. He'd hardly been able to sleep the previous night, lying awake in the dark, exalted, tingling, fairly fizzing with excitement. Even the appearance of the odious Marie Bain that morning hadn't dented his conviction that everything was going to sort itself out. The discovery that the malicious ex-cook had choked on a cake of her own making only added to Latch's hunch that some form of supernatural justice was finally being applied. Heaven knew, the Strega-Borgias had suffered some horrendous misfortunes of late, but if he wasn't mistaken, the scales were beginning to tip in their favour once more, their tide was beginning to turn. In his heart of hearts, Latch knew it was all going to be all right. Flora would—

He stopped himself in time, breathing heavily and halting beside a flooded rock pool. He didn't dare give voice to his growing suspicion that Damp had somehow found a way to be reunited with her beloved nanny, or to his hope – no, his *certainty* that both would return home safe. Here, on this misty shore, he was simply going through the motions, pretending to look for the child – for heaven's sake, if he'd *really* suspected that the two-year-old had gone for an unsupervised stroll by the lochside, he'd have called out the coastguard, the police, the marines, the navy seals *and* the air-sea rescue squad to assist him in his search. His reflection in the water of the rock pool grinned back at him, offering a brief glimpse of his secret joyous self – *Flora, my Flora* – before he composed himself, rearranged his features into an expression more befitting the temporary head of a ravaged household and strode quickly in the direction of StregaSchloss.

When Latch's footsteps sounded on the rose-quartz drive, a window on the first floor opened and Miss Araminta's head popped out.

'Don't worry about Damp,' he called up to her, noting how pale the young woman appeared, her face ghost-white against the honey-coloured stone walls of StregaSchloss.

Minty frowned and leant further out of the window. 'I was about to say the same to you—' She halted in mid-sentence and narrowed her eyes. To Latch, it looked as if she was about to say something more, but then she flicked him a brief smile, withdrew her head and closed the window.

Latch's eyebrows twitched, and he stood gazing up at the silent house, wondering to himself . . . Miss Araminta. It *had* been the right decision then, putting her in the Ancestors' Room, despite instructions from Signora Strega-Borgia to give the nanny the anaemic Lilac Room. Latch rolled his eyes. Adore his employer as he did, he had to admit that she had the psychic sensitivity of a mollusc. *Anyone* could see that Miss Araminta wasn't the type. The Lilac Room was for lady guests in cashmere and pearls; ladies for whom sorcery was something you put your teacup down upon; ladies who believed that Wicca could be purchased at a local garden centre. The same ladies who'd throw a hissy-fit if the ancestors were feeling a tad mischievous. No, Latch thought, the Ancestors' Room was not for the faint-hearted.

As for Signora Strega-Borgia's amazing lack of powers of observation – Latch had frequently had cause to bless his employer's ignorance about what was going on right under her nose. Baci was no eagle-eyed employer, terrorizing staff and swooping down to fret and fuss if anything was out of place. She sailed dreamily through her household, adored by husband, children and employees, serenely unaware of her surroundings, unmoved by the highs and lows of her spouse's Latin temperament and seemingly unperturbed by the domestic squalor afforded by living in the same house as three untidy children. Unfortunately, this lack of insight extended to her own affairs. Despite having spent many months on a course in Advanced Magic, Signora Strega-Borgia had all the magical talent of an enthusiastic schoolgirl armed with her first conjuring set.

Returning to the present, Latch wondered just how far his employer's lack of observational skills might extend. Was she likely to overlook the fact that Damp was missing? Latch suspected not. While Titus and Pandora were old enough to go off on their own for hours on end, Damp was far too young to be accorded similar freedoms. Wearily, he crossed the drive, rose quartz crunching under his feet. Unless he came up with a cunning plan, he would shortly have to explain to Signora Strega-Borgia that her littlest daughter had vanished. With a heartfelt groan, he imagined how *that* would go down. No. No, no and thrice no. It was simply too hideous to contemplate. Somehow, he had to come up with a convincing reason for Damp's absence. Wondering just how much time he had for this Herculean task, Latch stared off into the distance, his thoughts in turmoil. He frowned. Whose car was that in the distance, slowly negotiating the rutted track between Auchenlochtermuchty and Strega-Schloss? A taxi? As the vehicle drew closer, Latch waited to see who would emerge from the cab's interior to grapple with the gate to the StregaSchloss estate. After a long pause the driver's door opened and a figure leapt out, opened one of the rear doors and stood back to allow a passenger to struggle out of the taxi's interior.

A familiar figure unfolded itself from the vehicle and waited while the driver battled with the gate. A small moan escaped from Latch's mouth. Surely not yet? She was early. Horribly early. Why oh why hadn't she gone shopping in Glasgow as she normally did? Oh Lord, he thought, breaking into a run, his feet slipping on the lawn and skidding across paths covered in drifts of soggy leaves. Oh help, he thought, fleeing round the side of the house, out of sight of the taxi's passenger, who was waving cheerily at the departing vehicle and setting off for her home with a briskness of step at odds with her gravid appearance. Oh damn and blast it, he thought, his heel sinking into an ominously soft mound of earth which, judging by the stench, had been of recent evacuation. With no time for the niceties of shoe scraping or even removal, Latch bolted across the kitchen garden and flung himself into the house, yelling for assistance from anybody within earshot.

Silence rolled down the passages and stairwells of StregaSchloss, and the echo of his voice was swallowed up by walls several metres thick. The butler nearly slapped his forehead in frustration. No-one could hear him – or if they could hear him, they were choosing not to answer. Sprinting into the great hall, Latch seized the first object that came to hand and began to hammer the dinner gong with a golf umbrella as if his life depended on it.

Pandora lay on Titus's bedroom floor staring sightlessly at the ceiling, where several model aeroplanes dangled from threads so furred with dust they looked hand-knitted.

'I don't know what the photos prove.' Pandora's voice was weary, as indeed was its owner. Taking turns at the computer, Titus and Pandora had been combing the photo CD in search of clues about where the pictures had come from. That had been hours ago, and still they were none the wiser. The drop-down menus relating to all photo data had been wiped – all their locked files had names ending in *h_ex*, a fact which had caused Titus to waste endless hours running virus protection software and now, waiting for the disk to reload, Pandora was rapidly losing the will to live. She rolled over on her stomach and began morosely picking threads out of the carpet.

'I think,' she said at length, 'I – it's like everything's falling apart. Dad's gone, Mum's on planet New Baby, you say that Damp's missing, Latch looks like a ghost, Marie Bain's—'

'OK. Stop,' Titus interrupted. 'I get the picture.' He exhaled noisily and slumped back on his seat. 'Things change, Pan. Nothing stays the same for ever.'

'Yeah, but . . .'

'Could you quit picking holes in my carpet? You're acting like a – like a depressed moth or something. Look, for what it's worth, I'm pretty sure it'll all work out in the end. We *know* Dad didn't kill Mrs McLachlan, so sooner or later he'll be proved innocent and come home. Mum'll rapidly exit planet New Baby once it arrives and starts wailing all night long. Damp will . . . Damp will . . . Look, here are the photos at last.' And relieved to have something to do other than spouting faintly cheering platitudes, Titus turned back to his computer, only to emit a yelp of dismay.

'What?' Pandora rolled over and sat up.

'I *knew* it. I just knew it. I should *never* have tried to open anything with *h_ex* at the end of a filename. This is exactly like when my laptop got that weird virus last spring. Those were *h_ex* files too and they completely trashed my hard drive—'

'Let me see,' Pandora said, standing up and crossing to where her brother sat slumped, head in hands, rubbing his forehead and making small whimpering sounds. She bent over the ailing computer, and was about to start spouting her own faintly comforting platitudes when they both heard Latch's frantic summons on the dinner gong downstairs.

Here Comes the Night

The terrifying plunge into the waters of Lochnagargoyle had done nothing to improve Isagoth's temper, but oddly, as he wallowed and doggy-paddled for shore, the demon had a moment or two to marvel at how the unplanned swim had cured his migraine. This was before the salt water of the sea-loch began to work on his skin, and before he attempted to break all Olympic swimming records by windmilling through the waves for, in common with all demons, he was violently allergic to salt. He howled and shrieked at the two figures on the shore as he thrashed and boiled like a demonic waterspout.

Out of the north came a wind full of sharp little teeth, icing the pebbles of the shore and nipping at Damp and Mrs McLachlan as they shivered by the lochside. If the plummeting temperature was causing Mrs McLachlan to shudder, it was the sight of what Damp held out in her hand that really made her tremble with fear. Wrapped in Mrs McLachlan's arms, Damp was only dimly aware of her nanny disentangling the thread from her fingers, but that was perfectly fine by Damp. After all, she thought, she didn't need it any more; it had led her to exactly where she'd wanted to go. Then Mrs McLachlan gasped out loud, stiffened slightly and pulled back from the embrace to gaze intently into Damp's face.

The little girl smiled, unsure why her nanny was staring at her but swept along by a wave of utter joy at being reunited with her long-lost beloved.

'Och, my wee pet,' Mrs McLachlan whispered. 'What have you *done*?' Her eyes skidded sideways to where Isagoth's bobbing head emerged from the waves; he was shrieking something which, if his expression was anything to go by, was unlikely to be an invitation to come on in. 'This thread,' she persisted, her voice so sad, so full of foreboding and weary defeat that Damp felt her tummy tumble down to her toes in their rather dashing pink wellies. Uh-oh, she thought. I've done something very very not good at all. She closed her eyes and hoped that it, whatever *it* was, would simply vanish. Overhead, Mrs McLachlan talked about threads and Strega-Nonna and losing the way home and the trail of breadcrumbs in *Hansel and Gretel*—

'Not like it, that one,' Damp interrupted loudly. 'Horbil, horbil story. Not like it ginga bread either.' Her bottom lip gave a warning quiver and her voice grew louder. 'Not like it when you're cross with Damp. Not like it here. Horbil rocks. Nasty yuck water. Damp want to go home. Please?'

'Er' – Vesper cleared his throat – 'didn't you hear what the lady said? We can't go home now. You've got the *thread*. All of it. You were supposed to *follow* it from StregaSchloss to here, not *roll* it up and bring it with you. Your Miz Clachlan's right. It's like Hansel eating the trail of breadcrumbs. We're lost, girl. You blew it. We'll never find our way home nowww . . . Aaaaa—' With a stifled shriek, the tiny bat flung himself down Damp's fleecy top, clinging onto its zipper with his thumbs and squeaking with terror as he tried to shelter from the deepening chill. 'Return to your seats and adopt the b-b-brace position,' he managed. 'Do not p-p-panic, the trained cabin crew will assist you in the event of an emergen— Aaaargh, this *is* an emergency. Abandon ship, women and bats first. Mayday, mayday . . .'

The little bat was still issuing this piercing distress call when help came from a most unexpected quarter.

A wave of blackness swept overhead, bringing with it an invisible and choking ammoniac stench. Clutching Damp to her, Mrs McLachlan stared up into a sky so full of ragged black shapes that it was as if night had fallen. From the comparative safety of Damp's fleece, Vesper peered short-sightedly at the sky and gave a small sob of relief. Thank goodness. That ought to do it, he decided, stuffing both thumbs into his mouth and blinking rapidly. On the horizon, clouds the colour of a deep bruise came rushing across the darkening sky, crowding round the island like ghouls at an accident.

The ammoniac reek of bat-pee intensified and now, above the howl of the wind, Vesper could hear the leathery flapping of thousands of tiny wings; all of them chittering and squeaking in obedient response to his distress call; all of them at his command; all of them alarmingly vocal, thousands of bat-voices raised in a deafening tumult of sound . . .

. . . not one word of which Vesper could understand.

'To *me!*' he shrieked as, unheeding, the bats circled the humans, weaving ragged black loops and figures of eight in the air around them.

'Er, guys? Like, *hello?*' Vesper bawled as the bats screamed overhead. 'Listen to me, wouldya? Pay *attention.*'

By the loch a bedraggled figure dragged itself onto the rocks and vomited up a mouthful of seawater before staggering across the beach to where Mrs McLachlan and Damp clung to each other.

'Tell me,' the demon gasped, wiping his mouth

with the back of his hand and waving at the sky. 'These creatures. They yours? You summon them?'

Mrs McLachlan ignored him, watching as the bats circled overhead. A faint echo of something important was sounding at the edge of her consciousness. Bats. There were bats around the house. Around StregaSchloss. Something connected bats to one of the members of the family. What *was* it?

'Like, if you've brought them here,' Isagoth persisted, 'then that's tickety-boo. No problemski. On the other hand, if my Boss sent them to scope out what I was up to – well, pffff, then it's off to the Eternal BBQ for all of us, and just pray that S'tan likes his humans underdone . . .'

Barbecue? Mrs McLachlan thought distractedly. She loathed barbecued food; it reminded her all too vividly of a dark age when it was considered acceptable to burn witches at the stake. Consequently she refused to cook barbecued anything, much to Titus and Pandora's disgust. Her breath caught in her throat. Titus. Pandora. The *names*. And it was *Pandora* – she was the connection with the bats. It all came flooding back on a returning tide of memory: how the child had been out wandering the hills the previous summer and had stumbled across a colony of rabid bats living in a high coire. According to Pandora, these bats had a long-standing affinity with StregaSchloss and with witches in particular; if the family had need of their assistance, the bats would come . . .

'That's right,' a voice whispered. 'You needed, we came.'

Flora felt her skin prickle. Beside her, Damp was trying to soothe Vesper, who was having hysterics at his own inability to communicate with the bat-hordes.

'Lordy – he does go on and on, doesn't he?' the voice demanded in the same dry whisper as Vesper's squeaks grew ever more frenzied. 'Look. Let's cut to the chase, shall we?' A shape dropped down and landed with a soft thump on Flora's shoulder. 'We can't stay.' The voice sounded far closer now, cosy and intimate as its owner wrapped its wings round itself like a leather cloak. 'The rip in time between our coire and this island is only temporary. We must leave, and leave now. Are you with us?'

Isagoth was staring at Flora as bats settled on his outstretched arms. 'You think you can leave me behind? Think again,' he sneered, his voice almost inaudible in the din of beating wings. 'These mind-less mammals may well answer to you and your kin, but I can bend most creatures of the night to my will as easily as this.'

And to Flora's horror, the demon grasped a bat in each fist and squeezed. Almost immediately, he disappeared beneath a mantle of fluttering blackness as some of the bats of Coire Chrone obeyed his command and bore him up into the storm.

Here Comes the Don

Two heavyset bodyguards stood outside the double doors to the Hotel Bagliadi's most exclusive suite, the Maledictine.

'Eh. Fabbrizio.'

'*Si?*'

'Whaddya think he's doing in there?'

'*Cosa?* With the goat?'

'*Si.* And the candles.'

The bodyguards stared at each other and shrugged.

'Pfffff,' Fabbrizio opined, flicking an invisible speck of dust off the lapel of his suit before hissing, 'Enzo – 'f you know what's good for you, shutta your face. We're not paid to think.'

Both men scowled massively and returned to playing five-a-side football on their mobile phones.

'Eh. Fabbrizio.'

'*Si?*'

'Why a goat and candles? If I had the boss's money, I'd splash out. Have a – a leopard and a – a lava lamp—'

'What are you on about?'

'The boss. Goats and candles. Bit downmarket, eh?'

'Enzo?'

'*Cosa?*'

'Maybe the boss is fed up with alla the fancy eats in this hotel. Maybe he wants to singe a bitta goat's meat. How the hella should I know?'

Once more the men stared at each other and shrugged.

'Maybe he's summoning a d-d-demon,' Enzo ventured at length.

'Nahhh. Don'ta be ridiculous. I think he's having a candlelit dinner.'

'With a *goat*? Now you're being ridiculous.'

Behind locked doors, Don Lucifer di S'Embowelli Borgia stared in unalloyed dismay at the disembowelled goat lying on the hotel's charred silk carpet. Such an infernal nuisance. Why on earth the Devil couldn't use a mobile like everyone else was quite beyond his understanding. Every single time he – the most fearsome Mafioso in all of Italy, Don Lucifer di S'Embowelli Borgia – had to go through this ludicrous rigmarole of pentagrams, candles, goat's blood and incantations – when a simple country code followed by a ten-figure number would have been faster, easier and far less disastrous from the goat's point of view. With a disgruntled squeak, the Don slumped backwards onto an ottoman and waited for S'tan to respond to the summoning.

The Don's baleful meditations were interrupted by the arrival of a cloud of greasy black smoke which spiralled up from the gaping belly of the goat. The smoke thickened and spread out to form a wide column reaching from the floor to the ceiling as the temperature in the room plummeted to zero. The Don sighed and made a point of ignoring the curtains (billowing), his bed (levitating), and the water in his Jacuzzi, which was turning a bilious green and giving off sulphurous gases. Then came an angry hiss and a vast puff of scalding steam, followed immediately by the appearance of a corpulent man who stood astride the goat with a cleaver in one hand and a cook's blowtorch in the other.

Utterly confused, Don Lucifer slowly got to his feet. At first he hardly recognized Him, so vast had S'tan become. He was twice the fiend He'd been before, with dimpled arms folded across a belly which flowed up and over His cook's apron and overhung enormous thighs encased in black and white checked trousers. Don Lucifer frowned. Who was this lard-ball? Had they dared send him some overweight *underling*? Him? Don Lucifer di

S'Embowelli Borgia, Italy's most wanted gangster? Like, who *was* this bloated spectre anyway? If he'd wanted a cook he would've dialled down to the hotel kitchens and demanded one, not wasted hours disembowelling a goat by candlelight—

'WHAT,' the demon roared, 'IS IT. NOW? I'VE GOT A HOLLANDAISE ABOUT TO TURN INTO SCRAMBLED EGGS AND MY ROQUEFORT SOUFFLÉS NEED TAKING OUT IN A MINUTE. WHADDYA WANT?'

Don Lucifer peered at this apparition. It did, admittedly, *sound* a little bit like S'tan, but ... but ...

'OH, DO HURRY UP, ONE HASN'T GOT ALL DAY, YOU KNOW,' the demon continued peevishly. 'AND I CAN TELL YOU, PAL, YOU'RE SKATING ON THIN ICE. WHAT D'YOU MEAN BY KILLING ONE OF MY POOR INNOCENT GOATS TO DEMAND AN AUDIENCE WITH *MOI*? HMMMM?'

It *was* S'tan, Don Lucifer realized. Shrouded in lard, considerably less frightening, but still the unmistakable First Minister of the Hadean Executive. But – Don Lucifer reeled in astonishment – but what on earth had happened to Him? It was like opening the hood of a Ferrari and discovering a lawnmower engine idling within. Like ordering a steak and being served a tofu-burger. Now he noticed the smell – all around him, *everywhere*, every expensive square centimetre of Bagliadi air-space was filled with the stink of goats, making this oh-so-exclusive suite reek like a barnyard. At this rate he'd probably have to fumigate the top floor of the hotel when S'tan left. *If* He left.

'Yeek,' he managed, his voice squeaking pitifully, his hands groping in his trouser pockets for the notebook and pen he had carried ever since the bungled episode of plastic surgery had mangled his vocal cords and ruined his face for ever. 'Yeek squee ik ik yeep?'

'YOU CANNOT BE SERIOUS,' S'tan gasped. 'YOU *STILL* HAVEN'T MANAGED TO PUT YOUR HALF-BROTHER OUT OF ACTION? AFTER ALL THIS TIME? I *HAVE* TO MEET THIS CHAP – HE REALLY MUST BE QUITE A GUY, HUH?' Hugely amused by this, S'tan's belly wobbled and jiggled as He laughed in Don Lucifer's face, releasing a wave of garlic on His breath that caused the Don to reel backwards. Garlic? In Don Lucifer's dim understanding, weren't demons supposed to *hate* garlic? What on earth was going on? Still, Don Lucifer had an important favour to ask and it wouldn't do to offend his benefactor. He hunted for the right words and finally found the perfect way to phrase his request. 'Squee ee eekeee squee? Ee squee ik yeep? Eese?'

'OH FOR HEAVEN'S SAKE!' S'tan roared. 'MY *HOLLANDAISE*. LOOK, I'LL SEE WHAT I CAN DO ABOUT YOUR LITTLE PROBLEM. LUCIANO, WASN'T IT? HE DOES APPEAR TO HAVE THE LUCK OF THE GODS, HMMM? CONSIDER IT DONE. OR – CONSIDER IT *WILL* BE DONE, BUT ONLY AFTER YOU DO SOMETHING FOR ME FIRST.'

'Eeek?'

'YOU MIGHT HAVE NOTICED THAT I HAVE HAD A MID-LIFE CAREER CHANGE, HMMM? DON'T PANIC, I AM STILL THE SAME OLD NICK YOU KNOW AND HATE, BUT RECENTLY I FELT THAT I WAS GROWING SOMEWHAT STALE. BORED. AFTER ALL, I HAVE BEEN IN THE BUSINESS FOR SEVERAL THOUSAND AEONS, SO I DECIDED TO LEARN SOMETHING NEW. SOMETHING, DARE I SAY, *CREATIVE*? I HAVE ALWAYS BEEN SECRETLY ENVIOUS OF MY OPPOSITE NUMBER WITH HIS LITTLE PROJECTS LIKE, YOU KNOW — CREATING MANKIND AND THE UNIVERSE AND THE PERFECT ROQUEFORT SOUFFLÉ — ANYWAY, ONE DIGRESSES FROM THE POINT. I WANTED TO DO SOMETHING I ENJOY, AND FRANKLY, WHAT WITH ONE THING AND ANOTHER, THE ONLY THING I'VE BEEN ENJOYING LATELY IS FOOD. AND IN HADES, WELL, BETWEEN YOU AND ME THE FOOD THERE IS PRETTY HELLISH. BURNT TO A CRISP. EVERYTHING STINKS OF SMOKE — EVEN BREAKFAST — AND THAT'S WHEN IT OCCURRED TO ME. LEARN TO COOK PROPERLY. SO I DID. I TAUGHT MYSELF TO READ, I BOUGHT ALL THE BOOKS, I BOUGHT THE BEST EQUIPMENT, I WATCHED THE DEMOS ON TV, I WENT ON SEVERAL COOKERY COURSES AND NOW . . . WELL *NOW*, I TELL YOU — I'M *HOT*, I'M HIP, I'M HAPPENING AND I WANT MY OWN COOKERY SHOW.'

S'tan's yellow eyes skewered Don Lucifer in place, giving the mortal a timely reminder that overweight and outwardly transformed He might be; inside He was still the Arch-Fiend, S'tan the Earl of Earwax, His S'tainless S'teeliness, Beelzebub the Boss of Hades, First Minister of the Hadean Executive and Lord of Misrule.

'Eeek ik? Ike ek eep.'

'NO.' S'tan rolled the word around his mouth, managing somehow to invest this single syllable with not only marrow-tingling menace, but also several syllables unknown to humankind, so that the whole emerged as a vast swelling, breaking wave of sound that crashed over Lucifer's head like a sonic tide. 'NOAAOUGHEII,' S'tan repeated, then added, 'NOT A RADIO SHOW, YOU CRETIN. I WANT MY OWN TELEVISION PROGRAMME. DEVILLED FOOD. HOT AS HELL. FUN WITH FLAMBÉ. TOTALLY TOAST – I DON'T CARE WHAT IT'S CALLED AS LONG AS I GET TO COOK TO CAMERA.'

'Eeek,' Don Lucifer whispered. 'Eek ike onk eek ee-ee ike eep.'

'I DON'T CARE,' S'tan roared. 'USE YOUR INFLUENCE. USE YOUR MONEY – YOU'VE GOT ENOUGH OF IT. SO SPEND IT ON SOMETHING MORE INTERESTING THAN GOATS AND CANDLES. BUY A TV STATION. WHATEVER. JUST DO IT.'

'Eep.'

'EXCELLENT,' S'tan hissed. 'RECORDING TO BEGIN IN, SAY, TWO WEEKS? THAT'LL GIVE US TIME TO FIT IT INTO TRANSMISSION SCHEDULES IN THE RUN-UP TO SAMHAID—'

'Ike?'

'CHRISTMAS, YOU CRETIN. EUGHHHHH. THAT WORD. NOW I'LL HAVE TO GO RINSE MY MOUTH WITH NEAT GIN TO REMOVE THE TAINT OF SANCTITY. RIGHT, SCUM, WE HAVE A DEAL. YOU GET ME ON AIR AND I'LL SERVE UP

THAT BROTHER OF YOURS ANY WAY YOU WANT. ROASTED, TOASTED OR FLAMBÉD À LA MODE. TALKING OF WHICH, MY SOUFFLÉS ARE BURNING. TIME TO GO. BYEEEEEE . . .'

And in a cloud of sulphur so weak it smelled faintly of boiled cabbage, S'tan vanished from sight.

Jailhouse Blues

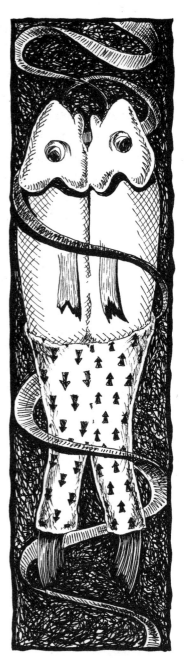

Prisoner 3/10/GLA/ MURD peered at the console in front of him and sighed. He felt awful: sick as a dog; stomach awash in acid; head throbbing; and as for his kidneys, they felt as if they'd been ground zero for a major battle between demons in hobnail boots and hippos in high heels. Luciano felt like death, and this, he reminded himself, was *before* he'd even begun to exercise in the prison gym. Whatever it had been that Malky and Big Bogbrains had encouraged him to drink, it had performed like a highly effective sledgehammer, laying him out cold and making sure that he felt completely flattened when he came to.

Unfairly, his cell-mates appeared to be immune to the drink's ill-effects, heaping their breakfast trays with mounds of congealed porridge and a stack of leathery toast which, to Luciano's hungover nasal sensitivities, smelled overwhelmingly of rancid margarine. The two criminals had proceeded to dispatch this unappetizing repast at top speed, chasing it down with several cigarettes thriftily recycled from fag-ends found in the previous evening's ashtrays. Luciano felt like a kipper when they finally left the smoke-filled cell and coughed along the corridors to the echoing, dazzling, testosterone-impregnated spaces of the prison gymnasium, where smoking was outlawed, unlike sweating, which was actively encouraged.

'Haw, youse,' roared a voice behind Luciano. 'Get a move on, there's a queue, eh no?'

Luciano spun round to see that this was the truth: standing cracking their knuckles in a line of muscle-bound menace were several prisoners, some with extensive tattoos, some with few remaining teeth and all engaging in warm-ups and stretches carefully chosen to remind a wuss like Luciano of his lowly weed-like status.

'Ah. Yeees,' he managed, turning back to the console and attempting to look knowledgeable.

SELECT A PROGRAMME

prompted the machine, scrolling automatically

through a tersely worded array of choices, none of which gave any indication of the true horrors in store for the novice treadmiller.

FAT BURNER
TOTAL FITNESS
BODY ATTACK
FLAB COMBAT

Luciano's heart sank, and then he spotted something that sounded at least do-able: 'ROLLING HILLS'. That didn't sound too painful. Right. He pressed a button and up came:

THANK YOU
BODY ATTACK ENGAGED
SELECT SPEED

Luciano frowned. He didn't *want* 'body attack', for heaven's sake. His body felt like it had recently undergone an aerial bombardment with major infantry action on the attack front. More of *that* he didn't need. He pressed the 'select programme' button several times. From under his feet came an ominous whine. To his horror, the console now read:

THANK YOU
LEVEL 19 ENGAGED
SELECT SPEED

Stifling a scream of dismay, he saw that the treadmill's levels of exertion only went up to level 20. And he still hadn't keyed in a speed. Maybe he could survive the rigours of level 19 if he chose a slug's pace? Hoping that he was unobserved, he repeatedly pressed the minus key under the speed button.

There. That ought to do it.

THANK YOU
65 K.P.H.
BODY ATTACK: LEVEL 19
BEGIN WORKOUT

Before Luciano could do anything to save himself, the treadmill whined into life. Under his feet the plate tilted and lurched upwards till he practically required crampons to remain upright on its alpine slopes. As the angle of the footplate steepened it began to move, at first slowly, but within seconds Luciano was scrabbling, running, sprinting, leaping, screaming and—

The treadmill spat him backwards, straight into the queue of knuckle-crackers, bowling them over like skittles and scattering them across the gym floor. Miraculously, he had escaped injury: as he spun shrieking into his fellow cell-mates, he'd had the good fortune to bounce into the marshmallow belly of Big Brian, whose lifetime's devotion to the product of the deep-fat fryer had endowed him with sufficient abdominal cushioning to qualify as a human airbag. However, Luciano was the only lucky one. The impact ruptured Big Brian's spleen, one of his meaty flying elbows broke Malky's nose, the other outflung arm connected catastrophically with the mouth of a police informer called Danny the Fox, and as Big Brian crashed backwards, his vast weight toppling like a felled oak, he landed on top of a frail little murderer whose name no-one could pronounce, and squashed him flat.

In the ensuing riot, no-one paid any attention to the blare summoning prisoner 3/10/GLA/MURD to the governor's office. No-one except for prisoner 3/10/GLA/MURD, that is. Everyone else just wanted mindless violence, revenge and a spot of recreational rending, biting and gouging. In the explosive atmosphere of a Scottish men's prison, it didn't take much to ignite the prisoners' tempers, and the sight of seriously injured bodies lying sprawled across the floor was a perfect excuse to get stuck in. Fists flew, recently healed noses were re-broken, cauliflower ears and black eyes blossomed like weeds. Manly grunts and squeals were punctu-ated with wet thuds and grisly crunches. Old scores were settled and new vendettas born. So merrily engrossed were the prisoners in their adoption of all things Neanderthal that it wasn't until several hours later that they noticed someone was missing from the bloodstained, bruised queue of criminals waiting in line to see the prison doctor.

'Aw, ma heed,' whined Malky, slumped on the floor beside the unconscious body of Big Brian. 'Ah need a painkiller, me.'

'Yoush got aff lucky, pal,' opined Danny the Fox, one hand over his mouth, the other clutching his front teeth, which had been an early casualty of the riot. 'Ah canny shee a thing right noo, ma eyesh are a' shwollen.' Indeed, the injured prisoner was sporting two black eyes, courtesy of a vengeful middleweight boxer who'd seized the opportunity to settle out of court. Hardly able to enunciate the words, he continued, 'Hash anyone sheen that wee Italian bloke who went fleein' aff the runnin' machine?'

'What – yon wee Mafia chappie?'

'Shhhh. Shut up. Wallsh have *earsh*.'

'Ow. So dae I, and both mines have got lumps bitten ootae them—'

A shadow fell across the queue and the injured men immediately quietened. A trolley bearing the flattened remains of Big Brian's last victim rolled past, casting something of a pall over the assembled prisoners.

'Aw jeez, that's no human any more,' stated Malky, turning away to demonstrate his vast reserves of empathy by gobbing on the floor. One of the prisoners seized the opportunity to ask about the missing Italian bloke with possible connections to the ... He tailed off in mid-query, suddenly remembering that he wasn't supposed to mention anything whatsoever to do with the Mafia. The guard pushing the trolley had no such scruples.

'What, you mean Don Borsher?' he roared, his voice echoing along the metal walkways and stone corridors of the prison; it bounced off cell doors and security blocks alike; ricocheting across the quadrangle outside until everyone within a two-mile radius shared in the joyous tidings that the prison had played temporary host to that wickedest of criminal types – a Mafia don.

'Aw, him,' the guard continued, giving a dismissive sniff. ''E's skedaddled, him. Shot the craw. Headit fir the hills.'

'Whaaaaa . . . ? He's *escaped*?' The prisoner could barely get the words out past his sagging jaw.

'Nawwww,' the guard grunted. 'Ah mean, he's gone hame. Released, he was. Case aginst him all fell apart. See, the chief witness for the prosecution was . . .' And with a lamentable lack of accuracy, the guard drew his finger across his own throat in the universally accepted gesture for 'murder by way of windpipe severance'.

This fiction met with a predictable response. The prisoners' eyes grew round – even those slitted from blows sustained earlier – their mouths dropped open and they effortfully and slowly put two and two together and arrived at a variety of conclusions, none of which bore any resemblance to the truth. However, the one fact upon which they all agreed was utterly and perfectly true.

That Italian chappie, whoever or whatever he was, was a lucky guy.

Dainty Dragoness

Peering round the moth-eaten damask curtains in Titus's room, Latch risked a quick look out of the window. He couldn't see Signora Strega-Borgia anywhere, but that might have been due to the fading light; outside, the skies were clogging up with browny-grey clouds from which a sleety rain was beginning to fall. Shivering, the butler turned round to face his co-conspirators.

'Well?' he demanded. 'What should we do? Cause the Signora hours of unnecessary anguish by telling her the truth, or try and keep up the pretence for a little longer?'

'But ... the truth – I mean, it's so weird. *Is* it true? Are you sure—?' Titus

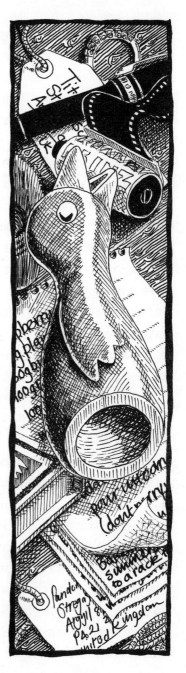

began, and then stopped, embarrassed, as Minty turned reproachful lavender-blue eyes towards him.

'I'm *sure* I saw Damp,' she said firmly, then qualified this with, 'Problem is, I don't know *where* that was. But I was given proof that it was real. Proof that what I saw really happened. Damp said – well, no, the woman *with* her said I was to look in the dresser drawer under the blackbird for a recipe for Titus's favourite food—'

'I do apologize, but can we please hurry this up?' Latch interrupted, turning away to stare out of the window again. 'She'll be here any minute now and we still haven't worked out what we're going to tell her about Damp.'

Rand yawned pointedly and muttered something under his breath.

'My favourite food . . . ?' Titus frowned, ignoring Rand and distracted by the proximity of Minty and by the fact that here he was, *towering* over her. Nannies, in his experience, usually towered over *him*. She smelled good, too, he thought, then forced himself to pay attention. 'Tell me then – what *is* my favourite food?'

Minty smiled. 'I checked. In the drawer. And there it was, tucked under a china pie funnel. It was handwritten on the back of a shopping list, and it said, *Raspberry muffins – makes twelve.*'

'Yes,' Titus whispered. 'That's *right*. I loved them. I'd completely forgotten. Mrs McLachlan used to

make them for me all the time . . . I . . . er . . . I . . .'
Oh, heck, he thought, I might just be about to burst
into tears here.

'Fascinating,' Pandora snapped, 'but if we could
just forget your stomach for once and concentrate
on Mrs McLachlan. This means— Oh my God –
don't you *see*, this means that Mrs McLachlan *is*
alive. I mean – *we've* seen her, Titus, but that might
have been because we so desperately *needed* to have
any hint, no matter how small, that she wasn't . . .
wasn't dead. But Tooth— I mean Minty really *did*
see Mrs McLachlan and Damp as well, so . . . so . . .
um, oh heck.' Pandora's shoulders sagged. 'But
we're still left with what on earth we're supposed to
tell Mum. I just don't see how we can pretend that
Damp is here. Mum'll want to see her.'

'Unless we said she was ill,' Titus suggested. 'You
know – something really infectious.'

'But not life-threatening,' Pandora said. 'Mum
would panic if it was dangerous. But what if . . .
what if . . . *Yes!* I've got it. What if Damp had something that was infectious, non life-threatening but
really dangerous for unborn babies? *That* would do
it. We could tell Mum that Damp was fine, but she
wouldn't be able to go near her—'

'German measles,' Minty said firmly. 'That's the
one. Harmless to almost everyone except unborn
babies—' She stopped and bit her lip. 'Bother. It's
only dangerous in the first three months of pregnancy
– d'you think your mum would know that?'

'Somehow, I doubt it,' Titus said. 'Even if she *does* know it, we could tell her that it's a new and virulent strain.'

'That really is very good,' Latch said. 'But are you all good enough at lying? Could you look your mother in the face and lie through your teeth? Forgive me for saying, but in all the years I have worked here, I've always been able to tell when you or your sister were being economical with the truth. Your eyes swivel about and you blush like beetroots. One look at your faces and your mother would know instantly.'

'If it's *really* infectious, we'd have caught it too,' Pandora said. 'We can say we caught it from Damp – poor us. That means we're all shut up together and Mum won't be able to see any of us. We can talk to her through the door, and if I absolutely have to, I can make my voice go all squeaky and pretend to be Damp.'

'I'm a rotten liar,' Minty confessed. 'Can I join you? After all, as your nanny, I'd be pretty likely to have caught whatever it is as well. And I could be looking after you, even though I'd be feeling pretty grim—'

'What about me?' Rand squeaked. 'Not only have I not got German measles, but that wax didn't work.'

'What?' Titus glared at him. 'What wax? I haven't given you any yet. Matter of fact, there wasn't any left when I looked. I meant to tell you. What wax d'you mean?'

'For God's *sake*!' Latch finally lost his temper and spun round from the window to glare at Rand. 'You, sonny, have a lot to learn. Right now, we're trying to come up with a plan to protect Titus's mother from the hideous discovery that her youngest child has vanished into thin air, while you, you selfish little toad, you're trying to hijack the conversation for your own ends. Time you got a grip, laddie. Just because your father has amply demonstrated that he's a moral midget doesn't mean you have to become one too . . .'

Rand's face coloured instantly, as if he'd been slapped. Unable to meet Latch's furious gaze, he looked down and exhaled noisily. Then, shaking his head, he visibly pulled himself together. 'Point taken,' he muttered. 'So . . . what d'you want me to do to help?'

Which, Latch decided, was probably the closest young Master MacAlister Hall would ever get to an apology.

Proving, were proof required, that she had the observational skills of an oyster, Baci had failed to notice the police excavations that had chewed up the path surrounding the moat and left it like a mud-slick. Perhaps she might have paid more attention to where she was walking had her thoughts not been so full of what she'd heard in her hotel bathroom that morning. How could Flora McLachlan have talked to her? Was she losing her mind, hearing the dead speak? Were aural hallucinations part and parcel of pregnancy? She didn't remember hearing things during previous confinements; in fact, quite the opposite – pregnancy had slowly filled her head with what felt like cotton wool and clouded her perception with an invisible veil. That was one of the things she loved about the whole birth thing, she reminded herself. It was like living in a bubble: pregnancy allowed her to float blissfully along, blown hither and yon, not really connecting with anythi—

'*Auuuk!* Watch out!' shrieked a familiar voice, as Baci suddenly found herself skating rapidly and uncontrollably through the mud towards the moat. The *empty* moat, her mind wailed, realizing all too late the significance of all the big yellow diggers, their buckets and scoops bent over the moat like vast birds at a watering hole. Except there wasn't any water in *this* hole, was there? Oh heck, she thought, bracing herself, this is going to *hurt*. She opened her mouth to scream – and was spun around to find herself skating *away* from the moat, this time with a partner. A partner dressed in very realistic crocodile skin, with arms that were regrettably too short to span her expanded waist-line, but a partner who was nonetheless very nimble on his fee— claws. Claws. Crocodile skin. Strong reptilian reek and row upon row of primrose-yellow teeth. Dear Tock, she thought, clinging on tight. How kind.

Scrabbling frantically in the mud with his claws, the crocodile managed to bring them to a halt, avoiding pitching them both face-first into a herbaceous border by using his tail as a rudder. They hung on for a moment, giggly with relief. Tock grinned up at his mistress, his nostrils drinking in her familiar smell of moisturizer, shampoo and, oddly for her, *lavender*. Gallantly extending a fore-leg, he offered to escort her inside, apologizing for the parlous state of the moat and surrounding garden as they walked together round the outside of StregaSchloss.

'It's a complete mud-fest,' the crocodile admitted, wondering if now was an appropriate time to raise the subject of funding for his moat renovations. Looking at Signora Strega-Borgia's pale face, he decided against it. Plenty of time later to explain that he needed unrestricted access to the Borgia bank vaults if he was ever going to build his dream moat. Together they picked their way carefully over a mound of broken flagstones, which the police had smashed with sledgehammers and dumped on the lawn. Baci heaved a sigh as she regarded her mangled garden.

'Those policemen seemed to take an unholy delight in making as much of a mess as they possibly could. I suppose there's nothing we can do about it either, especially now Luciano is in . . . in . . .'

'Don't,' Tock counselled, patting her arm and

half-dragging her towards the kitchen garden. 'Please, don't upset yourself. Think of your little baby. And look, there are your children welcoming you home.' The crocodile pointed up to the first-floor windows of StregaSchloss, where lights had been turned on since the daylight was fast fading and the sky was heavy overhead. He saw the waving silhouettes of the children in Titus's bedroom window and waved back, unable to see from this distance that their throat-cutting gestures did not signify hello, but meant something entirely different. A tiny feathery snowflake blew across his line of sight, closely followed by another and another. All at once the sky was full of snow. Tock shivered and clutched Baci's arm even more tightly.

'Come on. Let's get you indoors,' he said firmly. 'The children must be absolutely *dying* to see you.'

'Right, that's perfect,' said Pandora, peering at Minty with an artist's critical eye.

The nanny gazed in the mirror and groaned. 'I look *awful*,' she said, scratching her nose and pulling a face at her reflection.

'*Don't*,' Pandora commanded, 'you'll smudge them,' and turned her attention to Rand. 'Right, pal. You're next for the lipstick plague.'

Minty moved over to allow Rand some space in front of the mirror, then paused. 'But you're done already,' she said, gazing at his face, where a respectable crop of red spots had blossomed.

'No he's not,' Pandora muttered, sifting through a selection of Halloween face paints, Damp's finger paints and several of Tarantella's discarded lipsticks, all in similarly virulent shades of sugar pink. Holding up a tube of 'Deadly Nightshade', a hue rejected by Tarantella as being too poisonous by far, Pandora turned back to Rand.

'What?' she said, puzzled. 'When did I do that?'

'Do what?' he squeaked, aware that this was the closest he'd ever been to Titus's stunner of a sis—

'God, your *voice*. Honestly, at times you sound like Multitudina. I mean, did *I* paint all those spots on your face earlier, or are they home-grown?'

'You didn't paint these . . .' Rand poked his face gingerly, his reflection mirroring the dismay he felt at seeing his altered complexion. 'These are *real*. Hot, itchy, lumpy *and* sore. I tell you, some guys have all the lu—' He broke off abruptly.

'What *is* it?' Pandora had turned back to the mirror in order to apply dots of lippy to her own face.

'Er. Look, I'm trying my best not to freak out completely but—' Rand took a deep and wobbly breath.

'*What?*' Pandora demanded.

'The spots. They're *moving*. I mean inside. Under my skin. This is so weird. Titus – did this happen to you? With the' – he broke off to check that Latch was safely out of earshot – 'the wax,' he hissed. 'Did you get weird zits when you used it?'

Pandora finally worked out what Rand was talking about just as several of his spots simultaneously burst open to reveal what looked like springy coils of black wool underneath. Alerted by his sister's squawk of horror, Titus snapped out of gazing at Minty and swivelled round to see his fellow band-member rapidly sprouting a black rug across his entire face. Minty also turned and caught sight of Rand, who was doing a passable imitation of a werewolf: black fur erupted from every visible inch of his skin, and judging by the activity taking place beneath his clothes, every invisible inch as well. The nanny's eyes widened, rolled backwards – and with a little whimper of protest, she collapsed on the floor.

'Oh *really*,' Pandora said with disgust. 'What a complete and total lightweight.'

'Tea?' suggested Tock, one claw poised over the kettle.

Leaning against the towel rail on the range, Baci nodded. One cup of tea to warm her up and then she'd go and find the children. 'Can you smell toast?' she asked, sniffing the air several times.

'Now you mention it, yes,' Tock said, placing a cup and saucer on the table.

'That smell of *toast*,' Baci groaned, sniffing again. 'I couldn't swallow my hotel breakfast and I missed lunch too. Not good for the baby if I starve to death and besides, I'm *ravenous*.' She heaved herself off the towel rail and peered into the empty breadbin, sniffed several times in quick succession and frowned. 'It's coming from the pantry,' she decided, crossing the kitchen to investigate. Seconds later there was a shriek followed by an answering roar and a burst of bright light. Knocking Baci's cup and saucer to the floor in his haste, Tock ran to assist his mistress. He flung open the pantry door and was met by the unmistakable smell of burnt toast. In a corner, flushed with embarrassment, Ffup was trying to hide her paws behind her back. Her ingratiating grin was an orthodontist's assault course of uneven, yellow teeth; all flecked with black fragments of, presumably, burnt toast.

'Don't.' Ffup held up a paw to ward off any unkind comments, unfortunately forgetting that she'd skewered a slab of bread on each of her talons, all the better to facilitate multiple toastings.

'Oh, *my*,' came a languid drawl from the direction of the ceiling. 'Would you look at *that*. Oooo no, not me. I don't *do* carbohydrates. Not me, I'd rather eat bees, just as long as they're not *too* fattening.' Spinning down from the top of the pantry came Tarantella, flanked by her daughters Epicsaga and Anecdota, all three of them wearing identically aggressive red lipstick. Ffup's eyes narrowed and she shot the tarantulas an evil glare.

'At least I try to keep young and beautiful,' she muttered, extending her wings, giving a little shimmy and then refolding herself with a leathery creak. 'I mean, *I* haven't let myself go since *I* gave birth, unlike some I wouldn't care to mention . . .'

'Come *on*,' Tock insisted, crooking a beckoning claw at his fellow-beast and trying to persuade her to leave the pantry before Tarantella engaged first gear. 'Let it go. Just ignore her. Come and have some . . . some . . .' He dried up, aware that dieting dragons are notoriously picky about afternoon tea.

'Toast,' grinned Tarantella. 'Which reminds me, six loaves have disappeared down that dainty dragoness. *Six* loaves. Let's see – one hundred and fifty calories a slice, twenty-five slices to a loaf, that's six times twenty-five times one hundred and fifty . . .'

'That's twenty-two thousand, five hundred calories, Mum,' squeaked Anecdota smugly, and Epicsaga, not to be outdone, chimed in with, 'And *that's* probably the equivalent of eating ten kilos of lard washed down with a bucketful of double cream.'

Ffup didn't blanch, flinch or even twitch. She merely tossed her head, patted her belly meaningfully and wrapped an arm round her mistress's shoulders.

'Welcome home, pet,' she said, drawing Signora Strega-Borgia back into the light of the kitchen, slamming the pantry door and propelling her mistress towards a chair. 'Now, while dear Tock makes tea, let's you and I have some proper toast . . .' And rummaging in Nestor's changing bag, she triumphantly produced a small raisin-studded loaf, sniffed it ecstatically and then, before Baci could protest, sliced it into six slabs, popped one in her mouth – 'Fuel,' she explained indistinctly – jammed the other five onto her talons and, opening her mouth, cremated the lot.

Luciano Wises Up

Snow fell steadily, flake upon flake, blown in on a wicked wind, swirling around the chimneys of StregaSchloss, melting on the windows to slide down to the sills and blanketing the house's many roofs and turrets in white. Snow fell on the loch shore, smoothing over the pebbles and rocks, dissolving in the rock pools and completely obscuring the path between the loch and the meadow. Hedgerows turned white, fences disappeared and the sheer weight of snow brought down the telephone cables connecting the Strega-Borgias with the outside world. Later that night, snow would turn the mountains of Bengormless into a frozen Arctic wasteland, block the rutted track between StregaSchloss and Auchenlochtermuchty with a four-metre snowdrift, and bring all traffic in the west of Scotland to a complete standstill.

Unfortunately for Luciano Strega-Borgia, recently of HM Prison, Glasgow, no-one had thought to provide him with a weather forecast prior to his release. Nor had anyone thought to inform his family that he was being sent home. Now, with the phone lines down, it was too late. Standing with his thumb outstretched on a dismal, sleety road somewhere in the back of beyond, Luciano found himself beginning to think fondly of his nice, warm prison cell.

Cars slushed past, spraying him with dirty ice and snow-melt. The thin jacket he'd been wearing on the afternoon of his arrest was totally inadequate for keeping him warm as he hitchhiked home in a snowstorm. Bedraggled and miserable, he didn't look up when a car slewed to a halt in a lay-by ahead. Sleet stung his eyes, snowflakes melted and ran down the back of his neck and he could see his breath condensing in sad little puffs in the light of each passing car. Moreover, he thought, now he was utterly *ravenous*, wobbly with hunger – mainly because he'd been too hungover to eat breakfast; talking of which, he stank to high heaven of Malky's raw alcohol concoction. All in all, he was feeling just as miserable as it was poss—

'I say – is that *you*? Mr Borgia – heavens, man – what on earth . . . ?'

He heard a car door slamming and a torch was turned on, dazzling him, forcing him to lift a leaden arm to shield his eyes.

'I didn't recognize you. Terribly sorry. Just thought, Look there, Ludo, some poor devil's trying to hitch a lift in *the* most appalling weather. Come on, man, let's get you into the car – you must be frozen stiff.' And a tweedy arm was slung around his shoulders, delivering Luciano from the slush, the chill and the rapidly falling night.

His first impression was of warmth and a faint smell of pipe-smoke. He fumbled the door shut, sank into the embrace of a battered leather seat and saw a softly lit walnut dashboard in front of him. He peered at his rescuer, dimly aware that he'd seen him before somewhere.

'Ludo Grabbit,' the man said, thrusting out a hand to Luciano. 'We *have* met, but it was some time ago. Let me think, when *was* it? It'll come to me, but in the meantime' – a hip flask was pressed into Luciano's hands – 'drink, man – think of it as medicinal.' And this guardian angel of the highway turned round to root in the rear of his car, producing an old blanket that smelt decidedly doggy and, joy of joys, a dented tartan thermos which contained the nectar of the gods. Luciano nearly burst into tears of gratitude.

'Get it down you, man,' his rescuer commanded. 'Always roast and grind my own beans. Makes such a difference to the flavour – and water just off the boil, mind. Simply the only way to make a decent cup of coffee, don't you think?'

Luciano inhaled, drank, inhaled and drank again, his senses overloaded by the sheer joy of drinking real coffee after the vile poison dished out in its name in prison. *Real* coffee. At last. Now he believed he was back in the real world. He was wet, frozen, starving, desperate to see his family – but he was free. His shoulder muscles, held for so long in a defensive hunch, began to loosen and relax; his fists uncurled from their clench and a faint smile began to thaw the frozen planes of his face; the blank mask he'd been forced to adopt in order to survive.

To his horror, Luciano found his bottom lip beginning to quiver, his eyes filling with tears – Oh, God, he was *out*, he was safe, no-one was going to slip a sharpened spoon between his ribs as he slept or showered or— He shuddered, realizing he'd been unconsciously holding his breath, shuddered again and made himself exhale a tremulous lungful. He hadn't been so frightened since he was a child – he'd almost forgotten what fear could do. But in prison, cut off from those who loved him, from those he loved right back, he'd been petrified, literally turned to stone with terror. A sob welled up from his thawing heart, from the place where good strong coffee and malt whisky were working their benign alchemy. No, don't let me fall apart here, he pleaded. Not now, not in front of this kindly lawyer. No, pull yourself together, get a grip, Luciano.

Oh, bloody *hell*.

'That's it,' the tweedy angel murmured, refilling Luciano's coffee cup and passing it back along with a wedge of paper tissues and a stream of soothing platitudes. 'Don't hold back on my account. Better to let it all out. Why, you've been to hell and back, man. Read about it in the press.'

Luciano blew his nose in what he sincerely hoped was a manly fashion, cleared his throat a couple of times, took a deep swig from the hip flask – and burst into another bout of uncontrollable weeping.

'Takes a chap like that sometimes,' his companion said. 'You just have to allow yourself time, Mr Borgia. And don't be embarrassed. In my experience, real men *do* cry, especially when they've been wrongfully imprisoned.'

Luciano looked up. In the scant light from the car dashboard, he saw Ludo smile. 'I remember now.' The lawyer clasped his fists as if trying to grasp the memory before it slipped away. 'First time we met. It was a party, at your place, just after you'd met your beautiful wife, wasn't it?'

Life came flooding back to Luciano, reminding him of everything he'd so nearly lost: his family, his home, his position in the world . . . Of *course*. Ludo Grabbit, the estate lawyer, senior partner in the firm of Slander, Defame and Grabbit, W.S. It was all coming back now. Last time he'd seen Ludo was in StregaSchloss's candlelit ivory ballroom, the low lights masking the somewhat sagging ceiling and simultaneously hiding the brown stain left by a leaking stretch of guttering on the easternmost turret – Luciano reminded himself that nearly fifteen years later, he *still* hadn't attended to that repair; before sinking back into the memory of that evening, as he might sink into a warm bath.

They'd invited over two hundred guests, including Mr Grabbit, he recalled; wishing in their youthful innocence to reach out and share their joy at having found each other with everyone they knew. And everyone had turned up, blocking the road between StregaSchloss and Auchenlochtermuchty with a procession of vehicles of every colour, shape and vintage imaginable. Estate workers, Auchenlochtermuchty locals, landed gentry, the lobster fisherman whose boat had puttered up and down Lochnagargoyle from dawn to dusk seemingly ever since time began – they all came to wish the couple well. Ludibundus Grabbit, junior partner in the firm handling all StregaSchloss's legal affairs, had turned up with two drunken duchesses in the back of his ancient landau, producing a case of priceless Barolo as an engagement present. The young lawyer had swept Baci up in his arms, kissed her with evident relish and pronounced her the most beautiful woman in all of Caledonia, if not the world.

And she had certainly captured every heart in the room – save for one: that of Lucifer, Luciano's half-brother, whose blackened, shrivelled heart was immune to love of anything except money and power. Luciano had been astonished when his sibling had turned up at the party on a black motorbike, uncannily like the Bad Fairy in an perverse version of Sleeping Beauty. To Luciano's shame, Lucifer had behaved like a complete thug, pinching Baci's bottom, telling her to get him a proper drink when she offered him a glass of champagne, and demanding to know how much Luciano had paid for the engagement ring gracing her left hand. Lucifer cut a swathe through the throng of guests: fishermen and duchesses alike sensed something of the night about him; some taint of darkness that clung to his person like an inkblot on his soul.

Upon first clapping eyes upon him, Latch had marked Lucifer out as a thoroughly bad lot and had followed him around all night like a kilted shadow, afraid that the Italian gangster would attempt to make off with the silver spoons. In the event, Lucifer had been after far bigger prey that the mere contents of the cutlery drawer. Latch had found him upstairs, rifling through Luciano's private papers; rifling through them before attempting to set them alight, judging by the charred pyre of stocks and shares, bankbooks, bonds, gilts, cheques and even Luciano's stamp collection, all of them piled high in the library fireplace, doused in malt whisky from Lucifer's glass and beginning to crackle merrily. Latch had taken one look, rushed into the room, seized the first thing that came to hand and knocked Lucifer into the following day with a deftly swung reading lamp. Grabbing a soda siphon from the sideboard, Latch extinguished the flames, rescued Luciano's soggy personal effects and bundled *them up for later drying on the range. He then turned the siphon onto the body lying on the carpet and somehow managed to get Lucifer off the premises without alerting any of the guests raising their glasses to the happy couple downstairs.*

Luciano had been blissfully unaware of any of this drama – he'd only had eyes for his wife-to-be – and tactfully Latch had waited till the following morning before taking Luciano to one side to explain what had really taken place the night before. Even then, it hadn't sunk in. Not then, nor later, much later, when repeated cards, letters and e-mails went unanswered. Later still, when Lucifer had tried to kill Luciano and had sent a henchman to StregaSchloss to murder the family – yes, even then, Luciano had thought it was all about money. He hadn't even begun to suspect the depth of his half-brother's hatred for him. Later still, when Titus had tried to buy Lucifer off by signing over his inheritance of millions to his evil uncle, Luciano had been sure he'd never see or hear from his half-brother ever again.

Until a fellow-prisoner had died in a pool of blood with Lucifer's name on his lips, that is. Or indeed until his vicious cell-mates turned into completely fluffy bunnies at the mention of Don Lucifer.

And finally, as he sat in the semi-darkness, Ludo passed on the sad news of Munro MacAlister Hall's murder, offering his own services to Luciano without a word of reproach. Quote, unquote: you weren't to know, you poor souls, but MacAlister

Hall was up to his neck in dodgy practices. Law Society's been dying to do something, get him disbarred; think some of the law lords would have bumped him off themselves if they'd thought they could get away with it – kidding, Mr Borgia, ha, ha, my little joke – but seriously, he deserved everything he had coming to him. Rumour has it, just between you and me and the gatepost, old bean, MacAlister Hall fell foul of the Em Ay Eff Eye Ay, and was found in a dumpster out the back of a hotel sporting more perforations than a colander—

Luciano didn't say a word. He'd been so sure he'd never have to deal with his half-brother again, until now. Sitting in the front of Ludo's car, sipping whisky and wondering why he'd been so unbelievably dumb, Luciano realized his ordeal wasn't over yet. Somehow, he had to find his half-brother and put an end to this thing. Or else face the consequences.

A Blot on the Landscape

At first, when Latch led Rand into the kitchen, Baci thought that Knot had somehow given birth to a baby yeti, so furry had the boy become. Tock emitted a loud honk of alarm and leapt to defend his mistress, baring his teeth and lashing his tail from side to side in a virtuoso display of reptilian aggro. Ffup choked on a mouthful of toast and sprayed crumbs across the kitchen – much to the disgust of Tarantella, who dropped down from the top of the dresser to stare at this new arrival.

'What on *earth* is that?' the tarantula demanded, gazing at Rand's wildly gesticulating limbs. 'It looks like one of us. On steroids,' she added darkly, fascinated despite herself by the spectacle of a human hairball.

'Help,' the hairball squeaked, its voice muffled by an abundance of matted fur around its mouthparts.

'Hard to see how,' murmured Tarantella, recognizing the voice, but not its owner. 'What do you need? Hairbrush? Razor? Lawnmower? Strimmer? Overnight immersion in a vat of industrial-strength hair-remover? Wax. *That's* it. You need waxing. You know – melt, spread and rrrrrip. Problem solved, hmmm?'

Baci winced, and under his fur, Rand paled.

'Nnno,' he whispered. '*Not* the wax, please . . .'

While they waited for Minty to recover from her Rand-as-hairball-induced faint, Pandora tried to resuscitate Titus's computer. This consisted mainly of turning it off and on while pressing various combinations of keys.

'I don't think I've got enough fingers to do this,' she complained, both hands spread across the keyboard while she held down two more keys with her elbow. She glared at the monitor and in response it flickered, its hard drive emitted a series of lackadaisical clicks, as if summoning a pet dog, then, with a ghastly nails-on-blackboard shriek, it booted up and spat Pandora's disk of photos all the way across the bedroom.

'Uh-oh,' breathed Titus, retrieving the ejected disk and gazing at it in dismay. 'Oh *dear*. It's horribly chewed. Looks like it's gone ten rounds with a combine harvester.'

'I imagine that means I've lost the photos,' Pandora muttered, trawling through files on the newly awakened computer with little hope of finding her missing data.

'Just don't go raking through my – er – private stuff, right?' Titus said, turning back to where Minty still lay unconscious on the floor. After a pause he took a pillow off his bed and attempted to lift her head onto it. He couldn't bear the thought of all that golden hair spilling across the rarely hoovered grunge on his bedroom floor. Ughh. He didn't want her to regain consciousness and discover she had bits of fluff stuck all over her. Or worse. Mind you, he thought, his pillow wasn't exactly whiter-than-white; he tried to recall when, exactly, he'd last thought to launder his bed linen.

That was one of the problems about Mrs McLachlan having vanished. He found himself constantly missing all the things she did every day; the little things, none of which had anything to do with being a nanny but everything to do with making a house into a home. Things like laundry, like folding all his T-shirts. Perfectly. Like they'd been folded when he'd bought them. Little things like remembering to replace the bog-roll in the toilet. No-one seemed to do that any more. Things like hanging out the bathmat to dry – that way you didn't step out of the bath onto the towelling equivalent of the Thing From Fifty Fathoms With Added Verrucas.

He gazed at Minty, watching her eyes move from side to side as she dreamt. It wasn't just a question of being able to bake his favourite raspberry muffins, he thought, tears beginning to form in his eyes; it was *remembering* that they were his favourite food, writing down the recipe and tucking it safely into a drawer against the possibility that she might never return. He now realized that Mrs McLachlan had been passing her knowledge on to her unknown successor, sharing her baking secrets so that the children she loved would have some comfort after she'd gone. Titus stared unseeing at the body on the floor; remembering how he and Pandora had stood in the map room, holding their breath, every atom of their beings focused on the tiny fragment of vellum that bore the only evidence that their nanny had survived. He recalled that moment clearly – the colours of the map so vivid; the whole thing a little work of art. But back then he and his weeping sister had barely registered the skill of the mapmaker, hardly noticed the exquisitely drawn sea-serpents or the banks of pillowy clouds or the etched perfection of the foam and spume frozen on each impeccably limned wave. No. Titus and Pandora had eyes for one thing and one thing only. A little island; thrusting itself out of the loch where no island had ever been before; its shores pebbly, a tiny lochan in its exact centre, painted in a shade of blue identical to that of the unconscious Minty's eyes.

He checked; turned his focus out rather than in. The nanny was still out cold, the gentle rise and fall of her breath drawing Titus in an altogether different direction from the island in the middle of Lochnagargoyle—

Blinking rapidly, he forced himself to refocus. Obediently Titus's memory delivered up the blue lochan, the pebbly shore and a little campfire burning brightly, its hopeful flames a reminder that some unseen hand must have gathered kindling and logs; possibly even the same hand that had laid out Mrs McLachlan's clothes on a rock, all of them folded perfectly – these were the truths to which he had clung. Now, two long months later, fatherless and somewhat adrift in a sea of feelings he barely understood, Titus once again needed proof that Mrs McLachlan was alive.

The rational part of his mind cleared its throat, elbowed past the tearful child-like part and began to assert itself, pacing back and forth like a tetchy schoolteacher, lacking only a pointer and a blackboard to complete the picture of a pedantic pedagogue. Sure, Pandora had the photographs, but what exactly did *they* prove? These days everyone knew that you could make a photograph say anything you wanted it to say with the click of a mouse. Yes, yes, Minty had suffered some kind of seizure – psychotic episode – well, *hallucination* then

– call it what you will – but the fact remained that hearing portraits *speak* to her was only proof that the young woman was totally unsuitable for her current job. Who on earth had hired her? The same person who bought unicorn toe-jam off the internet and grated it over her children's dinners? And *what* could this person have been thinking of to put such an unstable character as Minty in charge of a vulnerable, bereaved toddler like Damp?

Unable to bear the direction in which his thoughts were taking him, Titus mumbled something to Pandora about going to the bathroom, promising that he wouldn't let their mother catch sight of him, swearing that he'd hide down the U-bend if necessary to avoid discovery. Pandora was too consumed by the intricacies of files and data retrieval to pay Titus much attention, Minty was snoring faintly and endearingly on the floor and Latch had taken the transformed Rand downstairs to see if anything could be done to return him to his normal state.

Titus sneaked out of his bedroom and tiptoed downstairs without incident. As he crept past the kitchen, he could hear Latch's deep voice explaining to his mother about the sudden outbreak of German measles, interrupted by shrill wails from, he presumed, the catastrophically altered Rand. Moments later, when he turned off the corridor and took the stairs to the level below StregaSchloss's central courtyard, all sounds faded to silence. Since summer, when Tarantella's daughters had hatched, the flagged passageway leading to the map room had become festooned with cobwebs, all of them lumpy, bumpy and unravelling like badly knitted socks. Shuddering with disgust, Titus crawled past on his hands and knees, preferring this indignity to the risk of becoming entangled in Tarantella's daughters' amateurish attempts at web design.

There were *hundreds* of them, he realized, knees aching with the wintry chill permeating up from the flagstones beneath him. And had the corridor always been this long? He crawled onwards, forcing himself not to scream as dangling skeins of spider silk brushed his ears, tangled in his eyelashes, stuck to his— With a sob of sheer relief he saw that ahead of him lay the door to the map room, standing slightly ajar, a faint light glowing behind it. Heart hammering in anticipation, Titus crawled in, praying that the web makers hadn't got this far. To his relief, not so much as a single cobweb spanned a corner cornice or dimly lit dado.

Feeling faintly silly, he stood up, aware that he'd still have to confront his arachnophobia and retrace his footsteps, or knee-shuffles, back along the corridor and upstairs. For the moment he was engaged in reacquainting himself with the peculiar atmosphere of this, one of the oldest rooms in StregaSchloss. Because of its location below the central courtyard, the map room had never been lit naturally. The combination of thick stone walls and no windows made the room feel muffled; thick with silence and acoustically dead. Indeed, the map room seemed to swallow sound whole, encouraging visitors to become silent and fall into a wordless reverie. This, added to the lack of daylight, had probably been the reason why it had rarely been used for anything other than maps. Successive generations of Strega-Borgias had avoided its cloistered confines, preferring the open spaces of any of the other ninety-five rooms afforded within StregaSchloss's generously proportioned walls. Here, unfaded by daylight, hung the family's collection of antique maps, most of which had been drawn by one of what Titus secretly thought of as the Great-Great-Etceteras – those endless ranks of old dead Strega-Borgias whose portraits hung in the Ancestors' Room. Come to think of it, hadn't it been the map-making Great-Great-Etcetera whom Minty had met? *Said* she'd met? Hallucinated? Dreamt—

Titus rubbed his eyes. What was he *doing* down here in the map room if not following a dream himself? If he and Pandora really *had* seen Mrs McLachlan's clothes carefully depicted in that antique map, then Minty could well have met her Apollonius the Geek.

The rational part of his mind retreated, muttering balefully to itself into a dark corner of Titus's head, allowing him to engage psychic hyper-drive and let his imagination soar unchecked. It *was* like dreaming, he thought. Like one of those dreams of flying when you were aware that flying defied the laws of gravity and was therefore impossible; but there you were, going ahead and doing it anyway. However, before he followed this dream to its conclusion, he *had* to check.

A single hammered brass lamp shone over the fireplace, illuminating the object he'd come to see. Titus stepped forwards, all the better to examine this most beautiful of all the maps in the collection. There was StregaSchloss, reduced to a postage-stamp-sized image; in this version of itself, missing the Georgian and Victorian additions – all the turrets and most of the chimneys hadn't appeared till years later, but in the century when the map was drawn, frequent sieges and battles meant that houses had to be built to withstand attack. Hence the central courtyard over the map room, in which to keep animals; the dungeons to store prisoners and supply the house with a source of water; the metre-thick stone walls to prevent the house being set alight; and finally, the moat surrounding the whole, a deterrent to all but the most determined invader. Titus's eyes tracked across the map; across the formal garden, its intricate yew hedging burnt during the oil crisis in the seventeen hundreds; the parterre, filled in now; the rose arbour; and then across the meadow, down to the loch and out, skimming across the water to the little island . . .

He must have made some sound then, some mew of disbelief, although he wasn't aware of doing so.

For a moment he was too intent on trying to breathe, to rediscover some measure of his equilibrium as, all around him, the room spun and those ever-so-solid walls moved in and out with each of his hammering heartbeats. Briefly, he thought he was going to pass out with the sickening cocktail of fright, grief and sheer horror. In the centre of the map an impossible black stain had appeared. It almost obliterated the island – the island where he had hoped to see some evidence of Damp and Mrs McLachlan. The black stain was *moving*, sweeping across the map like a cloud shadow, discolouring all in its wake. As it moved, it changed shape, from an ink-black arrow to a grainy spiral nebula, moving and shifting as it swallowed the island in the middle of Lochnagargoyle. Steeling himself to look closer, Titus stepped up to the map and searched for what he now hoped wasn't there.

Death at Sea

A wind that had ignored the shipping forecast howled and shrieked out of the north, snowballed down the west coast of Scotland and turned into a storm-force-ten gale as it hit Argyll. Despite this, the trawler put out to sea; its crew huddled below decks, relying on computers to plot their course out to the deep-sea fishing fields. The trawler's skipper was obliged to set out no matter how bad the weather was, frequently sailing into the teeth of almost biblical storms in the hope of landing enough fish to repay the bank loan he'd needed to buy the trawler in the first place. He looked up from another depressing set of sums he was scrawling on the back of his bank

statement, just as a particularly high wave made his tea slop over the rim of his mug and turned all his financial calculations into a damp smear. This, he thought, was the kind of night when some fishermen wished they'd chosen to study marine ecology rather than contributing to its collapse. This was the kind of night when the sea heaved and swelled like a living beast; each crest and trough bigger than the last; the deeps so deep they could swallow a man, his crew, his entire trawler (but not, alas, his marine mortgage) without so much as a ripple.

A white blip appeared on the screen in front of the skipper, causing him to catch his breath. He leant forward, keying in a command, knocking over his mug of tea as the image on the screen slowly changed. Now, pixel by pixel, came the picture of something floating off-stern, something on a collision course with his trawler. Without a second's hesitation he stood up, grabbed an oilskin and a loudhailer and headed outside. In the icy, blustery hell on deck, he staggered around like a drunken man, hand over hand along the railings, amazed as ever at the sheer raw power of the sea as it foamed and roared around him. With a frozen hand, he groped for the switch to turn on the floodlights and couldn't at first believe what he was seeing. A *boat*? This was not the kind of night to be out on a tiny tattered dinghy. What on earth were they playing at? He'd hardly seen it in the darkness. God Almighty, he'd nearly mowed it down – had the

men on board no sense at all? Three of them, clinging to the sides. Were they *blind* – or insane – or . . .
or what?

He raised the loudhailer to his lips, to tell them,
yell at them, swear, scream – he had no idea what he
was going to say to a suicidal raggle-taggle bunch of
sea gypsies – what *could* he say? Then all thoughts
of boats, of fish, of money, of anything other than

his baby daughter's face and his wife's eyes

all other thoughts were driven from his head. One
of the figures in the rowing boat turned to face him,
its pale eyes locking with his,

*please, not yet, let me hold my child once more, kiss my
wife, at least get to say goodbye*

and it opened its awful mouth to smile – at him – at
where he clung to the rail, frozen with dread.

'Later,' it said. 'Same place, another time though,
huh? Go home, you fool – don't you know you
could die out here?'

And laughing – *laughing?* – Death and his oarsmen vanished into the deep.

'Please don't be sleep,' Damp begged, tugging at
Mrs McLachlan's cardigan. The nanny lay on the
shore, face down on a little patch of snow-covered
sand in between two rock pools. Snow was

beginning to lie on her unmoving body; to powder her in white, just as she had once powdered her cakes and biscuits, sifting icing sugar over them until they too looked as if they'd had a light dusting of snow.

'*Wake UP*,' Damp bawled, pulling at Mrs McLachlan's shoulder, hauling at her, pummelling her, flinging her little arms around her nanny's neck; breathing in her face, stroking, patting, hugging, staring with increasing desperation at her silent, shuttered expression.

Beside Flora, with both legs so badly bent they must have been broken in several places, lay the demon Isagoth, the slight rise and fall of his chest the only evidence that he'd survived the journey. In the howling maelstrom of frenzied bats escaping the island, it had been uncertain if anything living *would* survive the flight. Like all air travel, it had come at a price. The bats of Coire Chrone were rabid, had been so for years. For humans, their bites were invariably fatal; for immortals like Flora and Isagoth, one or two bites caused slight feelings of tiredness; three or four, deep weariness; over ten, exhaustion; but any greater accumulation of bites caused a frighteningly deep narcosis. First Isagoth was dragged upwards, sucked out of sight by a gust of wind, his demented, gloating shrieks growing fainter and fainter as the bat venom overcame him. Next came Flora, silent and inert, raised horizontally into the darkening sky like a sacrifice to the storm. Then the wind took hold of her, her body angled upright and she spun round and round, faster and faster as, enveloped by a spiralling helix of bats, she was devoured by the storm.

Hunched into a tiny ball of fright, Vesper shuddered. To think *he'd* been responsible for summoning those bats. So bloodthirsty. He'd never liked the taste of blood himself. The fleshiest thing *he'd* ever sunk his teeth into had been a mango, and even then he'd had to spend the next week obsessively picking fibrous strands of the fruit from between his fangs and flossing repeatedly with a length of coconut fibre. Watching this multitude of his fellow-creatures latch onto first Isagoth and then Mrs McLachlan had been almost more than Vesper could stand. Petrified that the bloodthirsty hordes might accidentally bite Damp, he'd begged the little witch to pull up her landing gear and go; and she could forget the in-flight trolley service – due to the severity of the storm, the only thing they'd be needing on this trip were those handy little waterproof sick-bags. But Damp had refused to go. Despite all Vesper's entreaties, she had stood on the shore, buffeted by the wind – at times almost blown flat by the force of it – waiting until her beloved nanny had been overcome by the bats and hoisted into the sky. Only then had she allowed Vesper to lead her up into the storm.

And what a storm it had been. The noise was

unrelenting, battering at their ears like a mob baying for blood. The din made them deaf; it blunted all their perceptions and rendered them dumb with shock. Then, just when they thought it couldn't get any worse, the temperature plummeted so far below zero that the air snapped and crackled; the wind speed adding a whole new arctic dimension to the concept of 'freezing'. Fingers, wings, toes and claws – no extremity was spared, all burnt and stung. Vesper's eyes streamed and Damp's nose ran then froze in mid-drip. It became increasingly hard to breathe, as if even their hearts and lungs were beginning to slow for want of anti-freeze in the blood. The light had gone now and Vesper's ears strained to hear the squeaks of the bats of Coire Chrone, without whom he would have had no idea how to find his way home. Then the snow began; at first only isolated stinging flakes, then a flurry of hundreds, thousands, hundreds of thousands of needles of ice blown into their eyes and mouths by the vicious wind. Finally, to put the lid on their misery, the sharp ammoniac tang of bat-pee filled the air, burning their eyes and searing their noses with its inescapable bitter reek.

Howling with fear and outrage, Damp flew for her life. Vesper clung to her like a living compass, guiding and encouraging as they pitted their tiny bodies against the full might of the weather. Years passed, or so it seemed to Damp, her clock running rapidly backwards to once upon a time; then just as suddenly leaping forwards through time to give her a snapshot of something that hadn't happened yet, where she found herself sitting across a checked tablecloth from Mrs McLachlan, a single dark rose in a glass on the table between them.

She couldn't make out what the nanny was saying, so, embarrassed by her failure to hear, she looked down at her hands to where a silver thread wrapped round her wrist like a bracelet, one end disappearing under the tablecloth, the other twined round the rose stem and crossing the table to where Mrs McLachlan held it between her finger and thumb. Curious as to where the other end went, she bent to look under the table, finding, to her astonishment, not the stolid pillars of table legs and chairs, but a forest of tree trunks leading away into the distance.

She looked up, wondering if she should ask permission before getting down from the table to explore this forest, but Mrs McLachlan had gone, leaving three things behind on the tablecloth: a black marble, a tiny paint-brush and a burning salamander which, as Damp stared at him in wonder, seemed to sense the weight of her gaze and scuttled towards her, leaving a trail of singed foot-prints on the tablecloth behind him. The salamander stopped and looked up, his lagoon-blue stare infinitely sad, his whole being radiating loss.

'You're not her,' he stated reproachfully, the tablecloth smouldering around his fiery little body, 'And heaventh, but it'th freething,' he added, seemingly unaffected by the little flames licking round his brassy belly.

'Hello, snake,' Damp ventured, not entirely sure that she'd got this right, but wishing to appear friendly to this little beast.

'Oh, thigh,' the salamander groaned, rolling his eyes and coughing as smoke from the smouldering tablecloth swirled around him. 'I'm not a thnake, I'm a thalamander.'

'You're hot, hot, burny,' Damp pointed out helpfully, wondering if it would be impolite to pour the contents of the rose vase over the burning tablecloth. She could barely see the little creature for smoke and flames.

'Blatht. I theem to have thet the table on fire,' the salamander complained. 'Thuch a nuithanth.' And he vaulted down to disappear beneath the table with a swish of his flaming tail.

Damp lifted the now impossibly heavy, burning tablecloth and peered into the darkness beneath . . .

. . . and with a jarring, painfully bone-shaking crash, landed on the pebbly shore of Lochnagargoyle; no longer on the island, but home on the mainland, where she'd come from. As icy snow soaked through her clothes and her core temperature began to dip dangerously low, Damp tried her best to wake Mrs McLachlan. Calling her name, over and over, tugging at her arms, she found herself almost overcome with weariness. Her hands were numb with cold, her feet too and, ominously, she'd stopped shivering. Tucked inside her fleece, Vesper was too cold to complain, his tiny body hunched in a ball to conserve what little warmth he could.

Abruptly, Damp sat down on the snow and burst into tears.

'Not like it,' she sniffed, too tired even to wipe her nose on her sleeve in the hope that such revolting behaviour might sting Mrs McLachlan into wakefulness.

'Not *like* it,' she insisted, her voice hoarse and barely audible over the roar of the wind and the crash of the waves on the shore. 'Tired, tired girl.' And she curled her little body against that of her nanny, wriggling under an unresisting arm and trying to warm herself in the only way she could. Her eyes closed and, in the absence of any signs of disapproval from Mrs McLachlan, her thumb stole up towards her lips and popped into her mouth.

Snow continued falling, snow on snow, flake by flake claiming the three bodies on the beach and turning them white. Inside Damp's fleece, Vesper's autonomic system shut down all non-essential activity, plunging him into early hibernation. Squatting nearby in a little pool of snow-melt, the salamander slapped himself on his scaly forehead and gave out a howl of frustration.

'You *thtupid* people – you can't thleep here! Oh, for heaven'th thake.'

Flaming brightly, he ran up and down the length of Mrs McLachlan, trying desperately to set her alight and thus wake her out of this fatal slumber. 'You're going to die!' he squeaked, furious that the most his flames could achieve was to melt small patches of snow and send steam spiralling up into the gale. 'Help! Thomebody *do* thomething. Eth Oh Eth!'

As if in answer to his pleas, his words were washed away by a vast wave, its force drenching him and removing the crust of snow from the three bodies before cascading onto the beach with such force that it left a crater in the snow.

'*Jings!*' roared a voice. 'Oan nights like yon, ah'm awfy glad ah'm waterproof, eh no?'

Deafening slapping sounds accompanied this statement, then a vast eyeball appeared inches away from the stunned salamander.

'Whoo'r youse?' the voice demanded, the eye blinking, its pupil a huge pit of blackness in which the salamander saw himself damply reflected. 'Pleased tae meet youse an' aw that. Ma name's Neh . . . Ness, aye, right, but youse can call me the Sleeper.'

'Orynxth,' the little creature squeaked. 'Pleathed to make your acquaintanth.'

The giant eye withdrew and there were more slapping sounds, as if several enormous somethings were dropping onto the shore from a great height. With an effort, the salamander forced himself to burn more brightly, and in the increased candle-power managed to illuminate the owner of the eyeball and source of the voice.

A vast water-serpent towered over the bodies on

the beach, his long body arranged in five decreasing arches, the smallest of which was taller than any of the scrub oaks lining the shore.

'Aye, that's great, pal,' he roared. 'Jis' bring yon wee light ower here.'

The colossal beast bent over Mrs McLachlan and Damp, sniffing and snuffling over their bodies, as if in the darkness he needed to identify them by smell rather than sight. Obviously satisfied with the result of his enquiries, he picked both child and nanny up, tucked them into a vestigial pouch on his belly and turned his attention to the other body, that of the demon Isagoth.

'Thmellth nathty . . .' the salamander muttered, edging forwards to sniff alongside the Sleeper. 'Er, thcuthe me?'

The giant beast turned round, scattering snow and pebbles across the beach and slapping his tail into the water with a loud crash. Bits of flotsam were now embedded in his tender underbelly – a car tyre and, bizarrely, a blue rubber glove dangling like an alien udder from beneath the Sleeper's pouch.

'Look, pal,' he roared, 'ah'm due up at the big hoose fir ma dinner, so 'fit's awright wi' youse, ah'll take these wee craiturs up there wi' me. Drop them aff wi' their ain folk, eh no? Ah think the big yin's been missin' fir ages. They'll be pure dead chuffed tae get them back agin, eh no?'

Orynx nodded. He wasn't sure about the third

body though. Wasn't sure at all. In another lifetime he'd been enslaved by demons; even washed in seawater and blown clean in a gale, Isagoth still retained the faintest trace of the sulphurous reek of Hades. Fortunately, the Sleeper wasn't too impressed by his olfactory assessment of the unconscious demon either.

'Phwoarrrrr,' he pronounced, rearing back in disgust. 'That yin's gone aff. It's pure mingin', yon. No way ahm ah luggin' that aw the way up to the big hoose in the snaw and the dark, jis' tae have them chuck it in the compost. Let's go, wee yin, ah'm freezin' ma buns aff, stonnin' here.'

And leaving Isagoth to the mercies of the weather, the Sleeper plucked Orynx off the ground and placed the little creature on top of his enormous head, rearranged the passengers in his pouch and, undulating sinuously, headed in the direction of StregaSchloss.

Sweet Dreams

Tarantella's daughters watched with interest as a withered hand appeared, clawing its way over the lip of the freezer, all five fingers scrabbling for purchase on the smooth white metal lid.

'My goodness,' observed Emailia. 'And we thought *our* Ageing Parent was an antique . . .'

The lid to the freezer lifted slowly, falling open on its hinges as, inside, something large splashed around in what sounded like a tank of melted ice.

'Eughhh!' Novella leapt backwards out of harm's way. 'Water. Gag. Yeeeeurch. I'm out of here.'

Climbing out of the freezer came Strega-Nonna,

—— 313

wet, wrinkly, like a geriatric version of Botticelli's Venus arising out of her clam shell. The spider babies watched as the old lady removed several dripping bags of no-longer-frozen chips from beneath her feet, dropped them onto the floor and used them to cushion her landing as she half-climbed, half-fell out of the freezer with a dismayed yelp. Pausing only to check for breakages, she clambered to her feet and tottered off in the direction of the kitchen.

Tarantella's daughters picked their way fastidiously past the puddles left in Strega-Nonna's wake and scuttled after the antique ancestor, following her staggery progress past dusty, cobwebbed racks of wine from vintages long forgotten. After a catastrophic explosion in the cellar the previous New Year, Latch had restocked the racks with over two thousand bottles, some of which had been laid down at the beginning of the previous century. Consequently, the smell in the wine cellar was of old things: fading wine labels, wax-sealed corks and a faint, musty grapiness, where a cork had failed and allowed a bottle to drip onto the stone floor. Following Strega-Nonna's wet footprints, the spider babies paused at a particularly sticky patch – the sugary residue left when a bottle of exceedingly strong damson gin had steadily leaked its contents onto the floor over the previous two years. Tarantella's daughters were still at that stage in their lives where their avid desire for knowledge far outweighed their instinct for self-preservation. Like teenagers, the spiders had all come hard-wired with shameless curiosity, vast appetites and exceptionally sweet teeth. All they appeared to have inherited from their mother was her fastidious attention to personal hygiene. Consequently, when Anecdota found herself sticking to the floor as she crossed the dehydrated gin lake, she shrieked to a stop, delicately lifted two legs at a time and groomed herself as if her life depended on it. Very soon a wide smile crossed her mouthparts and she lurched, hiccuping, towards Emailia and Diarya, both of whom were regarding the sticky puddle with unalloyed disgust.

'Ladiesh, ladiesh,' Anecdota bawled. '*Chill*. Thish shtuff, I tell you, ish nectar of the godsh. Forget grooming, ladiesh. Jusht come on in and help your-shelvsh.'

Two minutes later, warm and fuzzy feelings began to overcome the spiders. Another two minutes later, a fly blundered into their company and prepared itself for instant annihilation, only to discover that the spiders were too inebriated to be bothered to sting it, wrap it and consume it at leisure. They reeled into the kitchen, rank of breath, unable to see straight, but affectionate, giggly and in a mood to party till midnight and beyond. Drunkenly, they rolled under the table, where they paused, shrieking with laughter, as the kitchen spun around them alarmingly. Above their heads the mood was far more sombre.

Strega-Nonna was becoming hysterical. 'I tell you, I've lost the thread – I cannot bring Flora back – I – I—'

'Seems to me you're a teeny bit confused, Nonna,' Baci said gently. 'Flora's been gone for a long time. Since the summer. But you weren't to know – after all, you were tucked up asleep in your freezer—'

'*No!* You don't *understand.*' The old lady nearly wept with frustration. 'Flora always goes away – and then I bring her back. Always. But I can't. Do you understand? I can't bring Flora back this time.'

'No, Nonna' – Baci's voice was soothing, the tone conciliatory – 'I *do* understand. None of us can bring her back. No matter how much we wish we could. Believe me, I do understa—'

'NO!' Strega-Nonna shrieked. 'No you don't. You can't understand. You keep on refusing to listen to me. D'you think that just because I'm *old* that means I'm stupid? D'you think I'm losing my mind? I've lost the *thread*, I tell you—'

'Telling me,' Latch murmured, and turned to confer with Signora Strega-Borgia under his breath. 'Signora, do you want me to see if I can calm her down? Tuck her up in bed upstairs while you deal with Titus's friend?'

'Oh, Lord,' Baci moaned, reminded of the hideously transformed Rand. 'It – he's in the pantry, been raking around in there for ages, trying to find a similar jar to the one he had earlier, but I've a horrible feeling that I know what it was he ate, and it wasn't what he thought—'

'You've got to help me,' Strega-Nonna insisted, turning from Baci and transferring her attentions to Latch. 'Flora is in terrible danger – she cannot return without the thread – she—'

The door to the corridor opened and Titus stood there, pale-faced and shaking. 'Mum – there's some-thing—' And half-falling, half-staggering across the room, he collapsed onto a chair and put his head in his hands. From under the table came an almost inaudible hiccup as Anecdota tried and failed to focus on all the legs now crowding under the table.

'Mum—' Titus began, then stopped.

Baci reached out to pat him, letting him know without words that whatever it was that ailed him, she would do her best to make things right, to make it all better, and then she remembered. 'TITUS!' she gasped. 'The measles. You shouldn't *be* here – near me – the baby—'

The kitchen door flew open and Pandora stood there, her lipsticked spots hideously apparent against her ashen face.

'My photos have gone,' she stated, then, catching sight of Rand emerging from the pantry, she gasped, 'Oh *heck*. You're turning into a spi— Mum? Can't you *do* something?'

Baci had one hand over her mouth, the other

outstretched as if to keep everything – everyone – in the room at a distance. Under the circumstances this was entirely understandable: two of her children were covered in the false rosy rash of an illness which Latch had assured her was fatal to unborn babies; Strega-Nonna was wetly hysterical; and Rand – Rand scuttled across the floor towards her, his eight furry legs ample evidence, if evidence had been required, that there was a whole world of difference between consuming acanthoid wax and the similarly spelled arachnoid version.

Just at that moment the lights flickered and went out and the door to the kitchen garden fell inwards with a loud crash. In a deafening roar, a voice informed them, 'Ah'm awfy sorry, but ah think ah jis' snagged ma tail in yer power cables . . .' And preceded by the brightly burning salamander, the Sleeper slid into the kitchen, bringing a blast of icy wind behind him.

'Were you born in a barn?' demanded Ffup, bounding into the kitchen with Nestor clasped under one arm.

The Sleeper quailed slightly, then recovered. 'Dinnae gi'e me ony a' yer grief, wumman,' he growled, punctuating this with what he hoped was a suitably manly snort. Haloed by snowflakes, he turned to face the assembled beasts, humans and spiders with an abashed look on its face.

'Aw, hen,' he mumbled, rearing over Signora Strega-Borgia. 'Ah'm that sorry, but ah've gone and trashed your wee door . . .' He bent forwards to pick splinters of oak from his belly, and paused, as if struck by a sudden thought. 'Aye, but look, see. Ah've brought youse all twa wee presents. Check these oot. Ah found them washed up oan the beach.' And unaware of quite how huge an effect this was about to have, he rooted in his pouch and produced his treasures for all to see.

Later, by candlelight, Latch crept into Mrs McLachlan's bedroom, hardly daring to breathe. Knees creaking in protest, he lowered himself into the wicker armchair by her bedside and closed his eyes for a moment to collect himself. His chest burnt with unshed tears and unbelievable relief that at last his beloved Flora had been returned to him. All those long months without her; all the nights he'd lain awake, wondering if he'd ever see her dear face again; trying to drag his thoughts away from the terror that he'd find her body washed up on the shore, broken and battered, lost to him for ever. His shoulders began to shake and, to his shame, he found himself unable to stop tears pouring down his face. Try as he might, he couldn't hold himself back any longer; why now, why *here*, he wondered; unable to do anything but sit by her bedside and cry silently, his whole person violently seized by feelings completely outwith his experience or control. The room shimmered in the candlelight as Latch sat beside the woman he loved more than life itself and wept himself dry.

A hand touched his and his eyes opened. He must have fallen asleep, dozed off in the chair, how long had he—? Confused, disorientated, he saw first Titus, then Pandora standing beside him, gazing down to where Flora slept. Clearing his throat, Latch stretched and stood up slowly, his long legs cramped with his vigil by Flora's bedside. As if a veil had lifted from his eyes with the return of his beloved Flora, he now saw that the children looked like wraiths in the candlelight. Although man-sized, Titus had the bruised eyes of a lost boy and Pandora looked as if she hadn't slept since the day her nanny had vanished. Latch's heart squeezed with pity as he realized how orphaned Titus and Pandora had become by losing their Mrs McLachlan. They'd hidden it well, he thought, watching as Titus's eyes filled up with tears, watching Pandora's hands shake as she covered her face. He reached out and drew them both into his embrace.

'Is she . . . ? Will she be . . . ?' Pandora began then, unable to continue, she buried her head in Latch's shirt and sobbed.

Titus shook like a reed, racked by huge choking sobs. 'I just – I just remember looking at all her sensible shoes,' he whispered into Latch's shoulder. 'And – and thinking she'd n-never – n-never fill them again . . .'

'And her bed,' Pandora wept. 'I used to go and

curl up under her quilt b-b-because I could smell her lavender soap under there – but – but then—' A fresh burst of weeping all but obliterated Pandora's next words, but Latch felt his own eyes prickle as he heard the child gasp out, 'It *faded*. I – I – I couldn't reach her – I began to f-f-forget what she w-w-was like.'

Outside the window, the storm howled and raged as gales battered the stone walls of StregaSchloss.

'When will she . . . ? How long before . . . ?' Pandora began, then stopped herself.

It didn't matter, Latch realized, looking at Flora's dear face and feeling a wave of absolute joy at the thought of all the happiness to come. He too had wondered when would she and how long . . . but it didn't matter at all. What was important now was the simple fact that she was back. Home again. Safe.

'And I'm never letting you go again,' he whispered. 'Not without me by your side.'

In an antique porcelain candleholder by Baci's bed-side, Orynx the salamander curled himself into a little ball and glowed faintly. Hanging upside down from one of the bars of the headboard, Vesper narrowed his eyes and muttered, '. . . and if you think you're replacing *moi* as Damp's familiar, you can think again, dude.'

The salamander ignored this completely, his light dimming by not one watt in response.

'I'm her main man,' Vesper continued. 'Her *numero uno* first lootenant. I'm her shadow. I, like, er, stick to her like a tick, like glue, like a glove, like a . . . like a . . .'

Orynx yawned, rolled his eyes and glared up at where the little bat dangled above Damp's head. 'Oh, pleath,' he sighed. 'Cut me thome thlack. I'm not out to trethpath on your patch. I'm here for Thomeone Elth Entirely.'

Damp sighed in her sleep, pressing her back into her mother's tummy, stretching happily under a heavy arm. Inside Baci, Someone Else Entirely opened brown eyes, wriggled luxuriously in the darkness and fell asleep once more. Vesper folded his wings and glared at Orynx then, deciding that he offered no threat whatsoever, the little bat launched into the lullaby with which he'd soothed Damp to sleep ever since they'd first met.

'Cabin crew, doors to manual and crosscheck. We will shortly dim the overhead lights for landing—'

'Thpeak for yourthelf,' muttered Orynx. 'The only dim thing round here hath wingth and thqueakth a lot.'

'Please return your upright to the tray position and extinguish all seats—'

'Vesper?' Damp groaned, but before she could finish, Orynx interrupted with a terse, 'Pleath. Thut up.'

Titus and Pandora sat guarding Flora for a while, as

if they feared she might vanish again if their attention were elsewhere. Around them, Strega-Schloss slept, the sounds of the house settling into the night and forming a familiar symphony composed of the ticking of cooling radiators, the creak of contracting roof trusses, the whistle of water in pipes and the prolonged wail of baby dragons wanting to be tucked in by Mum, not Dad.

'Na, na, na,' came Nestor's distinctive wail. 'No wantit. Not likeit. Want Mummmaaaaa.'

'Aw, come oan, son. Yer mammy's havin' a bath. Jis' snuggle doon and let Daddy get some sleep, eh no?'

'Na. Hot. Not likeit hot. Scratchy. Not likeit jaggy.'

'Look, smout, when youse're thousants a' years auld like yer dad, youse'll be aw jaggy an' hafta shave an' aw. An' a right pain in the bum youse'll find it as weel. Noo settle doon, eh? Ah'm no gettin' oot a' bed tae have a shave the noo, right?'

'Na, na. No wantit. MUMMMMAAAA.'

There was a crash, the sound of vast feet taking the stairs down to the dungeon three at a time, a roar, a scream, a brief argument – then heavier thudding feet taking the stairs to the upstairs bathroom five at a time, followed by the slam of the bathroom door and a prolonged buzzing sound as the Sleeper applied himself to Luciano's electric shaver.

Moments later the smell of toast filled the house.

* * *

In the mushroom, Rand lay face down on his bed, vowing that if he ever got himself out of this mess, he'd always pay close attention to what it said on the label, even if the label only happened to be stuck to a can of beans. Who'd've thought a couple of letters in the wrong place could have had such a catastrophic effect? Acanthoid – arachnoid – he still could hardly tell them apart. With a heartfelt groan he rolled over and clapped a hairy leg to where his forehead used to be. Mrs Borgia's totally pathetic attempts to return him to his normal teenage self had only resulted in reducing him to normal spider size. Before Titus almost stood on him, she had helpfully pointed out that the only way to break the wax's enchantment was for him (yes, *him*, Rand MacAlister Hall) to weave a counter-spell in spider silk (like, *how*?) during the next waxing (like, yeah, Rand thought, nice touch of irony there) of the moon. So . . . let's see, that gave him, what – about three weeks to learn how to spin spider silk? Oh yeah, like *that* was going to happen. Furious, he pummelled his pillow with all eight legs and screamed out loud. God. It was just *so* unfair. Now, instead of being transformed into a bloke with a deep voice and a sprinkling of hair on his chest, he was a spider with a deep voice and hair all over his chest, his face, his legs, his legs, his legs . . .

A peal of laughter came from behind his bed, making him spring onto all eight legs and rapidly check all around. There it was again, and more than one voice by the sound of it. Not threatening, though. Just girls. Vastly amused girls. Hang on a minute, though. He was a spider, right? Girls weren't too keen on spiders, were they? If they saw him, these girls would probably go, 'Ewwwww,' before trying to squash him flat. Better run for cover then. Rand scuttled across his mountainous pillow and vaulted over the cliff-edge of his mattress, falling straight into another world entirely, but one which looked suspiciously like heaven to him.

Seven pretty young women were slung under the bed, two dangling from the springs and waving at him, one coyly peeking out from behind a discarded sweet wrapper on the carpet and four linking their legs and surrounding him in a circle of feminine charm.

'Ooooh,' they chorused. 'Aren't you just yummy? Look at all that *fur*. Mmmhmmm. Step this way, big boy.'

Rand blinked in disbelief. This couldn't be happening to him. Dimly, he tried to recall what little he knew of a spider's life cycle. Wasn't there some catch? Some problem with being male?

'Erm . . . ah,' he managed.

'Oooh. That *voice*,' breathed Epicsaga. 'Come and talk to *me*, gorgeous.'

'No, *me*,' demanded Emailia, batting her numerous eyes at the bewitched Rand.

'Oooh, I want to have his babies,' sighed Diarya. 'Hundreds of them, just like him.'

'No, *me*,' insisted Emailia.

What *was* it? Rand wondered, sinking backwards into a harem of long legs, shining eyes and widely smiling mouthparts, dimly aware that somewhere, way off in the distance of his memory, a warning bell was ringing.

Still Me Inside

Titus woke up, stiff, sore and decidedly crumpled. Pale dawn light illuminated the sleeping shape of Mrs McLachlan beside him and, on the other side of the bed, Pandora, also fast asleep. Latch was slumped across the armchair, the rhythmic sound of his breathing indicating that he too was sleeping soundly. Tiptoeing downstairs to make himself some breakfast, Titus discovered that Minty had got there before him. The nanny stood propped against the range, a cup of coffee in her hands and a puzzled expression on her face when she caught sight of him.

'Morning,' he mumbled, hauling open the cereal

drawer and immediately slamming it shut as he remembered that it still contained the same weevil-infested bag of muesli that had been the sole cereal on offer at StregaSchloss ever since Mrs McLachlan had gone.

But, Titus thought joyously, she wasn't gone any more. She was upstairs, sleeping, healing – whatever she had to do to get better – and once she recovered . . . Guiltily he stifled this happy thought, trying to throw a psychic blackout over it, lest Minty read his mind and see how happy he was that her predecessor had returned. For, he realized, as a blush crept across his cheeks, Mrs McLachlan's return meant that they now had two nannies, not one. The young woman bending down to retrieve something from the baking oven; this girl with lavender-blue eyes – she would have to go. Titus's heart sank. With the best will in the world, they only needed one nanny at StregaSchloss. However, he thought, they *were* missing one cook. A smile hovered round his mouth as a whole world of delicious possibility opened up in front of him. Minty didn't have to go. At least, he sincerely hoped she didn't. She was funny, brave, resourceful and clever – not to mention stunningly beautiful; *not* that beauty had anything whatsoever to do with it.

Minty straightened and placed a baking tray onto a wire rack in front of her. Tendrils of steam curled up from whatever it was she'd just taken out of the oven and Titus was struck by how much she seemed to *like* cooking. She was brilliant at it, obviously quite obsessed by it in fact. Her seventeen suitcases, rucksacks and trunks, which he'd effortfully dragged upstairs to her bedroom, had proved to be full of recipes, whisks, pans, cookie cutters, loaf tins, tube moulds, icing bags, pizza cutters, jam thermometers, soufflé dishes and enough ramekins to remodel Tock's moat in fluted white porcelain should she so wish. She'd even brought seven cook's aprons *and* ten pairs of oven gloves too. I mean, he thought, you don't waste your money on all that stuff if you hate cooking. Do you? He gazed at her, unaware that he was staring.

Minty removed her oven gloves and smiled at him. 'Muffins,' she explained. 'Raspberry ones. Apparently they're Titus's favourite. Any idea where he is?'

Titus frowned. What was she on about? He was here, in front of her, wasn't he?

'Er . . .' he ventured, his voice emerging with distinct adolescent squeakiness. It was then that he remembered. That wax. That stupid, stupid wax. It had worn off, stripping him of his 'enhanced features' with no warning, leaving him beached, blushing and – damn it – a boy again. 'Um,' he began, wondering how on earth he could even begin to explain. It's me, he wanted to yell. It's still me in here. He nearly howled with the indignity of it all. I'm still Titus, even though I'm a lot younger than you've come to expect. Just because I look different doesn't mean my feelings have changed. Oh bloody hell, he thought miserably, she was now regarding at him, not as an equal, but like someone you had a duty to look after. Some . . . some *kid*. He looked down at his feet, suddenly aware that his dad's trousers now hung in folds around his ankles, and that the sleeves of his shirt dangled beyond the tips of his fingers. He'd shrunk somewhere between bedroom and kitchen, shrunk back to being a kid again. Titus was assailed by a feeling of such acute bleakness that he had to grab the worktop for support and take a deep breath.

Phwoarrr, that was a bit better, he thought, taking another breath. Hmmm. And another, and another. Wow. Those muffins. They smelled sensational. A thought occurred to him – admittedly a somewhat unworthy thought, but given the circumstances, an entirely understandable one. After a very brief struggle with his conscience, he decided to go for it. Smiling appealingly up at Minty, he said, 'Actually, would you like me to take some muffins up to Titus? He's not really himself just yet . . .'

Heavy snow had continued to fall overnight, forcing Luciano to abandon all hope of returning home until daybreak. Briefly, he'd entertained desperate notions of skiing home, or borrowing snow-shoes and walking or even hiring a helicopter and being airlifted to StregaSchloss. Good sense had prevailed and he ended up spending a passable night curled up in a quilt on an ancient Chesterfield in Ludo's study. Dusty leather-bound law books lined the walls and Ludo's vast desk was buried beneath tottering piles of torts, tracts, tomes and hundreds of model soldiers, for, as the lawyer explained, war games and strategies were his passion. Which was why, Ludo said, pressing a hot-water bottle into Luciano's hands before turning in for the night, he would be more than happy to assist in the finding and eliminating of Luciano's half-brother, Lucifer.

'Elim – elim – eliminating him?' Luciano's face paled in the flicker of light from the log fire. 'But – but surely that means we would become as despicable as him? If we descend to the level of going around cold-bloodedly killing people then we're . . . we're . . .'

The lawyer laid a restraining hand on Luciano's arm. '*If* we descend to the level of cold-bloodedly killing your half-brother, then you, your wife and your children all might stand a chance of surviving to see another year. Otherwise . . .' Ludo didn't over-dramatize this point by doing anything so crass as drawing a finger across his throat; instead, allowing the silence to speak for him, he left a considerable pause before he patted Luciano on the arm, bade him goodnight and headed to bed.

To his own astonishment, Luciano slept. Convinced that a combination of the day's events, the subject matter of his conversation with Ludo and his understandable impatience to return home to his family would all conspire to render him sleepless, he was pleasantly surprised when waves of exhaustion rushed towards him the moment he lay down. Ludo's battered leather Chesterfield was deeply comfortable, the hiss and crackle of logs in the fireplace soothingly reminiscent of campfires in his youth and the shadows cast by the flames onto the ceiling were those of hundreds of model soldiers, all steadfast and all fighting on his side. Moreover, someone had been decent enough to replace all the bones in his body with warm Play-Doh and plate his eyelids with lead. Gratefully, Luciano let go.

Overnight, Argyll had been transformed into a scene from an Advent calendar. Waking in the dazzle of low-slanting sunshine, Luciano was at first totally disorientated – home, prison, where? – and then brought back to his senses by a distant waft of real coffee. Across the study a set of clean clothes had been laid out on a button-back club armchair, plus a towel, bathrobe and a well-thumbed copy of *The Art of War* by an author with an awful lot of military awards after his name. This, when opened, had a yellow post-it note stuck to the title page. It read:

L

*Help yourself to bath/shower/coffee/-
breakfast/whatever you need.*

*'Mi casa è su casa', huh? Hope you slept
well. Sorry to abandon you, but I've got court
at 10. Have a think about what we discussed.
If you're game, you might find this volume of
some use. Otherwise, I'd strongly advise you to
consider finding a bodyguard and going into
hiding with your family.*

*Trust me, Luciano, he's not going to give up
now.*

Whatever you decide, let me know?
Yours
Ludo

Luciano took a deep breath. Sunshine glinted off the ranks of model soldiers and dappled the floor with lozenges of light. It was time to go.

An hour later he stopped at one of the gates which barred the entrance to the StregaSchloss estate. Some comedian had changed the sign that had warned trespassers about the dangers of straying onto the land between this gate and the distant loch. Now the sign read:

WARNING
~~BEWARE OF THE DRAGON~~
~~bewair of the trantuler~~

~~BEWARE: LOW STANDARDS~~
~~OF LITERACY PRACTISED HERE~~
~~bewair: children mite run out~~
BEWARE: HOPE SPRINGS ETERNAL

Underfoot, the snow was thawing rapidly, dropping off the leafless branches of the chestnuts and retreating to all but the highest peaks of the Bengormless range. The air smelt cold and clean; in the distance he could see his house silhouetted against the loch. A thin thread of smoke trickled out of one of the chimneys. Luciano shaded his eyes against the sun and calculated that someone, probably Latch, had just lit the fire in the library. He was afforded a brief vision of himself, curled on a sofa in front of that same library fire and surrounded by his beloved family. This was no vision of a hysterically happy reunion, more of its peaceful aftermath; a relaxed vision, comfortable, cosy: Titus immersed in a computer manual, Pandora in a book as thick as a doorstep, Damp breathing heavily over a picture book, Baci chewing the end of her pen as she puzzled over the crossword, and himself . . .

Checking that the book was safely zipped into the pocket of the jacket he'd borrowed from Ludo, he pulled up his collar and stared into the light. Later, he decided, banishing thoughts of his half-brother to the back of his mind. There would be time for all that later.

Up ahead, a figure detached itself from the broad mass of the house and stood still for a moment, as if trying to work out who he was. Then it waved, and Luciano waved back, his feet breaking into a run, his voice cracking with the joy of saying her name. His daughter began to run towards him, her hair flying around her like a flag to welcome him back home.